KILLER STYLE

STELLA KNOX SERIES: BOOK TWO

MARY STONE

STACY O'HARE

Copyright © 2022 by Mary Stone

All rights reserved.

No part of this book may be reproduced in any form or by any electronic or mechanical means, including information storage and retrieval systems, without written permission from the author, except for the use of brief quotations in a book review.

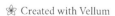 Created with Vellum

DESCRIPTION

Evil never goes out of style.

Special Agent Stella Knox thought she'd seen it all in her two years with the Nashville PD. But after two weeks at the FBI, she's already witnessed more than she could have imagined, including her newest case. The bodies of two women have been found in an alleyway, both missing one arm, one leg, and all their fingers and toes.

Now, a third woman is missing.

Shasta daisies artfully arranged over the bodies and at each crime scene indicate the work of a serial killer. But every victim is unique, with nothing to connect them. They are all different ages and different ethnicities, with different upbringings and different lives.

With nothing to link the victims, preventing the next murder is nearly impossible.

Anyone can be next.

When a fourth person goes missing, the clock is ticking...and Stella and her team are already running behind. Can they find the killer before another mutilated body turns up or will one of them become part of their unsub's fantasy?

Chilling and engrossing, Killer Style is the second book in the new Stella Knox Series by bestselling author Mary Stone and Stacy O'Hare—a puzzler that will make you realize anyone can be a killer...no matter how harmless they seem.

1

I'*m going to die.*

Kati Marsh's chest ached. Her breath scraped the inside of her throat, and the muscles in her thighs burned. The stitch in her side was worse, though. So much worse.

She couldn't run anymore. She just couldn't.

Too exhausted to even be pissed at herself, Kati dropped to her haunches and was promptly ambushed from behind. As the huge weight knocked into her back, she fell face-first onto the grass.

Claws raked over her skin. As she rolled onto her back to fight off her attacker, a wet tongue slid over her face.

Gross.

"Juno...stop!" Kati pushed the giant Rottweiler away. The dog collapsed next to her, tongue lolling as she panted quick, hot breaths into Kati's face.

"Come on, Juno. You can't be tired. You've got twice as many legs as me. C'mon, girl."

Attempting to be a good example, Kati pushed herself up and grabbed Juno's leash. In response, the black and brown dog rolled onto her back, legs in the air.

"You big lug. Was that all you wanted? Here." Smiling, Kati rubbed her dog's tummy before giving her broad chest a good scratch. "Now, come on. You're supposed to protect me out here. You could at least *look* like you know what you're doing. Can you give me a growl? Come on. A small one."

Juno lifted soulful, black eyes to Kati. She stood, blinked twice, then pushed her side against Kati's leggings and flopped onto her back again.

Kati pulled her feet out from under the dog. "Useless. All looks and no bark. Or bite."

Knowing Juno would follow, she began to walk, needing to cool down and let the fire in her thighs ease. Right on schedule, Juno trotted at her hip. "To be fair, some people are scared of Brodie too. In this day and age." A cloud of sadness gathered around her, and she fought back the rise of emotion that came each time she thought of the racism her boyfriend still endured. "You'd have thought they'd have grown out of that by now. He's an even bigger softie than you."

She scratched Juno's broad head with both hands. "And that's why I love you both *sooo* much. Come on. Almost there. Let's sprint to the end."

Kati broke into a run, hoping her body would be more cooperative this time. Though she regretted the third taco she'd eaten earlier, she always enjoyed her evening jogs in the park with its wooded trails and cool air. Running gave her time to think. Gave her something to escape to, be proud of. Especially in a home where very little she did was a source of pride.

"Come on, girl."

Racing away from those depressing thoughts, Kati picked up speed. Face intent, Juno matched her stride for stride, the hard muscles in her shoulders flexing with each movement. Kati understood why many people hesitated at the sight of the muscular dog. Her Rottweiler looked intimidating as hell, but she had the disposition of a cuddly kitten.

But why would anyone be frightened of Brodie? People, like her parents, were judgmental of her boyfriend's shoulder-length dreadlocks and dark skin without taking the time to get to know the book under the cover. It was crazy. Brodie was soft and quiet and loving, a true gentleman in a world filled with jerks.

Reaching the end of the trail, she slowed her pace to a walk again, but not because the stitch had returned. She simply wanted to stretch and breathe in the fresh Tennessee air. Nashville had become as polluted as most big cities, but here, she felt removed from that. She gloried in the peace surrounding her as the sun moved closer to the earth.

Lowering her arms from a deep shoulder stretch, she examined her hands. The ring finger of her left hand was bare. Was that going to change soon? She wasn't sure.

Brodie had been acting a bit strange lately, especially when he'd asked her to keep Wednesday night clear. He'd also asked what her favorite cupcake was. It wasn't her birthday for months yet, so why had he needed to know that? And why had he been so nervous when asking her? His hands had been shaking, but a huge smile had broken over his face when she'd said Wednesday was all his.

Unless she'd misread the signals, Wednesday would be a very special day indeed.

Resisting the urge to pull a Julie Andrews twirl right there, she bit back her burst of excitement, not wanting to get her hopes too high.

Scanning the horizon, she realized the sun was lower than usual at this part of her run. Unless she wanted to crash into a tree later, they'd better go. "Come on, Juno. It'll be dark soon. Let's head for home."

Picking up speed, they made good time on the last mile.

Kati was smiling as she and Juno left the wooded trail and headed up the hill toward the small lot where she'd parked. This was always the hardest part...trudging up the steep incline after a hard run.

On the grass verge marking the entrance to the parking area, a man sat on a folding chair behind an easel. He must have been about sixty. His wild, brown hair was gray in patches, as though his head wanted to try every color it could find. He looked to be in good shape, though. Muscles rippled in his arms as he dipped his paintbrush into paint.

When he looked up, Kati jolted, knowing he must have caught her staring. She needn't have worried, though. His attention wasn't on her but on the setting sun at her back.

Circling around, Juno rubbing against her legs, Kati turned and took a few moments to breathe in the sight herself. This was the real reason why she ran in the evenings. It was cooler, sure, but witnessing the miracle of the sky changing colors, the hues and shades merging and melting across the horizon, was the perfect way to end a busy day.

It must have been the same for the artist. He'd been there at the same time over the last couple of weeks, capturing the majestic Tennessee evenings on his canvas.

Kati couldn't blame him. The scenery was beautiful in this park, especially as the dying sun darkened the green leaves and spread a lilac wash across the sky. She really wanted to see how his painting was coming along. He must almost be done by now. She hadn't dared ask, though. Artists could be touchy about the creative process. She'd just let him be, enjoying nature and art in his own way.

The man smiled as Kati and Juno made it to the top of the hill. He dabbed at the canvas before lowering his brush and lifting a hand in greeting. "Good evening. Isn't the sky extra beautiful tonight?"

Kati followed his line of sight. High on the hill as they

were, he had a spectacular view of the trail snaking into the woods, the curving trunks of the poplars and the beech trees as they faded to black. Above them, the sky was lined in shades of purple and crimson, and the bottoms of the high cirrus clouds had turned burnt ochre.

"It really is."

"But then, isn't every sunset beautiful?" The man's chuckle reminded Kati of her grandpa's, making her smile. "Even the best of us are just daubers compared to the artistry of Mother Nature. And she's more productive too. She churns out a new work of art every night."

Kati wanted to give him a hug. "But you put on canvas what nature has created. That's art too."

He beamed. "Well, I'd like to think so." The man sat back from his easel and smoothed his hair. It sprang right back up. "You talk like someone who appreciates art."

Perceptive.

Once upon a time, Kati painted or sketched every day. She wasn't sure how comfortable she felt talking about her love of painting, but the man seemed warm and friendly. And he was a working artist.

Juno lifted her nose in the air, searching for some scent that only canines can detect. Kati scratched the dog's ears, considering how much of her story she wanted to tell.

Screw it. What could it hurt?

"I do." That came out wrong, so she corrected herself. "I did." When he appeared to be puzzled, she rushed to explain. "I was planning to major in art history in college."

"But?" There was no judgment there. Only genuine curiosity.

"But…" Kati sighed. "My folks pushed me toward accounting. Much more secure, they said."

The man smiled and gave a small nod. He checked the sky again and dabbed his paintbrush near the top corner of his canvas. "I can't blame your folks for that. Not much job security in art." He tapped the handle of his brush against his chin. "But maybe accounting is kind of an art too. The more creative you can make your accounting, the more your clients pay, no?"

"Oh, I don't know about that." Kati mentally shuddered as she imagined getting an unexpected visit from the IRS. "Getting creative with numbers sounds more dangerous than artistic."

Wrinkles fanned out from the painter's eyes as he chuckled. "Some of the greatest artists were considered a bit dangerous, getting told they were too creative in their lifetimes. Van Gogh. Monet. Picasso. Henry Darger worked as a janitor and died in poverty. His works sell for three-quarters of a million now."

Henry Darger?

"You sound like a real connoisseur. Are those your favorite artists?"

The man swished his paintbrush in a jar filled with grayish water. "Oh, yes. You can't go wrong with the impressionists and the modernists and finding outsider art is such a thrill. But there are some very talented local artists around here too. Do you know Gary Glenderson? Or Liz Richards? Darwin Rhodell or Sofia Benson?"

All those names were familiar, but she hated to admit that she was so out of touch with the local art scene. Kati couldn't name one of their works. She couldn't put their faces with their names. "I've heard of all of them, but I'm sorry to say that I've allowed myself to get so busy with my job that I haven't experienced the joy of seeing their work."

"Oh, that's fine." He capped the gray water tightly before running a cloth down the brush. "I'm just an old man with far too much time on my hands, and I like to spend it at art fairs and galleries. But you should check them out sometime. They really are amazing talents."

"Thanks." Kati made a mental promise to take the kind man's advice. "I'll do that."

The artist's neck popped as he turned his head to inspect the area around them. The sky had darkened, turning the purples a navy blue and almost hiding the trees entirely. "Well, light's gone. Guess I'm done for the day. You have a good night now."

He opened his paint box and tucked his brushes inside. Peeking over his shoulder, Kati's mouth sagged open as she caught a glimpse of his canvas. Glowing bands of mauve and lilac and plum slashed by curving, black lines of trunks and branches made Kati's heart ache a little.

If she had carried on with art, would she have been able to paint like that? She wanted to think so, and to hope that she hadn't entirely lost her chance. "Well…it was lovely speaking with you. Have a good evening. C'mon, Juno. Let's go."

But Juno didn't want to go. She was still sniffing the air and pulling on the leash, wanting to inspect the artist more closely. Her stubby tail was like a tiny windshield wiper set on high.

"C'mon, Juno." She blushed when the dog disobeyed and tried to pull her closer to the artist. "Sorry…I really need to get her some training." She tugged harder. "Juno, stop it. Let's go."

The artist only chuckled and held his hand out for Juno to sniff. The dog got even more excited, making the man laugh harder. "I think she likes me."

Well, I'm not liking her very much right now.

Giving a sharper tug, Kati lowered her voice like Brodie taught her to, forcing some command into it. "Juno. Stop. Come."

Juno ignored her.

The artist opened his box and pulled out a mostly eaten sandwich. "I'm betting she's smelling the ham. May I?"

Anything to get Juno to listen. "That's very kind of you. I swear I don't starve her."

"She certainly looks very well taken care of." He winked. "But don't we all want a treat sometimes."

Kati grinned. "I guess so."

Holding the bite of sandwich out on his palm, the artist seemed pleased at how gently Juno took the offering. "She's a good girl, isn't she?"

Proud to her toenails, Kati nodded. "She sure is. Needs some manners, but she's still a pup officially. Just eleven months old."

"Gracious. I can't imagine how big she'll be when she's fully grown."

"Her parents weigh more than me, so I imagine she'll be that big someday soon." Kati tugged on the leash. "Well, we'll get out of your way so you can get packed up before it's fully dark." She was relieved when Juno didn't fight her this time. "Have a good evening."

The man picked up his painting, holding the wet canvas facing outward while tucking his easel under his arm. "You, too, my dear."

Stepping toward her car, Kati glanced back to see the man clutching his box of paints and chair in his free hand. As she watched, the easel slipped from under his armpit and now leaned against his leg. Without a free hand, he was trying to hook it back up with his elbow.

Crap.

She couldn't leave him to struggle like that, so she back-tracked. "Here, let me help you. I'll take that." Wrapping the handle of Juno's leash over her wrist, she took the easel from under his arm, allowing the man to stand straight and lift his painting higher off the ground.

"Thank you. That's very kind. My car is just here."

Only when she was halfway to his vehicle did she think how odd it was that she was willing to get this close to a person she didn't know, especially in such an isolated area. Her parents had tried to scare both Kati and her sister half to death about talking to strangers. Their warning rang in her head.

She pushed the thought out as soon as it entered. She always carried a bottle of mace in her pocket. And there was Juno. The dog might be a big lug, but Kati was sure that, if push came to shove, Juno's muscles and sharp teeth would shove back.

Besides, this old guy looked harmless, with his wild artist's hair and arms packed full of gear.

Kati followed him past her own car to a gray Volkswagen parked under a poplar close to the steepest side of the hill. The man leaned his painting against his leg, then fumbled in his pocket for his key.

"Nope. Can never find the darned things. Head like a sieve." He set his paint box on the roof of the car, then dug into his other pocket. "There we are."

He unlocked the doors with a click, opened the back passenger's door, and waited for Kati to slide the easel on the seat before placing his chair and paint box on the floor behind the driver's seat. Finally, he slipped the wet canvas on top, using clamps to hold it in place.

She watched him closely, appreciating the system he'd created for transporting a wet canvas back and forth.

"Thank you so much." He closed the door and shot her another beaming smile. "You've been so helpful. I don't suppose you want to see a finished piece? It's no Turner. I can't claim any of that Englishman's genius, and it's certainly no Monet, but I would very much like your opinion."

Kati glanced at her watch. Time was getting on.

Stop being such a baby.

Sure, it would be entirely dark soon, but her car was just there, and Juno was by her side. And she did want to see a finished piece. The painting he'd worked on for the last couple of weeks was so colorful and beautiful.

"Sure. I'd love to."

The man's beaming smile made her doubly glad she'd accepted as he held up a finger. "One moment. Just one minute."

With a bit more spryness in his step, he hustled to the trunk, opening it with the push of a button. A few seconds later, he lifted a 24x30-inch canvas out and set it on the ground, leaning it against the fender.

As Kati took half a step back to admire the work better, he began prowling through his trunk again. She was too distracted by his work to pay attention to what he was doing, though.

Wow.

She had thought that she was doing the man a favor by agreeing to see his picture. Now, she began to think he had done her the favor.

A large wave that reminded Kati of Hokusai's *The Great Wave of Kanagawa* dominated the portrait. But while the famous painting was blue and gray, the spray recreated as grasping fingers, this wave was soft and warm, the white foam rolling in front of an orange and red sky.

Kati crouched in front of the canvas. The paint had been laid on thick. He must have used a spatula to create those ridges in the foam.

What had she been thinking? Of course she should have

gone to art school. Accounting was so dull. She should have never let her parents—

Juno pulled at the leash, knocking Kati over. From where she'd draped it around her wrist, she didn't have a good grip and the handle slid off her hand. Before she could cry out or say a word, Juno bolted toward the artist, jumping...jumping...

"Juno!"

Kati scrambled to her feet just as the artist reared his arm back and threw something she couldn't see into the woods. Juno darted after the object like a flash, racing down the steep hill for her prize.

"Juno! Get back here."

But the dog was already out of sight, her black body lost in the dark woods.

That was when Kati realized just how dark the evening had become. And how alone she was.

She started after Juno, but only made it two steps before pain like she'd never known stopped her in her tracks. A thousand wasps seemed to sting her at once, but she couldn't yell, couldn't say a word. Frozen to the ground, her brain rattled in her skull as she tried to understand what was happening.

That's when hands gripped tight around her arms, and she was falling...falling but not onto the hard cement. She was in the artist's trunk.

The energy of the night shifted, leaving her dizzy. Kati couldn't process the speed, couldn't figure out what had gone so wrong.

Something soft landed on her face. A piece of cloth? His hand pressed it over her nose and mouth, gripping tightly.

"Hnnn. Hnnn!"

She couldn't speak. The cloth stank of alcohol and disinfectant and something else she couldn't name.

Panic exploded from her chest and flooded her shaking muscles. She gasped, dragging in more of the cloth's stench. She scrambled to pull the cloth off her face, but her fingers only landed on the man's wrist. His grip was strong, stronger than seemed possible for his age. Her own grip as she pulled and scratched at his hand felt incredibly weak.

Spots dazzled her vision.

He pressed harder, his grip tightening. And the smell. It seemed to drift up behind her eyes and suck any remaining strength from her arms.

Juno!

Kati willed her dog to come back, to save her. Where was that dog when she needed her the most?

When the Rottweiler didn't reappear, Kati tried to catch the man's eyes, to somehow plead with him. But he was a heavy shadow among shadows by this point. She was never going to stop him.

No. Please, no.

"Rock-a-bye baby on the treetops. When the wind blows, the cradle will rock."

The man sang the lullaby while Kati's muscles relaxed further. She could still think, barely, but she could no longer move. And soon, her brain was numb, too, drifting away on skies of lilac and ochre.

The man's grip loosened. "There we are now. All calm."

Calm? Yes, so calm.

Her wrists were yanked together and something sharp bit into them—same with her ankles. And another cloth was stuffed into her mouth.

"I am sorry about this, but it's just in case your little sleep wears off too soon. It's so hard to know how much to use. Now, you lie right here."

The man glanced to the side, his eyes widening in alarm.

Juno? Where's Juno?

Blackness surrounded her the moment he slammed the trunk lid closed. A second later, the car rocked as he slid inside. The engine roared to life, the vibration jarring her head.

No. No. No.

The words echoed in her mind as her body shifted and swayed from the movement of the vehicle. Rocking...rocking...

Rock-a-bye baby, on the treetops.

It was Brodie's voice singing to her this time. He had a beautiful voice, and she loved to lie on his chest and feel the deep timbre vibrate her cheek as she listened.

When the wind blows, the cradle will rock.

Would she ever hear his voice again? Ever feel him slide a ring on her finger?

When the bough breaks, the cradle will fall.

Sorrow filled her soul at all she'd miss with him. With Juno. With their future family.

And down will come baby, cradle and all.

2

─────────

Special Agent Stella Knox's nerves were singing as she took a seat in the Nashville Resident Agency briefing room of the FBI. She wasn't on tilt because her boss, Special Supervisory Agent Paul Slade, had just called the team in to discuss another case. And it wasn't because she was exhausted from the Cherry Farms serial killer paperwork the entire team had spent their Saturday morning completing.

No.

Less than five minutes ago, Agent Mackenzie Drake had pulled Stella aside to share what she'd learned about the death of her father. But before she could share more than a few words, SSA Slade interrupted, ordering them both to the conference room where they now sat.

Stella mentally rewound their brief discussion and played it again…

"I've been digging around, trying to find info about your father. About his murder."

Stella's pulse picked up speed. She gripped Mac's arm.

Mac lifted a hand. "Hey, don't get too excited. I haven't found anything about him yet, nothing that you don't already know."

Though disappointment wanted to take a bite from her, Stella closed her eyes. Taking in a long breath, she willed her heart rate to slow. Of course. She couldn't possibly think Mac could crack the case so quickly. "Right."

Mac was still staring at her intently. "It's about your dad's partner."

What in the world? *"Uncle Joel?"*

"Uncle?" Mac shot her a quizzical grin. "Really?"

Stella jabbed her with an elbow. "Yeah, Joel Ramirez. He and my dad were best friends for years."

Mac rubbed her ribs and chewed on her bottom lip. "Right. He was killed too, though, wasn't he?"

Stella nodded. Everything that had happened the previous week vanished. All that mattered was Mac and the information she might have uncovered. "Yeah. Just like my dad. I miss him. Why?"

Mac glanced over her shoulder and lowered her voice. "Well, you're not the only one who's missing him."

Before Mac could explain, Slade had called them into the briefing room.

What had Mac meant? Who was missing him? As far as Stella knew, Uncle Joel had no family at all.

Stella's insides burned to know.

Beside her, Mac yawned so wide that Stella got a good view of her tonsils. "Wish I'd grabbed another coffee before heading in here."

Coffee?

Stella didn't need coffee right then. Her mind was doing cartwheels, reaching for all the possibilities of what Mac had tried to tell her.

As an agent in the cyber crimes division of the FBI, Mac knew how to dig for information in ways that Stella didn't. That's why she'd enlisted Mac's help. Well, that was only part of the reason. The two had become fast friends the moment they met two weeks back, when Stella joined the Nashville team.

Less than two weeks.

In under twelve days, Stella had helped crack her toughest case to date and had even survived all the paperwork. Since today was a Saturday, she'd come in early to get the final forms filled out before going home and enjoying the rest of the weekend.

That wasn't going to happen now. The report and the research would both have to wait. A new case had already landed.

Slade stood at the front of the room, his gaze sweeping over each agent until the team fell into a hushed silence. Once all the attention was on him, he cleared his throat. "Sorry to ruin your weekend, but I've just had a call from Sheriff Allen Lansing down in Morville County. They've got two bodies. Both women." Slade rested his hands on the table and leaned forward. The effect made the forty-five-year-old SSA look like a hawk about to dive at prey. "They're both missing one arm, one leg, and all their fingers and toes."

Caleb Hudson released a low whistle. "That's some trophy hunting."

"Yeah, wouldn't want to see those hanging over the fireplace at the lodge." Martin Lin grinned as he leaned back, linking his hands behind his head.

"Guys." Chloe Foster gave Martin a stare that could have broken rock. "We've got two dead women. Show some damn respect."

As Martin's cheeks turned pink, and he lifted a hand by way of apology, Stella wanted to pat Chloe on the back for that verbal smackdown. Most law enforcement officers used macabre humor to ease stress during situations where control was difficult or not possible to obtain, but this was a conference room, not a crime scene.

"Thank you, Chloe." Slade straightened. "The bodies were found next to a dumpster in an alleyway near the small downtown part of Berthar Lake."

"A dumpster. Jesus." Hagen Yates shook his head as he wrote the details in his small pocket notebook. "Some people. But why can't that sheriff's office handle this? They think the missing body parts suggest a serial killer?"

"That would be my first thought." Ander Bennett rubbed the blond curls on the back of his head. "Dismemberment sounds like a serial killer's signature to me."

"Could be someone trying to hide evidence, which would make it more M.O. than signature," Stella countered. "We had a case my first year as a cop. Somebody found a body in a lake. It looked like a drowning at first, but when we pulled out the corpse, we found it didn't have any fingers. The cuts were clean, like someone had taken a machete and just hacked them all off in one chop."

Ander raised an eyebrow. "Not a serial?"

"Nope." Stella's blood heated at the memory of the grue-some murder. "Turned out the victim was a junkie who had tried to steal from a dealer. As the dealer strangled him, the victim scratched the killer's face and arms. The dealer thought there might be evidence under the nails, didn't know which ones, so he just cut them all off. Fed them to some pigs in the end."

Martin shook his head. "Thanks, Stella. I brought a ham biscuit for breakfast. Think I'll skip it now."

Stella nearly laughed out loud but managed a shrug instead. "If that thought turned you off breakfast, Martin, you're going to be pretty hungry throughout this job."

"Let's focus." Slade clapped his hands, drawing the atten-tion back to him. "We don't know why the body parts are missing yet. Could be the killer's signature. Could be trophy hunting or, as Stella says, it could be someone trying to hide evidence. We don't know, and we're going to find out. But that's not why the sheriff called us."

"So, what's his story?" Hagen folded his arms and focused his green eyes on his superior.

"His story, as you put it, is that he's got two bodies but three missing persons."

"Jesus." Hagen hung his head. "The clock's ticking already, huh?"

"And we're already behind. The bodies have been identified as belonging to Tiffany Wright and Darlene Medina-Martinson. Both were from Berthar Lake, and both had been missing since June fifth. Kati Marsh of Morville County went missing three days ago."

Slade tapped a button on the remote for the projector, and a picture appeared on the screen behind him. Two bodies were posed faceup, side by side in a narrow alley. Slade used a laser pointer to indicate the woman on the right. "This is Tiffany Wright. Thirty-five, married. Two children."

Tiffany's eyes were closed and sunken in her pale face. Bright orange curls, just like Danielle Jameson's two seats over, sprang out around Tiffany's head like a copper halo. They matched the freckles dotting her face, her shoulders, and arms. Or what was left of them. Her left arm had been severed at the elbow, as had her left leg halfway down her thigh. Both her remaining hand and foot were missing their digits.

Slade pointed to the other victim. "Darlene Medina-Martinson. Also thirty-five, married, no kids. The two were childhood friends. Met for a drink and never came home."

Darlene's eyes were also, thankfully, closed. Her straight, brown hair stopped just short of her shoulders. Her skin was unblemished and so bronze that it glistened in the camera's flashlight.

The stumps on the ends of both women's limbs were covered by carefully arranged white flowers. More flowers hid their breasts and pubic areas.

Stella closed her eyes and opened them again. She thought she'd seen it all in the two years she'd spent with the Nashville PD. In less than half a month at the FBI, she'd already witnessed more than she could have imagined.

Were these images worse than the pictures she had seen last week of teenage boys with their heads caved in, slashed with a sword, and locked into poisoned paralysis? She wasn't sure.

Her stomach wasn't churning like it had last week, though. Maybe she was growing used to these scenes. She hoped not. This wasn't something she ever wanted to grow used to.

This arrangement of bodies was certainly more bizarre. More organized. More artistic.

Slade clicked the button on the remote again, and a woman's face appeared on the screen. She had wavy, black hair and green eyes framed by thin, arching eyebrows. Her high cheekbones narrowed toward a small chin set below a wide smile that creased the edges of her eyes.

Stella liked her instantly. She looked so happy, so carefree and approachable, a friendship waiting to happen.

Slade tapped the screen. "Kati Marsh. Twenty-three. Unmarried, no known connection to the other two victims. She had a habit of taking her dog for a run at a local park around sunset."

Caleb groaned. "Sounds dangerous."

"Dog's a Rottweiler. Not the kind of thing you'd want to mess with. Even you, Caleb. Dog was found in the park. When animal control tried to contact Kati, she couldn't be located. The police found her car the next morning. Notice the flower."

Slade pushed the button again, and Kati disappeared. In her place was a picture of a blue Ford Focus parked in an elevated lot surrounded by trees. Under the windshield wiper was a white blossom.

Hagen leaned toward the screen. "Do we know what kind of flower that is?"

"It's a Shasta daisy," Stella answered before Slade could. "They grow all over the place this time of year."

Martin nodded. "Like pretty weeds."

"Like a pretty signature." Stella studied the placement of the daisy. "The perpetrator used the Shasta daisy to cover the injuries to his victims. Even though they grow everywhere, we shouldn't ignore the fact that it's been deliberately placed at an abduction site."

"I miss you raising your hand." Martin smiled, taking the sting out of his comment.

Slade narrowed his eyes. As always, it was enough to bring silence.

"Sheriff Lansing thinks that Kati may have been taken by the same person who killed Darlene and Tiffany. He wants us to help before it's too late. Caleb, Martin, I want you two to stay here and hold down the fort. Triple check that the Cherry Farms paperwork has been completed, and be ready for the calls that will probably be coming in. You'll have to follow them up and see if there's anything worth tracking."

Martin didn't look pleased. "Yes, sir." The other three simply nodded.

Slade turned to the next table. "Dani, Mac. I want you to do a regional search for missing persons cases. These might not be the first victims. Let's make sure that other law enforcement agencies didn't miss anything that could be related to these abductions." Slade nodded at Ander. "You're with me. Hagen, Chloe, Stella, you head out to the Morville

County Sheriff's Department. Grab your day bags. You'll be staying out there until we're done."

The briefing room filled with the scrape of chairs being pushed back along the tile floor. On the way out, Stella grabbed Mac's arm. She wasn't sure when they'd next get a chance to talk. She led her friend into the breakroom and pulled her behind the vending machine.

"What were you going to tell me earlier?" Stella's voice was low but urgent. "About someone else missing Uncle Joel?"

Mac glanced over Stella's shoulder. They were alone, and no one was coming, but she still lowered her voice and leaned closer. "Joel Ramirez." Mac squeezed Stella's shoulder.

Stella braced for the news.

"That was an alias. His real name was Matthew Johnson."

She hadn't braced hard enough.

The room swirled, and Stella shook her head to force it to stop. "What? Matthew Johnson? Who the hell is Matthew Johnson?"

Mac searched Stella's face, her green eyes thoughtful. She didn't want to share the next bit of news, Stella realized.

"Look, I don't want to stir anything up."

"Tell me." Stella heard the sudden fierceness in her own voice.

Mac's sympathetic glance caused a flutter in Stella's chest. It was the same expression doctors made when they were about to deliver news that would change your life.

"Matthew Johnson was Joel Ramirez. Ramirez was his cover name. He worked undercover in Memphis, but he was actually from Atlanta. He even had a family there."

How many times had she called her father's partner "Uncle Joel"? How often had he put an arm around her, invited her to tell "Uncle Joel" how her day had been or whether there was any boy at school worth a crush? How many mornings had "Uncle Joel"—this guy, this stranger—picked up her father from home and driven him out to some of the most dangerous places in the city?

Stella placed a hand against the wall. She needed to touch something solid, to believe that not everything was going to crumble around her, not everything was going to come crashing down.

Did her father even know? Had "Uncle Joel" lied to him too? Or had her father lied to her about his friend?

Who the hell was he?

"There's more." Mac pressed her lips together. "There's no death record for Matthew Johnson."

How? Why?

"So...did he even die that day in Memphis?" Stella searched for the right questions to ask. "Or did he go back to his family?"

Mac shrugged. "I don't know."

"If he did die, does his family in Atlanta know anything about his murder?" Stella stopped. A whole new world of things she didn't know opened in front of her. "And do they know anything about my father's murder?"

"Well, now." Mac blew out a breath. "That's something worth finding out. I guess we've still got more work to do."

"Oh, Mac." Stella hugged her new friend tightly. "Thank you so much. It's a huge shock but also incredible."

Mac patted Stella's back. "Hey, I'm just getting started. We're going to get there, Stella. I promise. It's all going to work out."

Stella stepped back and forced a smile. No, it wasn't all going to work out. Her father had still died in the line of duty. That wasn't going to change. But for the first time since that terrible, black day, she could see a little light in the distance and a path toward it.

Once this new case was solved, maybe she could find

Uncle Joel's—or Matthew Johnson's—address in Atlanta. Maybe she could even take a couple of days and drive down there.

Maybe she was going to find out what really happened to her father at last.

But, first, she needed to find out what happened to Kati Marsh.

3

Hagen Yates rested one knee against the floor as he tied, and retied, the lace on his shoe. Stella and Mac were just around the corner, and although they had been talking quietly, he had managed to pick up every word.

And what the hell did he just hear?

Joel Ramirez wasn't real? He had a family in Atlanta? He might even still be alive?

The thought sent his heart racing and his fingers fumbling. He didn't give two damns whether Joel Ramirez had a family in Atlanta, another in Florida, and a third in Burkina Faso. But if he were still alive…well, that was something else altogether.

Joel Ramirez had worked the Memphis crime scene for years. He had been undercover alongside the people Hagen's dad had been hired to defend in court. If anyone knew who had ordered the hit that had left his father bleeding to death on the courtroom steps, it was Joel Ramirez.

Hagen wanted to sprint around the corner, grab Mac by the lapel, and demand to know where this guy was. He wanted to grill Stella until she told him everything about her "Uncle Joel."

But...but asking them, even politely, would mean opening up. It would mean telling them about his own mission, his own goal, about the fire that raged in his chest whenever he thought about finding the people responsible for his father's death. And he wasn't prepared to do that. Not yet, anyway.

Let Stella do the work. Let her follow the lead quietly, meticulously. He'd help if he could. A little here, a little there. And once she got close, he'd leap out and take the vengeance his father's murder had demanded all this time.

Something twisted in his guts.

His plan wasn't entirely fair. He knew that. Stella had managed to pick up a lead that he hadn't come close to finding. In less than a month, she'd made more progress than he'd made in years. He hadn't thought of looking at Ramirez while Stella and Mac had headed straight for him.

But she had her own reasons for searching, and they were good reasons. As good as his.

Damn, they were smart.

This could be the break he'd been waiting for.

Maybe they could do it together. Maybe he could just get close to her and find out what she knew about Memphis and Joel Ramirez. Track down that sonofabitch—*he has to be out there, he has to be*—and avenge their fathers' murders together.

Didn't Stella deserve to find the people who murdered her father too? Didn't she need vengeance as well?

What right did he have to put his revenge above hers?

Two fathers. Two murders. Two acts of vengeance. A perfect partnership.

He pulled the knot on his shoe tight and stood. That partnership would come. Mac was right. It would all work out. One way or another.

But first, they had a case to solve.

THE DRIVE to Morville County Sheriff's Department took Hagen, Chloe, and Stella no more than forty minutes. It took Slade and Ander a little less. They were already in the entrance hall waiting alongside the sheriff when the other three agents turned up.

Slade introduced Sheriff Allen Lansing to his agents. The sheriff gave Hagen, Stella, and Chloe a short nod but didn't smile or extend a hand in greeting. Lansing looked no more than a decade older than Hagen, though responsibility had already pushed his hairline up his temples and given his black eyes a tired, rigid stare. His face was as serious as granite.

"This way."

He set off through a narrow corridor lit by a flashing fluorescent tube. Hagen glanced at Stella. She shrugged and followed.

They reached a conference room that was smaller than their own room at headquarters. The blinds on the windows were creased and stuck at strange angles. The carpet was stained, and the air had a faint odor of old coffee and stale sandwiches.

Sheriff Lansing didn't bother to turn the lights on. Even as Hagen was still taking his seat, he launched into the briefing, covering much of the same ground that Slade had in his morning's account.

This presentation, though, lingered a little longer over the corpses of the victims. While Slade had been content to show the agents how the bodies had been arranged, Sheriff Lansing included the morgue shots that revealed the pink fat under the stumps, a half-circle of white femur visible between the muscles.

Hagen eyed the pictures with gritted teeth. What kind of monster were they dealing with here? What kind of person would do such a thing to two women? He only unclenched his jaw when those pictures gave way to images of Kati Marsh and the woods where she disappeared.

Sheriff Lansing pointed at the picture of the Ford Focus. "And this is Kati Marsh's car. The Shasta daisy on the windshield is the same type we found on the bodies of Tiffany Marsh and Darlene Medina-Martinson."

Hagen's shoulders relaxed. Now came the assignments. He hoped Slade would send him to the woods with Stella to look for clues. She'd been effective and professional in the field yesterday when they'd caught the Cherry Farms killer. He could trust her. And an environment like that might just be calm and quiet enough to get her talking about her father and his best friend, Joel Ramirez.

Sheriff Lansing pulled another picture onto the screen. Hagen sat up straight.

What the hell's this?

It was a photo of a man. Thin stubble dotted his upper lip, and his hair was mostly gray. He was much older than the victims and of Asian descent. For a moment, Hagen assumed Sheriff Lansing had mixed up his presentation images and accidentally shown them pictures from a different case. But instead of turning off the screen, the sheriff continued as though nothing had changed.

"Hu Zhao. Sixty-eight years old from Hazelhead Hills. That's just up the road here. He was reported missing by his daughter, Min Zhao."

"Why weren't we told about this?" Slade's voice was tight, controlled, but his eyes said more than words ever could.

Hagen tried not to smile. If Slade exploded at Lansing's lack of communication, that might be mildly entertaining. It was a Saturday, after all. Didn't he deserve some entertainment?

Sheriff Lansing rubbed his chin. "It just came in while you were on your way over. That's why I've been a bit...brusque. Sorry about that. We still don't know if Hu Zhao is connected, but we're treating him as an endangered missing person. His daughter is insistent that something is wrong. He's not a young guy, he has severe arthritis, and he rarely goes anywhere other than his home or to the family cabin. That's where he was supposed to be today. The car's there. He's not. We've issued a Silver Alert—"

"He doesn't fit the victim profile." Stella's tone held the same skepticism Hagen thought the rest of them must have felt. "So far all the victims are young women."

Sheriff Lansing nodded. "Right. That's what I figured. But I spoke to his daughter, and I asked her if she found any white flowers at the cabin. She said there was a Shasta daisy on the kitchen counter."

"Jesus." Chloe leaned back and planted her boots on the seat opposite her. "We've got another one?"

The sheriff glanced at her feet. He paused, then ignored the way she was sitting. "Maybe. Like I said, we can't be sure. Hu Zhao's a local author. He's quite well known around here, and Min says he's keen on flowers. He could have picked one of those daisies up and left it on the counter."

Sheriff Lansing rubbed his chin again. Hagen wondered if the sheriff hadn't had a beard once and only recently shaved it off to knock some years off his face. He looked like he was hitting the age when you had to think about that sort of thing.

"But I'm worried," the sheriff continued. "Worried enough to include it with the other victims, at least for now, and send some people out looking."

"I agree." Ander tapped the briefing room table. "The appearance of that flower can't be a coincidence."

Hagen was less certain. If those flowers grew everywhere, then the presence of one in the kitchen could well be a coincidence. And this Hu Zhao was so different from the other victims. He was a different sex, different age, different ethnicity. A completely different life. If the person who had taken Kati, Tiffany, and Darlene had also taken Hu, they seemed to be choosing their victims entirely at random.

Slade stood, iPad in his hand. "All right, let's get visuals. Sheriff Lansing, I'm going to need a printed map of the area, pictures of the victims. Some sticky notes."

"Right away."

Hagen leaned back in his chair. Now, they'd start to see the case come together.

HALF AN HOUR LATER, Slade had finished creating his murder board, with a map of the area on one side. A blue pin marked the spot where Tiffany and Darlene had been found. A green pin stabbed the parking lot next to the woods where Kati had vanished. A yellow pin to the east of both spots identified the cabin where Hu Zhao should have been writing his new book.

Hagen tried to ignore that pin. He left enough room in his head for doubt, but he'd be less surprised if Hu Zhao turned up safe and sound, having taken a long walk to avoid an overprotective daughter and stir his creative juices.

Pictures of the victims, of Kati's car, and of the Shasta daisy—that cheerful-looking white flower that was so popular in the area—made up the other half of the board.

The last pictures to go up on the board were close-ups of the victims' mutilated limbs. The room had fallen eerily silent when Slade attached them. When he stepped back, they added a grimness to a board that was otherwise colorful, floral, and in the placement of the victims' bodies, even symmetrical.

Stella spoke first. "Why those limbs?"

Hagen answered with his own question. "Why those victims?"

"Answer both those questions, and we'll have our killer." Chloe lowered her feet from the chair and stared at the board. "Maybe we should focus on the bits we can't see. The missing arms and legs. What's he doing with those parts? How is he even storing them?"

Ander stretched his back. "Caleb thought he was trophy hunting. That sounds right to me. Though how you can keep them is beyond me. Unless he stuffs them in the freezer alongside the pork chops and last season's venison."

"They're all different, though, aren't they?" Stella pointed at the pictures of the stumps. "Tiffany's a redhead with skin covered in those dark freckles. Her friend, Darlene, looks like she spent too much time in a tanning bed."

"That's a natural tan"

Everyone looked at Ander, amused expressions on their faces.

Ander frowned back. "What? I can't know about tans? If it were fake, you'd get marks around the eyes. From the goggle thingies."

"Right." Stella rolled her eyes and turned back to the photos. "Kati has an olive skin tone somewhere between Tiffany and Darlene's. I wonder if their skin tones even matter."

"I think you guys are barking up the wrong tree here." Sheriff Lansing rested the tips of his fingers on the table with an *are you all crazy* expression on his face. "This area's pretty mixed. Even if the killer was picking people at random, I doubt he'd hit the same skin tone twice."

"But that's the point, Sheriff." Hagen tried to keep a note of exasperation out of his voice. "Killers don't usually pick their victims at random. They have a plan. They have their own project. They choose who they kill for a reason. I know this guy looks like he's just pulling names out of a hat, but I'd be surprised if we don't find a method behind his madness."

"Maybe you should add 'florist' to that note." Stella's voice contained more than a hint of resignation. "The killer also seems to know his flowers."

Slade hesitated before grabbing another note and wrote *florist?* and added it to the board. "So that's where we are. We've got two female victims, another one missing, and a middle-aged Asian man who may or may not be connected. We've got missing limbs and perhaps some sort of floral link. Although, frankly, Stella, that does seem like a reach. Sheriff Lansing? Anything you want to add?"

Sheriff Lansing ran the back of his hand against the bottom of his chin. "No. I think you've got everything, and I'm grateful you're here. I'm really worried about Kati Marsh and Hu Zhao, and I have no clue how we're gonna stop this guy before he hurts them."

Slade faced his agents. "Stella. Ander. I want you two to head to the restaurant where Darlene and Tiffany were last seen. See what you can learn. Find out if they spoke to anyone or if anyone tried to speak to them. Two pretty women drinking alone? You might just land something. When you're done, head to the area where Kati's car was found. See if you can find something that forensics overlooked."

Hagen set his jaw and released it. So, Ander would be with Stella on this one. That would probably make him happy. Never mind. He was sure he'd have plenty of other opportunities to talk to her about Joel Ramirez.

"Hagen. Chloe." Hagen snapped to attention at the sound of his name and returned his focus to Slade. "I want you to talk to Kati Marsh's parents, Darlene's husband, and Mark Wright, Tiffany's husband. Maybe the women had complained about someone bothering or threatening them."

"What about Min Zhao? Hu's daughter." Chloe was already halfway out of the chair. "You want us to talk to her too?"

Sheriff Lansing lifted a hand. "Let's focus on the two women and Kati. Hu might still be nothing. Let's give him some time to show up."

A shout came from outside the conference room, just loud enough to be clear. "Tiffany," a man bellowed. "My Tiffany."

Slade threw Sheriff Lansing a look. Footsteps pounded down the corridor before the door was thrown open. A deputy stood in the doorway, his cheeks flushed. He ignored everyone else and talked directly to Sheriff Lansing.

"Sorry to interrupt. We've got Mark Wright at the desk, and the guy…he's losing his damn mind."

The shouts came again. "Tiffany! Tiffany. How could you let this happen to her? You were supposed to protect her. You were supposed to do your damn jobs."

Sheriff Lansing took a deep breath. "I'll deal with him. I'll see if I can calm him down before you guys speak to him."

Hagen watched him leave. He didn't envy Sheriff Lansing's task. Mark Wright had lost someone close to him. Nothing was going to calm him down ever again.

4

The arms filled the white space of my canvas as if they were made to rest there. Tiffany's right arm, pale as a cloud and as freckled as a forest trail, gripped Darlene's earthen and unblemished golden limb, covering the unsightly cuts I was forced to make.

Such firm friends. Now touching for eternity. The beginning of the unity circle.

It was hell itself to weave Tiffany's fingers over Darlene's amputation, but once the limb had released itself of the rigor mortis, I'd bent her fingers around it. Now, they'd never let go. You'd need to apply force to tear them apart, and who would do such a thing? Who would possibly want to separate these two beautiful creatures?

Not me. I'd frozen their friendship.

I laughed out loud, enjoying my wordplay. Because they *were* frozen. I had to work with gloves in that room, which made the whole thing more difficult. There were times when I'd worried about manipulating Tiffany's fingers so hard they would snap clean off.

That would have been such a waste.

Closing my eyes, I thought back to the rest of Darlene's fingers, wishing that I'd been able to use each of them in my art. A couple of them didn't work for the composition I'd envisioned, though, and needed to be disposed of.

I was quite proud of myself for thinking of feeding one of them to that sweet Rottweiler, instead of burying it in the woods as planned. I hoped Juno enjoyed her tasty treat.

The whole takedown had worked quite marvelously, which was how I knew absorbing Kati's life energy into my canvas would be blessed by the gods.

I'd first seen Kati and her lovely pup ten days ago while painting a sunset. She'd just appeared, like the lovely angel she was. And I'd known.

When she came back the next day and the next, I could feel her soul crying out for release…even if she didn't know it yet.

They never did.

I entwined the last two fingers and stepped back to admire my work. It was coming along nicely. The togetherness. The tones. The attachment.

We are all the same.

That was what I had said as I worked. And it was my reaction then when I saw Darlene and Tiffany's arms side by side, holding each other's hands.

We are all the same.

Rrriinggg.

Smiling at the perfect timing, I glanced at the monitor inside the freezer room that'd been activated by the doorbell. My gallery remained locked at all times, but I'd left instructions for visitors to ring the doorbell if they wanted entrance.

A couple was standing outside. His gray hair was parted to reveal a wide, bald patch on the top of his head. Hers was dyed mostly blond. Her hand rested lightly in the crook of his elbow, and they stood so upright, so elegant.

Beautiful people. All people are beautiful. We are all of us a work of art.

Pulling off my gloves, I touched the intercom button to let them know I was on my way. After leaving my coat hanging inside the freezer, I made my way through the corridor and through what used to be the dining area to the front door. It always amused me that my studio and my gallery used to be a restaurant. People used to come here to feed their stomachs. Now, I nourished their souls.

They were so friendly, the couple. Californians looking for something bright and colorful to hang in the guest room of their vacation home. Something not too challenging, not too controversial. Just pretty.

Nothing wrong with that.

You couldn't put too much beauty into the world.

I showed them one of my pastorals, all shades of green and fading blues. It held just a hint of sadness. The dying of the day and the lightening of the pasture as summer gave way to fall, all symbolized through the use of bluebird feathers. I had found the bird already dead in the park and thought it a waste to leave those beautiful blue feathers behind. That was nature. Death always gave way to new life and new creation.

Relocking the door behind them after they left, I felt a pang of longing for the painting that was now under the buyer's arm. It always happened that way...the sadness, even though I was also very pleased that others could enjoy my work.

It had been a long morning, and I was due for a lunch break. Linguini, and perhaps some stir-fried dumplings in my apartment above the gallery. But first, I needed to check on my pieces—the latest, generous contributors to my artwork.

I took the key from my desk, unlocked the steel door by the freezer, pulled back the deadbolt at the top and bottom, and headed down the steep, concrete stairs into the basement.

There they both were, still tied to their chairs, staring at me over the cloth covering their mouths. I'd rather not gag them, but I had no other choice. They should have been free to talk to each other, to bond, but I didn't trust the sound-proofing. I'd pasted some black foam to the back of the door and on the ceiling and walls, but I still couldn't be sure it would block the sound as much as I wanted.

Better to stay safe now that I was this far ahead. Better to keep them silent.

"Hnn. Hnnnn."

Kati tried to speak as soon as she saw me. She shook in her chair, struggling against the ropes binding her. Her fore-head was creased, and her cheeks were red. That angry look didn't become anyone. So unattractive.

And she was such an attractive woman, a mixture of a young Sophia Loren and Audrey Hepburn in their prime. Like a burnt auburn that still showed traces of the reds and yellows from which it had been mixed. Such a rare tone.

She didn't understand. That was the problem. She couldn't really. She hadn't seen what I was doing. From her position, she couldn't fathom what an honor it was just to be involved, how her contribution to humanity would be one of the most selfless acts of love anyone would ever make.

That she would die not knowing how much she had given would only make her generosity even more beautiful.

I took a granola bar from the shelf, pulled down her gag, and pushed it into her mouth. She was probably hungry. That had to be why she was so angry.

She stared at me as she bit into the bar. Was that a look of gratitude? I thought it was until she spat the grains at my face and told me to…well, I wouldn't repeat what she said. The language was not beautiful, not full of peace and love. Quite the opposite.

I wiped my face and filled a bottle of water from the sink in the corner. Perhaps she was thirsty.

She spat the water back at me too. "You monster. You're evil. How could you? Look at him. How could you do that to an old man? Look!"

That was another problem. She had been quiet and calm until I'd brought her company. She was frightened, of course. I couldn't blame her for that. She'd begged to be untied, pleaded with me to let her go, promised not to tell anyone. But there had been no anger and no hostility.

She changed after I carried in Hu. She didn't understand. She thought he was weak because he was old. He wasn't. He looked weak, and he *was* old. But his age was just part of his beauty. Hu was a pillar of strength.

I'd seen a video of him practicing Tai Chi in his garden. He moved with such grace, one leg raised, bent at the knee. One arm swept high above his head, pushing his vital force through his body to the tips of his fingers.

He'd bring so much of that energy to my project.

I tried to explain. "He's a beautiful work of art. He's not weak. He's as strong as a wave, as immovable as a mountain. He's perfect. Just like you, Kati."

Her body shook and tears brimmed. I studied her as jumbo-sized teardrops spilled down her cheeks, drenching her gag, and I knew she'd been touched by my words.

"Please." The whiney voice wasn't beautiful. "Please just let us go."

I sighed and pulled up her gag. If only she understood. It would stop so many complaints and save so many tears.

Hu's face was a little paler than when I'd brought him in the previous day. His color worried me. I hoped he wasn't sick. I wouldn't want a sickly pallor in my work. Everyone had to be vibrant, healthy, and full of life when they made their contribution.

I pulled down his gag and offered him some water. He drank and didn't spit it out, but there were tears in his eyes.

"What's the matter, Hu? Why are you so sad?"

He lifted his sad eyes to mine, brown and liquid, like silt washing at a levee. He pulled his head away from the bottle.

"How can you do this? How can you do this to *me*? We were friends. I liked you!"

A spark of frustration caught in my chest. Him too?

"You're a writer. An artist. How can you not understand that I've chosen you *because* you are such a good friend, such a good person? It is your humanity, your grace, your kindness, not just your skin, that will bring so much to my work."

Alarm flared in his eyes. "My skin?"

I patted his arm. "Don't worry. I'll incorporate you tonight, and then you'll understand, my dear, dear friend. In this world or the next, you'll understand everything."

Those big, sad, brown eyes went wide. "No. Please. Let me go. My daughter. She's waiting for me. She—"

I pulled the gag back up. Too hard. His head jerked back, bumping against the wall.

Forgive me, my friend. It was just a moment of frustration.

Why did they have to make this so difficult? Why couldn't they see the beauty that they were helping to create? Perhaps I should have expected this reaction. Death could be hard. When my dear, sweet Diana had her life taken away, I...

My fingers trembled. I had to bite my bottom lip to stop the cry that wanted to come out so very much.

I mustn't go there. I mustn't let those ugly notions in.

I pushed off the thought, refocusing. *Think about the work, its meaning, its message.*

The melancholy fell away, and my heart sang with renewed purpose. I would add Hu next. His eyes were wearing me down. I'd work on him this afternoon.

First, lunch. Then I would get to work.

5

Stella stood next to Ander at the entrance to Patty's Pub and Grill at Berthar Lake. The place was mostly empty at noon on a Saturday. Only a handful of couples were nursing their beers, flipping through their phones, and chatting over burgers and fries.

Stella assumed the place looked very different after night fell. It wasn't hard to imagine each table full, music blaring, and glasses raised while laughter shook the ceiling. She could picture Darlene and Tiffany enjoying a girls' night out. The thought even made Stella fancy one herself. She'd enjoyed the drink she'd had with Mac the previous week.

Could drinks with a colleague become routine? Could she build any deep friendships in this new job? The thought gave her both a chill and a warmth somewhere inside her belly. Who knew where such attachments might lead? Stella only knew how much they hurt when they ended.

She needed to focus. She needed to solve this case so she could find out who Matthew Johnson was. Mac had really outdone herself with that chilling nugget of information. Stella certainly owed her a drink for that.

Ander nodded toward a server who was just leaving the bar, two giant plates and two tall glasses of beer balanced on a tray. She was slim and comfortably dressed in leggings and a bar t-shirt, her blond hair pulled back into a neat ponytail. "Let's start with her."

Fine by Stella. The woman looked as good a place to begin as any.

Ander was leaning against the bar when the server finished her rounds. She sized him up and smiled, interest lighting her eyes.

Stella couldn't blame the woman. Ander was tall and well built. His blond curls fell in ringlets just above his shirt collar, which was as far as the FBI would allow him to grow it.

Mac had called him "Thor" the night they'd shared a drink, and Stella hadn't been able to stop laughing for almost five minutes straight. He was something of a Scandinavian god, she agreed. Just give him a cloak and a hammer, and he'd be saving the world from alien invasions.

The server wasn't the first woman Stella had seen turn red when she spoke to him. She slid her tray onto the bar and pushed a lock of hair into her ponytail. "Hey there. What can I get you?"

Ander pulled out his ID. "Answers. I'm Special Agent Ander Bennett, and this is Special Agent Stella Knox. Can you tell me who was working here last Saturday night?"

The server's face fell. She picked the tray back up and tucked it under her arm. "Yeah, that was me. And I've already answered all the cops' questions. Like I said, I didn't see nothing, didn't notice nothing. And the security cameras here…" She pointed to a camera hanging from the ceiling near the entrance. It looked old enough to require film. "They're just for show."

"Listen, I get it." Stella glanced at the server's name badge.

"We don't want to take up too much of your time, Becky. We know you're busy. That's why we came now when the place is quiet. We just need to learn as much as we can about the night those two women went missing."

Ander shot her a winning smile. "Please. You'll be doing me a big favor."

Good lord.

Stella wanted to roll her eyes as Becky bit her bottom lip and shifted her weight closer to Ander. Her fellow agent's curls and toothy grin sure did their job. Becky rested an arm against the bar next to Ander's and gazed at him through mascara-caked eyelashes. "What do you need to know?"

"How about your last name?"

Becky practically preened. "Long. Do you need my digits too?"

"Please."

Stella jotted down the number as Becky rattled it off, hoping to all that's holy that she'd never acted this desperate in front of a man.

Ander removed his phone from his pocket and showed her a picture of Tiffany and Darlene. These weren't the images they'd seen at the briefing. Ander had pulled them off Tiffany's social media site on the way over. They showed the two women sitting on a porch at sunset, two glasses of wine on a table in front of them.

"Do you remember seeing these women in here last Saturday night?"

Becky placed her hand over the back of Ander's and tilted the phone toward her. "Yeah, I remember them. Sat by the wall over there." She pointed with her chin toward a table for two that stood under a stringless electric guitar hanging on the wall. "I served them. They were living it up, if I remember right." Her hand lingered on Ander's for a few seconds.

Stella bit back a smile at the woman's audacity. "Do you remember what you served them?"

"Oh yeah, hun." Becky leaned forward on the bar, pressing her breasts against the wood. Stella kept her gaze straight at Becky's face rather than her "assets." Ander's head, however, seemed to shift more than normal.

The server smiled. "They were having a wild time. Started with a couple of large margaritas and a jumbo plate of nachos. Followed that up with a pitcher of margaritas. They didn't eat much of the nachos. Wasn't much left in the pitcher, though."

"How long were they here?"

Becky barely glanced at Stella as she answered her question. "Oh, I don't know. A couple of hours, maybe. It was a busy night, and they were having a good time." Gaze focused on Ander, her voice dropped to a smokey octave. "Know what I mean?"

Ander flashed a grin. "Not entirely. What does a good time mean to you?"

Stella stopped herself from kicking Ander. Barely.

"Well, to them, it meant laughing a lot and loudly. Joining in on the choruses with some of the singing. No voice for it, but that never stopped anyone in here."

When she batted her lashes, Stella almost laughed. *Does that really work on men?*

Apparently so, because Ander seemed riveted by the woman.

"What does it mean to me, Special Agent Ander Bennett?" She sidled even closer. "Well, I'd want some special company to feel that I'd really lived up the night."

Stella exhaled slowly. Patience was necessary. Also, nachos. Her stomach growled. "Can you get us some nachos and a couple of bottled waters, please?"

Both Ander and Becky looked startled, but the server

recovered quickly. "Sure thing, hun. Just a sec."

"Nachos?"

Stella patted her belly. "I'm hungry, and I thought I should eat something before your flirting made me lose my appetite."

Ander laughed. "Gotta work with what you've got, Knox. Didn't you learn that in the PD?"

"Yeah, Bennett. Brains. I work with those."

He was still grinning when Becky returned a few minutes later. Either the service in this place was good, or the food had been sitting out a while. Inspecting the plate, she decided on the former.

"Did anyone bother Tiffany and Darlene?" Ander asked. "Did they talk to anyone?"

"Not as far as I could tell, hun." Becky resumed her bust-enhancing pose. "They just had a good time, the pair of them. And it was mostly regulars here that night. They're all good people. Just come round for a few drinks. Maybe there were a few new faces here, but no one strange if that's what you mean."

"So, no one stood out in particular? No one caught your eye?" Stella popped a tortilla chip laden with queso, jalapeños, carnitas, and tomatoes into her mouth. The chips were a little stale but, otherwise, she perked up as she crunched down.

For some, her eating while interviewing a potential witness might come across as unprofessional, but she'd learned that doing something so human during times like this lowered the witness's guard, making it easier to question them. Plus, she was really hungry.

Becky shook her head. "No. There was a group of young guys. They spent most of the night playing darts. I don't think they spoke to anyone else. There was a couple who looked a bit too dressed up for this place, if you know what I mean. Like they'd made a bad choice for an anniversary dinner. And there was some older guy sitting by himself in the corner. Drank coffee and just did a crossword puzzle."

Ander frowned. "Is that usual?"

She wagged a hand in a so-so gesture. "We get them sometimes. Guys who live alone. Just want to be around people on a Saturday night. He was nice, this guy. Friendly, you know?"

"How so?"

"Getting jealous there, big guy? He was just polite, chatty. Full of compliments but without being creepy. I kinda felt sorry for him. Gave him a free plate of nachos." When Becky patted Ander's forearm, Stella covered her amusement with another nacho.

Then it hit her, and she swallowed quickly. "A free plate of these?" Waitstaff didn't often give free food to customers, not unless there was something special or unusual about them.

"Yeah. It seemed to make him happy."

"Where did you say he was sitting?"

Becky indicated an empty table in the corner. It wasn't far from where she'd told them Darlene and Tiffany had sat. "He was sitting over there."

Abandoning her food, Stella pulled out her notepad. "Can you describe him?"

Becky lifted a finger in the direction of a couple who was calling for their check. "He was late fifties? Early sixties? I don't know. Graying, brown hair. Kinda wild and frizzy and overgrown. Medium build. Unmarried. Listen, I gotta get back to work."

"How did you know he wasn't married?" That seemed like an odd thing for Becky to add to the man's description. "Did he tell you or wasn't he wearing a ring?"

Becky's cheeks pinkened. "He was wearing a ring, but he

told me his wife had died a few years ago. I felt sorry for him."

Interesting. Or was it? Was it normal for an older widower to charm a pretty woman into noticing his marital status and giving him free food?

Must be one charming dude.

"Don't suppose you got his name?"

"Didn't ask, and he didn't offer. Not sure when he left either. I took a quick smoke break, so I was in the back for a few minutes. He was gone before I returned. Actually, both he and the two women were gone when I got back."

Stella pushed the nachos away. "They skipped without paying the bill?"

"No." Becky glanced at the area where Tiffany and Darlene had been seated, as if hoping the visual cue would jog her memory. "They left a hundred on the table. The man left a twenty, which was way more than the cost of the coffee."

"They left together?"

Becky shrugged. "I was in the back, remember, so I didn't actually see any of them leave. Just grabbed the cash off both tables and rang them out."

"Think you'd recognize him again?" Stella mentally crossed her fingers. "Pick him out of a lineup? Describe him to a sketch artist?"

"I dunno." Becky held up a hand and took a step back. "Look, it's pretty dark in here at night. Boss likes it that way. For the mood, you know? And so people can't see what they're eating."

Stella eyeballed her plate, questioning her life choices.

While her stomach roiled, Ander picked up the line of questioning, flashing the server another beaming smile. "Think you could try?"

Becky practically melted back into the bar. "Maybe."

Stella wanted to gag. Wiping her fingers off with a napkin, she pulled a card from her pocket and hopped off the barstool. "We'll be in touch to schedule time with a sketch artist."

Becky shoved the card into her apron without looking at it, her gaze fixed on Ander. "What about you, big guy? I don't get your number?"

As if he were a magician, a card appeared in Ander's hand. "If you think of anything, big or small, that might be helpful in this investigation, please let us know."

Becky gazed at the card for a full ten seconds before slipping it into her pocket and giving him a saucy wink. "Sure will." Sighing, she ripped a page from her order pad and headed over to the couple, who were now waving frantically.

Tossing a twenty on the bar to cover the ten-dollar nachos, Stella snagged her water and headed outside. She'd drained half the bottle by the time Ander caught up. "So, what do you think?"

Ander wrinkled his nose. "If she calls, I think I'll tell her I'm washing my hair."

Stella managed not to laugh, but just barely. "Yeah, I can see how that would keep you busy. But it's not what I meant. A lone guy. In a bar on a Saturday night. Charming enough to impress a waitress he'd never met before. She says no one stood out, but that sounds like someone standing out to me."

"Maybe. Could still be nothing, though."

"Yeah." Stella took a deep breath. "But it's...whoa."

In a crack next to the bar's front step was a small pile of white flowers held down by a river rock.

Ander was on them in a second. Pulling out his phone, he took several pictures before donning a latex glove and placing the flowers and rock into an evidence bag.

Holding the bag up to the light, he glanced at Stella. "Or it could be something."

6

"There it is."

Hagen released a long breath of air as Chloe pulled to a stop, hitting the brakes hard enough to propel him into the windshield if his seat belt hadn't locked him down tight. When Chloe drove her black Dodge Durango, Hagen tried to spend as little time in the vehicle as possible.

Catching his breath and releasing his grip on the handle, he covered his distress by examining the Marsh family's home. The place reminded him of the house he'd grown up in. It was just a simple, one-story ranch, but the lot was large enough to accommodate two houses. The lawn was neatly trimmed, and the front porch spanned the length of the house, the cane sofa and swinging wicker seat as pristine looking as the house's white façade.

There was money here. And comfort. And now, pain.

Chloe was already halfway to the door, her heavy boots and black t-shirt as out of place as a basketball uniform at a bankers' convention. Hagen caught up just as the door opened.

Carolynne Marsh was almost a head taller than Chloe.

Her fair hair had mostly faded to gray and fell to her shoulders in a largely unbrushed mess. Her cheeks were puffy and red, and dark mounds had grown under her eyes. Hagen didn't need to ask if he and Chloe were in the right place.

They showed Mrs. Marsh their IDs.

The distraught mother peered over Chloe's head toward the SUV. "Have you found my Kati?" Her face fell when it became clear that Kati wasn't in the back seat, waiting to spring out and surprise her mother.

"Not yet." Chloe slipped her ID back into her cargo pants. "Do you mind if we come in, Mrs. Marsh? We'd just like to ask you a few questions."

Carolynne pressed a tissue under her nose and led Hagen and Chloe through a tidy living room with white carpet as deep as the soles of Hagen's shoes. In the kitchen, Harry Marsh sat at the island. His phone was in his hand, his glasses perched on the end of his nose, and his short, gray hair stood up at one side as though he'd spent the morning with his head in his hands.

Carolynne showed them to seats next to her husband. "They're from the FBI, honey. But they haven't found her yet."

Harry glanced from Hagen to Chloe and back again. He lowered his phone onto the counter and cupped a fist in his hand. "Then what are you doing here? She's not hiding in the house. Shouldn't you be out there looking for her?"

As if her husband's anger fueled her own, Carolynne leaned forward, her eyes sharp as drills. "What does it mean that the FBI is involved? Don't they only call you if things are really...?" A tear fell, and she swiped it away. "What aren't you telling us?"

Hagen kept his expression calm, caring, professionally neutral. "Mrs. Marsh, it means that both the sheriff's department and we are taking your daughter's disappearance very seriously, and we have teams of people looking for her now. Special Agent Foster and I are here to ask questions that may help narrow down the search."

"Now, look. I don't—"

Harry placed a hand on his wife's arm. At her husband's touch, her mouth snapped shut and she lowered her gaze. Harry directed his focus at Hagen, ignoring Chloe. "Go ahead. Ask what you want."

Clearly not appreciating being ignored, Chloe took the lead. "In the days before Kati's disappearance, did she seem agitated at all? Did you have any arguments? Any signs of depression? Any issues with friends or family?"

Carolynne planted both fists on the marble countertop. "Young lady, I don't know what you—"

"We have to ask." Hagen opened a clean page in his notebook. "We need to rule out the possibility that she's just gone off for a few days by herself."

The woman bristled. "She would never do anything like that. She—"

Harry rubbed his wife's arm and tapped the back of her hand. Once again, Carolynne fell silent. "Everything was fine with Kati. And she would never go away without telling us."

Carolynne snorted. "And she'd certainly tell that Brodie. I can't imagine her going off without telling *him*."

"More's the pity." Harry returned to cupping his fist again, gripping it until his knuckles turned white. "She has a boyfriend. Brodie Stanley. I hope the FBI has people checking *him* out. That's where you should be looking. Not wasting your time with us."

As Hagen made a note of the name, Carolynne jabbed a finger on the island in front of her husband. "Nasty piece of work. Didn't I tell you, Harry? I told you he wasn't right for her. Didn't I say?"

Harry pressed the heels of his hands into his eyes. "I

know, dear. You're right. I agree with you completely. He's not right for her at all."

"No, he's not. Not our sort." Carolynne's nostrils flared, one side of her lips curling up in contempt. "What sort of friends would a man like that have? Who on earth would she have been mixing with?"

Chloe's gaze was intent on Kati's mother. "What's wrong with her boyfriend?"

"He just…he just isn't right." Carolynne drew her back straight. "He's not the right kind of man for our daughter."

The muscles in Chloe's jaw tensed as she wrote something in her notebook. Hagen wondered what she was writing. It wasn't likely to be a positive impression of this couple. Something was off here. What did they have against Brodie Stanley?

He and Chloe would have to find out. In the meantime, he wanted to move the conversation on, get whatever he could out of the people in front of him.

"We'll take a look at Mr. Stanley. Anything else? Did she mention anything that made her worried? Anyone suspicious hanging around her apartment? Or at work?"

"No, nothing like that." Harry set his jaw. When he spoke again, it was as though he were pushing out each word individually, as though he'd much rather say nothing at all. "Everything has been fine. She's been doing great since she left college. She has a good job. We were a little worried about that, weren't we, dear?" He looked at his wife, who nodded enthusiastically. "But she's on a good career track now. We helped find her a great little apartment."

"We always try to help our children." Carolynne lifted her chin. Clearly, this was a point of pride. "Always. Her little sister too. We try to guide our girls onto the wisest path. Do you two have kids?"

Hagen shook his head. Chloe ignored the question.

"Well, if you had kids, you'd know what I mean." Carolynn resembled a teacher lecturing her classroom more than a worried mother. "It's not easy. It's not, is it, Harry?"

Harry reached for his wife's hand again. "It certainly is not. I just about talked myself blue in the face persuading Kati to study accounting instead of that go-nowhere path she wanted." He snorted. "History of art? Well, what are you going to do with that? That's a hobby, that is. Won't give you a career. She's certainly grateful now, though. Making good money. Soon as Lanie gets back, we'll have the same talk with her."

"How old is Lanie?" Chloe held her pen over her notebook.

When Harry hesitated to answer, Carolynn rolled her eyes. "She's twenty."

"Is she here? I'd like to speak to her. Sisters sometimes tell each other things they don't tell their parents."

Hagen tried not to smile. Chloe was on the right track. He also had a feeling those sisters would tell each other a lot that they wouldn't tell their parents.

Contempt lifted Carolynne's lip again. "Well, you'll have to call Nicaragua and hope she can get reception. That's where she is, out in the jungle somewhere, on some humanitarian mission or something. Like we don't have enough problems that need fixing right here. Half the country's going to the dogs, and she has to fly to Nicaragua to feel good about herself?"

Damn. Would nothing these girls did make their parents happy?

Hagen made a note. "Okay, thanks. I doubt we'll need her, but I'm sure we can track her down if we do."

If the poor girl wanted to be found. She'd probably tried to get as far away from her parents as possible.

When the doorbell rang, Harry was off his barstool and striding toward the door before the chimes finished ringing.

Hagen glanced at Chloe. She shook her head. If something had happened, if Kati had turned up, they would have been informed first.

"Oh, it's you." Harry's voice was a mixture of disappointment and anger.

Kati's father returned to the kitchen trailed by a handsome, young man with dreadlocks that reached his shoulders.

With an icy sharpness in his stomach, Hagen knew what the Marshes had against their daughter's boyfriend. And judging by the low grinding coming from Chloe's teeth, so did she.

These damn people were racist assholes.

While Hagen seethed over this knowledge, Harry addressed his wife, turning his back on the young man. "Says he wanted to check up on us. Make sure we're okay."

Carolynne folded her arms, her nostrils flaring wide. "Does he? Well, Agents. Looks like Brodie saved you a trip. You said you wanted to speak to him. Here he is."

The young man ignored the woman and focused on Hagen and Chloe. "You two with the FBI?"

"Yeah." Introducing them both, Hagen showed Brodie his ID. Chloe did the same.

Brodie examined each badge carefully before handing them back. "I'm glad you're here. Can we talk?" He glanced at the Marshes. "In private."

The kid didn't need to ask twice.

"Of course." Hagen and Chloe slid off their stools.

"Now, just one minute." Harry was on his feet as well. "Whatever he's got to say, he can say in front of us. This concerns our daughter."

Chloe touched Hagen's elbow. "I'll see you out on the porch. Let's go." She left the room, Brodie trailing behind.

Hagen swallowed a curse. It was nice of Chloe to leave him alone with these two. Real nice. But her choice was probably wise. She was less capable of hiding her feelings than he was and much more likely to explode.

"We need to speak to him in private. If he tells us anything we think you need to know, we'll inform you."

Without giving the couple a chance to argue, Hagen followed Chloe out onto the front porch. A silver Nissan Titan idled in the driveway. The broad head of a black and brown Rottweiler stuck out an open window, pink tongue on display.

That must be Juno. Good. Glad the dog was with this young man instead of the hate-filled people inside.

"Sorry for interrupting you guys in there." Brodie's dark eyes housed so much pain it was hard for Hagen to look into them for too long. "I just thought you should know something about the family, is all."

Chloe leaned against a post. "I think we've got them figured out."

Brodie's straight, white teeth were brilliant against his dark skin, but the smile didn't last. "Yeah. They don't do much to hide it, do they? Most people round here, they're not like that. This whole area's changed over the last decade or so, and just about everyone else has been fine about those changes. This is a good place to live. It's just Mr. and Mrs. Marsh. Everyone knows about them. You can ask the neighbors. They're all sick to death of them and their dumbass ideas."

Sympathy was a living thing in Hagen's chest. "Just your luck to date *their* daughter."

Brodie took the statement seriously. "It is. I feel lucky every day. Kati is beautiful and kind and caring and strong.

Heck, I don't know where it all came from because it certainly didn't come from them. Her sister's the same. That's why she headed out to the wilds of Nicaragua. I'll be surprised if she ever comes back. She wanted to get as far away as possible."

"I can understand that," Chloe said quietly. "How long have you guys been together?"

"About three years. We met in college. She was studying accounting, and I was in the engineering program. We had a math class together. She was struggling, and I helped her out a bit, and..." Brodie shrugged.

Damn. Hagen felt for the guy while detesting Kati's parents more by the second. "So, for three years, they've seen their daughter date a Black guy?"

"And hated every minute. They argued all the time. I think that was why Kati got that dog. She wanted something that just loved her unconditionally." Brodie's smile lasted a bit longer this time. "Juno's a big softie. Not much of a guard dog, though. Man, I just hope Kati isn't suffering because someone hates her parents."

Something moved out of the corner of Hagen's eye. The window next to the door was open an inch. Pressed up against the glass, hidden behind the linen drapes, was the face of Carolynne Marsh.

"You've got to be kidding me." Looking like her head was about to pop off, Chloe motioned for Brodie to follow her off the porch.

Hagen waved to Carolynne, tempted to add the bird. "If you could just give us a little privacy, ma'am. If we need any more information, we'll come back in."

Carolynne's face turned bright red before the curtain fell and she disappeared into the house.

This line of questioning for both the Marshes and Brodie was only just beginning. Hagen and Chloe still needed to establish their alibis and dig through the skeletons in their closets.

Hagen and the team couldn't get tunnel vision. Just because Kati Marsh went missing at the same time two bodies were found, didn't mean the person who killed those women took her.

Worldwide, a woman was killed by a family member or intimate partner every eleven minutes. The two people in that house, or even the nice young man standing next to Chloe, couldn't be overlooked as potential suspects.

Yeah...they still had a lot of questions to ask.

Hagen followed them down the driveway toward the car as Brodie's cryptic statement rolled over in his mind.

"Man, I just hope Kati isn't suffering because someone hates her parents."

Hagen hoped Kati wasn't suffering for her parents' sins too.

He hoped she wasn't suffering at all.

7

"I'm strong. I'm powerful. I'm confident. I can do anything."

Stella stood at the end of the trail in Morville Pond Park and imagined she was a twenty-three-year-old woman who had just finished a workout. A run always filled Stella with energy. The tired, aching muscles would come later, but whenever she finished a five-mile run, she was on top of the world. Surely Kati Marsh would have felt the same way.

"Add a Rottweiler to your side. How do you feel then?"

Ander stood alongside her, hands buried in his pockets. Kati's car was a dozen yards away, still parked in the lot and surrounded by police tape. One search dog combed through the undergrowth nearby, while a second was farther up the trail. So far...nothing.

Stella rested her hands on her hips with feet apart. "I'd feel damn near invincible. So, what could make me lower my guard? How could someone kidnap me?"

"Maybe that was the problem." Ander scanned the edge of the woods. "Maybe she was too confident. Maybe she got complacent and thought she could take on anyone, especially with a Rottweiler by her side."

Stella stepped closer to the edge of the lot, stopping just before the land dropped into a steep descent to the tree line. There was nothing in the bushes lining the parking lot. If there had been, forensics would have found it already. They had to be overlooking something. Some clue that Kati's attacker left behind.

"I don't think so. Look." She gestured to the cement covering the parking lot. "What do you see?"

Ander frowned. "Nothing."

"Exactly. You come off a run, full of energy, endorphins pumping. You get attacked by a big guy, maybe two. You take off, or you put up a fight. You might not win, but you're not going to do nothing, not with all that adrenaline already running through you. There's no sign of a struggle here. No broken branches. No blood. Nothing. It doesn't make sense." She held up a finger. "And no fur off Juno either."

"You're thinking it was someone she knew."

"Maybe." Stella strolled away from the trail, following the route Kati would have taken back to her car.

Ander followed her. "Or maybe she was taken by someone who looked safe. An old person. A woman. Maybe even a kid."

"That's possible, if a woman or a kid were working with someone else. Doesn't happen often, though."

Who else would take a woman off her guard? What kind of stranger would a woman be willing to speak to in a secluded area? Who could charm her enough to do that?

Stella stopped walking and chewed her bottom lip. Hadn't they just heard about someone like that? "What about an older guy who comes off super friendly and harmless? Maybe even a bit lonely. Someone charismatic enough to get a waitress half his age to give him free nachos?"

Ander blew out his cheeks. "I see what you're thinking. Yeah, that's an option, I guess. He sees her out here. He looks so innocent. They spark up a friendly conversation, and... whammo. With a single blow, he knocks her out...and gets eaten by a Rottweiler."

Nuts. Ander was right. The dog. How did the attacker get past Kati's big-ass dog?

"Maybe the dog isn't as tough as she looks. I've known pit bulls that would have sold their owners to human traffickers for a tummy rub."

Ander linked his hands on top of his head. "But would the attacker have known that? He sees a woman with a dog that looks like the spawn of Satan. Is he really going to risk messing with that?"

"Hmm. Fair point."

"Even if the attacker had been charming enough to lower Kati's guard, his sweet manner wouldn't have worked on the dog, especially once the attack started. So, how did the attacker fool Kati and deal with the threat of the dog?"

Stella closed her eyes again and tried to imagine the scene. Kati coming back from her run, sweaty, tired, but pumped. That big dog bouncing at her side. Some old dude asks her for help, and...

And what?

The answer had to be here. It had to be.

Stella opened her eyes and stood directly in front of Ander. He was almost a foot taller, and the contour of his biceps was visible under the sleeves of his shirt. "Imagine you want to attack me. You're going to knock me out and drag me away. But I've got a big-ass dog right here. Its head comes up to my hip, and its got teeth like a dragon. What are you going to do?"

"What am I going to do?" Hagen scoffed. "I'm going to check myself into a psych ward."

Stella lowered her head and laughed. Ander's answer was reassuring, even if it wasn't very helpful.

"Okay. That's…good to know. But now, imagine you've escaped from the psych ward, and you're looking for your next victim before they catch you and toss you back in. You see me. You know you look harmless and can turn on some charm. But you also believe that as soon as you make a move, the dog will tear you to bits. How do you get rid of the dog?"

Ander took a deep breath. "Maybe we should ask Hagen. He's the dog guy."

"Hagen's not here. C'mon, Ander. You never had a dog?"

Ander rocked on his heels. "Yeah, we got one for Murphy once. A rescue pup. He took it with him when my ex left."

Stella winced. She'd just wanted to get Ander thinking about Kati's dog, not bring up personal memories. "So, you know dogs. What makes a dog leave its owner?"

"It depends on the dog, right? Some dogs will run off at the first sight of a squirrel. Others will chase any ball they see. Some will only move for food, and it had better be a piece of steak, rare. A well-trained dog wouldn't even do that." Ander pointed in the direction of a search dog sniffing its way across a grass verge. "Try to send a dog like that away, and it will just pull up a chair and laugh."

"Yeah, but according to what we've learned so far, Kati's dog wasn't a police dog. She was less than a year old and used to chasing sticks and running after balls."

Stella walked back to the edge of the trail. Maybe the dog was a big coward and ran away as soon as the attack started? Or maybe Kati sent her away so the attacker wouldn't hurt her? Neither of those options seemed very likely, though. An attack severe enough to have triggered either of those responses would surely have left traces.

But what if the attack wasn't spontaneous? What if it was

planned? Suppose the attacker came prepared with some-thing to distract the dog. He wouldn't need to hurt her. He'd just need to get the dog away from the girl, far enough away to do whatever he wanted.

Far enough away. That was it.

Rushing over to where the hill was the steepest, she imag-ined herself throwing a ball or even the steak Ander had mentioned. The tree line appeared to be less than twenty yards from where she stood, but that was as the crow flies. If the ground were flat, a dog could run twenty yards or so in a few seconds.

But, if she tossed that ball from up here, the dog would need to scamper down the hill, find her prize, and then dig deep to make it back up the incline. How long would that take? Long enough to subdue a young woman?

Her gut said yes.

"They're looking in the wrong place."

Ander's eyes narrowed. "Who is?"

"The search dogs. Come on." Glad her shoes had good tread, Stella started down the hill, with Ander right behind. "What if he threw something to distract the dog? Under normal circumstances, the average person could throw a bone or ball or whatever, what, twenty or so yards?"

Ander looked at her like she was crazy. "I can throw double that."

She rolled her eyes. "Work with me here. What if our unsub threw something to distract Juno from up there, and it landed down here? By the time the dog made the round trip, I think our bad guy could have had enough time to take Kati by surprise."

Ander eyed the terrain and shrugged. "It's possible." He stuck two fingers in his mouth and whistled at the closest search team. "Bring a dog over here."

When the team arrived, the muscular German shepherd's nose still on the ground, Stella explained their theory. "Can you search a circumference of about thirty yards around the lot?"

"Absolutely." The handler gave the order, and they were off.

Stella watched them go, praying to any god who would listen that they found something that might lead them to Kati Marsh.

The beautiful dog was all business as he searched every inch of the area they'd indicated. Stella scratched her head as the shepherd moved farther into the woods. She was a terrible judge of distance, but thought they were a good twenty yards deep. Could the charming nachos-eater have thrown something this far? Would the dog have gone after it if he did? Was the nachos-eater even involved?

Maybe they were reading this all wrong. Maybe *she'd* gotten it wrong.

Dammit.

Just when Stella was about to give up hope, the dog's entire demeanor changed.

Ander saw it too. "I think he's got something."

Please don't be Kati.

Stella's stomach was in knots by the time the dog plopped onto his butt, his gaze glued to his handler. She knew different dogs were trained to alert in different ways, and she hoped the animal's behavior was a positive sign.

"Agents, I think we got something."

Heart beating hard in her chest, Stella jogged toward the handler. After pulling on a pair of gloves, Ander combed his hands through the clump of woodland phlox, his long fingers separating the stems and disturbing the blue, star-shaped flowers.

"What the—"

He stepped back, one hand still pulling back the plants.

Stella peered over his shoulder and saw exactly what had made the dog so excited.

A human finger.

8

"Let's hope this guy is easier to be around than the last pair."

Hagen grinned when Chloe slammed the car door with a little more force than necessary. They'd spent the past couple of hours conducting deeper interviews of the Marshes and Brodie Stanley and were lucky to have escaped the Marshes' home without Chloe being physically removed in handcuffs.

From the look on her face, she hadn't shaken off her distaste for the couple's bigotry and judgment quite yet. Hagen couldn't blame her. He hadn't quite shaken it off himself. Worse, after submitting themselves into their dark world of hatred, Carolynne and Harry had been of very little help in the end.

After attempting to pick apart the couple's alibis, Chloe and Hagen had asked for any records they had access to, including Kati's credit cards and bank account statements, as well as her phone records. It had been a long shot that an adult woman's parents would have those types of passwords, and neither of the Marshes did.

Brodie, however, had been a fountain of information,

providing passwords to Kati's cards and accounts, as well as the password to her phone's backup cloud. It wasn't as good as having the device itself, but it was better than nothing.

Since Kati was an adult, they'd still need to secure a warrant to officially start digging through the records, but the passwords would save them time once that warrant went through. Hagen had already given Mackenzie Drake a heads up. If anyone could find even the slightest bit of information to help them on their quest to find Kati Marsh, it was the cyber specialist.

"Can we keep the Marshes on our persons of interest list on principal?"

Hagen grinned. "I wish, but that would mean you'd need to interview them a couple more times, remember?"

The look of abject horror on his partner's face had him laughing out loud. He stifled the sound, remembering that they were standing on the sidewalk of a man who'd recently lost his wife.

Reading his mind, Chloe's expression went neutral too. "What do you think we'll find inside?"

At the rate their luck was going, Hagen wouldn't hazard a guess. "Expect tears. Lots of tears."

Chloe shot him a wry grin before pressing her finger on the doorbell. "Yeah, you guys aren't very good at controlling your emotions."

The Martinsons lived in a two-story craftsman-style home with a low-slung roof and a small, boxy front yard surrounded by a chain-link fence. The grass was overgrown, and the place appeared to be the only one on the block not littered with tricycles, rubber paddling pools, and plastic slides.

Heavy footsteps approached the door, which swung open to reveal a tall man with a wide stomach and a brown beard in need of a trim. His thinning hair was gelled straight back, and lines of pink scalp peeked out between the comb marks. The sleeves on his plaid shirt were rolled up to his elbows.

He scowled at Chloe, who was barely level with his shoulders. "Yes?"

Chloe didn't bat an eye. "Joshua Martinson?"

"Yes?" Joshua Martinson's voice had already grown sharper.

Well, there went Hagen's theory. No tears but lots of attitude. Why? They weren't out collecting souls.

"We're from the FBI." He flashed his ID and introduced them both. "We need to ask you a few questions."

"Well, it's about damn time. Don't know what the hell's been keeping you. What do I pay my taxes for, huh?"

Leaving the door open, Martinson stormed back into the living room and fell heavy into the corner of a gray sofa.

Chloe glanced at Hagen.

He replied with a single raised eyebrow and headed inside. It was days like this that made Hagen glad he carried a gun.

The house was dark, and the blinds mostly closed. The coffee table held three empty takeout boxes that leaked soy sauce and stone-hard rice. News about a demonstration in Chicago that had turned violent three nights before was blaring from the television. That station, apparently, still considered the events newsworthy.

Chloe pointed at the screen. "Can you turn that off for us, please, sir?"

Martinson jammed his hand down the side of the sofa. When he pulled it out, he was gripping a remote control. With a small pop, the screen turned black.

"Don't even know what you're doing here. You should be out there talking to Mark. That's who you should be talking to. Could have told you that days ago. Would have saved you a lot of time."

"You mean Mark Wright? Tiffany's husband?" Hagen took out his notebook. This interview wasn't going the way he'd expected at all. Either they were about to get a useful tip, or Darlene's husband was spraying shrapnel in every direction.

What the hell was making him so angry? Where were the grief and shock? Some people really did react to loss in very strange ways, but this…?

"Yeah, I mean Mark Wright. He knew what was going on. Damn near encouraged it. Wouldn't be surprised if the whole thing just turned him on, the freak."

Hagen glanced at Chloe, who seemed about as confused as he felt. If Martinson's anger disturbed her, she didn't show it. "What did he encourage?"

Martinson pushed himself to his feet and walked around the sofa to the corner of the room. "Oh, you know." He eyed Chloe from the top of her short hair to the bottom of her black boots. "*You* know. Yeah, I'm sure you do."

While Hagen was still connecting the dots, Chloe went from puzzled to intense in a second. Her eyes were fixed hard on the man across from her. Was Hagen about to get a demonstration of Chloe's famous roundhouse kick? Part of him hoped so. The other part dreaded the paperwork and Chloe's inevitable suspension.

Not that this guy didn't deserve a boot to the face, but Hagen doubted that he was worth the trouble. The way he was going, though, he might talk himself right into it.

"Do you want to fill *me* in?" Hagen took a step forward, ready to put himself between them if necessary. He wasn't sure who he was protecting more, Chloe or Martinson.

"Oh, those two. Darlene and Tiffany. Best friends forever." His voice went up a few octaves as he attempted to mimic his dead wife. "Best friends, my ass. They weren't just friends. Uh-uh. Not those two."

A large part of Hagen wanted to interrupt the rambling,

but he let the man go on. Maybe he'd work himself into a lather enough to say something useful.

"The way they were always giggling and laughing, walking arm in arm, whispering sweet nothings like they didn't have husbands." Disgust crossed Martinson's features. "Heck, Tiffany had children, not that she gave a damn. Hadn't been for her, I might have had some too. Maybe Darlene would have paid me some attention more than once a damn year."

"Are you saying that Darlene and Tiffany were a couple?" Chloe asked the words casually, but Hagen could see the fire in her gaze. They'd already dealt with a pair of racists. Were they now facing a homophobe too?

"A couple?" Martinson spat out the word. "I wouldn't call 'em that, but I knew they were in love with each other. Moonin' like a couple of lovestruck teenagers. Shame of it. Man, we should have moved out of here years ago. Used to be a good place, once. 'Til all these new folk moved in, bringing their big city ways with them. Damn moral corruption is what it is. Everywhere you look around here now."

Chloe took a step closer to Martinson. Hagen's pulse shifted up a gear, and he prepared to act if needed.

His partner's voice remained surprisingly calm and even. "Sir, my understanding is that Darlene and Tiffany were childhood friends. Is it possible that you're misreading the—"

"The hell I am!" When Martinson jabbed a finger at Chloe, Hagen mentally girded his loins. This was going south and quickly.

Chloe didn't move, though. She wouldn't unless Martinson actually touched her.

Smart girl.

"And I'll tell you something else," Martinson raged. "I'm sure that my Darlene wasn't the only one. That Tiffany probably had a whole string of lovers. Men, women, you name it.

I'll bet that's what this is all about. I bet one of them got jealous or something. Maybe Mark finally grew a pair and decided to do something about it. Hell, I wouldn't blame him if he did."

Slow him down. Show him what he's saying. Let him see what he's accusing his wife of. Once he can see how ridiculous he's being, maybe he can move from anger to acceptance.

"So, let me get this straight. You're saying that your wife, Darlene, was in love with her childhood friend, Tiffany. You're saying that Tiffany cheated on her husband with multiple lovers, including Darlene. And you think that either one of her lovers, or Tiffany's husband, murdered them in a jealous rage. Is that right?"

Martinson laid two heavy hands on the back of the sofa, glaring at Hagen. "Are you deaf? That's exactly what I'm saying. Or are you too stupid to understand? Man, no wonder this country's in the mess it is when they let idiots like you in the FBI."

A flame roared to life inside Hagen's chest, but he tamped it down to the warm but steady glow of a candle.

Anger wouldn't help him solve the murder of this man's wife and her friend, nor would it help him find a missing young woman.

He'd let Martinson spew his anger, watching him closely. Either he had turned his grief toward blame and rage, both of which would eventually burn out, or he was using anger to hide his own guilt. With that kind of temper, it was no wonder Darlene had looked for friendship and warmth outside the home. And with that kind of anger, what else was the widower capable of doing?

Hagen needed to find out.

"Your wife and Tiffany were last seen at a bar on June fifth." Chloe had reclaimed her composure too. "What were you doing while they were out?"

"I was watching the boob tube right here."

"Can anyone verify that?"

He curled a lip. "Yeah, a buddy called around eight thirty and we shot the shit."

"We'll need his number." She moved on before he could give her any more grief. "Your wife and Tiffany went to a restaurant near Berthar Lake. Was that outing a special occasion? Do you know what their plans were that night?"

Martinson glared at her. His fingers dug even deeper into the top of the sofa. "Yeah. They were on a hot damn date."

That was enough. It was clear to Hagen that they weren't going to get any further here today.

Chloe was right. Men could be pretty emotional sometimes.

Hagen tucked his notepad away. "Listen, Mr. Martinson. We can question you here, or we can take this to the station and put this interview on record. It's up to you. Here or there? What's your choice?"

Martinson's mouth worked up and down, his face growing redder by the second. "Do I need a lawyer?"

Hagen lifted a shoulder. "Do you need one? It's certainly within your rights."

And just like a balloon losing air, the bluster seeped out of the man. "No, I don't need one because I didn't do nothing to nobody."

Offering Martinson a smile he had to force onto his face, Hagen indicated a chair. "Then please have a seat and answer our questions."

On legs that seemed to be made of wood, Martinson did what he was told.

Not that it did much good.

An hour later, Hagen trudged after Chloe to her Durango, mulling over all they'd learned, which wasn't much. On the bright side, the man had promised to print out copies of the credit cards statements and bank accounts Darlene had access to. He'd also given them permission to access their cell phone records.

It wasn't much, but it was a start.

"You know, if it weren't for those white flowers on the victims' bodies, as well as on Kati Marsh's car and in Hu Zhao's kitchen, I'd be inclined to think Kati and Hu's disappearances had nothing to do with Tiffany and Darlene's murders. Flowers aside, for this pair, I'd be thinking domestic."

Chloe nodded. "That guy's the sort, all right. Certainly a lot of drama going on between the Wrights and the Martinsons."

"What do you think, though? You think he was right about his wife and Tiffany?"

Chloe glanced back at the house. "No. I think those women were nothing more than old friends who loved, trusted, and enjoyed each other's company." She unlocked the door of the SUV but paused before slipping behind the wheel. "And I think that asshole needs to spend a very long time in therapy."

9

M ark Wright's living room was small but clean. A pile of embroidered coasters sat on one corner of the coffee table. On the shelf below, near-pristine multiple copies of *Architectural Digest*, *House Beautiful*, and *Elle Decor* were stacked in a neat pile.

A dust-free bookcase ran the length of the wall, its shelves displaying silver candlestick holders, a collection of porcelain angels, and a dozen framed family portraits of Tiffany, Mark, and two small girls. In one, the redheaded children were playing on swings. In another, they posed in identical dresses.

Only two elements in the room broke the order.

The first was a wicker basket by the door with Barbies and Bratz tossed in without a care.

The second was Mark Wright himself. He sat in the armchair facing the sofa, his elbows balanced on his knees, his head held in his hands. He lifted his face and scraped his nails down his unshaven cheeks.

As sad as the man was, it was a welcome change to the attitudes of the Marshes and Joshua Martinson. For the first time that day, Chloe thought she might not be tempted to smash a person's face in.

"I'm sorry about earlier. At the station. I...I just lost it."

"That's okay." Chloe was glad to finally meet a person she didn't want to mentally murder. "We understand."

"If you could thank the sheriff for having one of his men drive me back. It was kind of him."

"Of course."

Hagen came in from the kitchen holding two cups of coffee. Wright took two coasters from the pile and placed one in front of himself and the other in front of Chloe.

"Thank you for making this." He took his mug from Hagen. "Sure you won't take one yourself?"

Hagen passed the other cup to Chloe and sat next to her on the sofa. "No, I'm good, thanks."

Chloe sipped her coffee. Instant. That explained Hagen's reluctance. He was such a snob. "Mr. Wright, can you tell me how things were at home in the weeks before Tiffany died?"

Wright appeared lost in thought for a moment. "Fine. Great. I mean, you know, as good as always."

"No big arguments? No work troubles?"

"No. Nothing special. Tiffany had just landed a new client. She is..." he swallowed hard, "she *was* an interior designer. A new project always made her excited. My work was the same as always. And the girls were..." He fumbled his mug while setting it down but steadied it with his other hand before the coffee spilled. "Oh god, the girls. They're with my mother. I still...I still don't know what to tell them."

Chloe lowered her gaze. She was sitting closest to Wright. Should she pat his arm, stroke his shoulder? Do something to let him know he wasn't alone? Someone else would probably have done that. Stella might have. Dani certainly would have. Not her.

She sipped her coffee and waited for Wright to recover.

He pulled a tissue from his pocket, blew his nose, then lifted a framed picture from the shelf next to the armchair.

"They're four and six now," Wright continued. "They're going to have their whole life without their mother. It's just not fair."

He was right. Life wasn't fair. The two girls deserved to grow up with their mother's love, her warmth, her protection. Some scumbag had taken that away.

"They won't forget, but they will be okay." Hagen's tone was surprisingly soothing. "Eventually. What about Tiffany's relationship with Darlene? They were old friends, right?"

"Oh yeah." A smile played at his lips but didn't hold. "They went way back, those two. Darlene was the maid of honor at our wedding. They were always texting each other, talking on the phone maybe four, five times a week."

Hagen nodded. "And they met up often?"

"Not as much as they used to before the girls came along. But they'd get together at least once a month. Girls' night out."

"You didn't mind?"

Wright shrugged. "No. Why should I? I shoot hoops some evenings with the guys from work. We get a beer afterward. Same thing. Keeps us both sane."

Chloe had her own line of questioning, but Hagen was doing well. He was driving Wright neatly into the area that Martinson had found so troubling. And the reaction was so different. The women's friendship didn't seem to bother Wright at all.

"When they met up, did they always go to the same place?"

"No, I don't think so. They had some bars and restaurants they liked, but I don't think there was a pattern or anything. It was more about meeting up than finding a place."

"And who knew where they were going that night?"

"Don't know." Wright pinched the bridge of his nose as if he could force names out of his brain. "Me and Joshua. I don't know if they told anyone else. No reason they would. Nothing special about that place. Or that evening."

After Hagen had asked some additional who, what, and when type of questions, Chloe put down her coffee. Her partner had been nudging nicely, but it was time to take the bull by the horns. She leaned forward and fixed her eyes on Wright. "We spoke to Darlene's husband before we came here. He isn't as relaxed about Darlene and Tiffany's relationship as you are."

"That guy." Wright fell back in his chair and dug his elbows into the corners as though he could climb into its depths and never leave. "He's such a..." He snapped his mouth shut, his teeth grinding together so hard Chloe could hear them squeak. "He and Darlene were having trouble. They'd been having trouble for a while. He thought it was because the girls were so close, like their friendship left no space for their marriage. It's a load of crap."

"He told you that?"

"Yeah. Jeez. Said he thought they were a couple, that they were madly in love and just using us for cover." Wright laughed. The sound was out of place in that house, as though someone had emptied a bag of coal onto the living room's white carpet.

Chloe held his gaze. "And what was your reaction when he told you that?"

"At first, I told him he was crazy. He was totally nuts. But he kept at it. Annoyed me after a while. Eventually, I got fed up, told him to keep his fat mouth shut or I'd shut it for him."

Hagen lifted a single eyebrow. "He's a big guy. Was that wise?"

Wright's shoulders practically touched his ears. "Probably not, but I figured he's just an insecure bully, you know. Push him back hard, and he'll fall right over. He shut up after that."

"Did Mr. Martinson ever tell Tiffany what he thought directly?"

Wright scoffed at her question. "No, but I did. She thought it was hilarious." The smile played at his lips again, lasting a bit longer this time before falling away. "I dunno, though. Joshua was getting himself worked up, but I don't think he'd ever hit Darlene. She'd have been out of that house like a rocket if he did, and he knew it. But, sometimes, he just looked like he was on the edge of doing something stupid." A haunted expression crossed his features. "I used to worry sometimes when Tiffany visited."

Chloe's breathing became shallow. "You thought seeing them together might just tip him over the edge?"

"I thought…" Wright sighed. "I don't know. He was too frightened of losing Darlene to do anything to her. I was worried he might do something to Tiffany but…who knows?"

Chloe hated to keep pressing the subject, but she needed a straight answer. "So, *you* don't believe that Tiffany and Darlene were a couple?"

His lips lifted and held this time, which transformed his otherwise serious countenance. Small dimples even appeared near the corners of his mouth. "Not a chance."

"You seem pretty certain about that."

"One hundred percent certain. That asshole's just paranoid."

Chloe nodded. The next question sat in her chest like a rock, but she had to ask it. "What about someone else? Could Tiffany have had an affair with someone other than Darlene?"

Any remnants of Wright's smile disappeared as he stared at Chloe. "Tiffany? Who with?"

"Mr. Martinson mentioned—"

"Joshua again! Jesus Christ." He leaned forward, resting his arms on his knees and interlacing his fingers so hard his knuckles turned white. "Look, Tiffany was friendly. She had a smile for everyone. She hugged her friends, and she'd touch your arm when you were talking. That sort of thing. For Joshua, that meant she was sleeping with half the city. But he's nuts. No, Tiffany was not having a damn affair." Wright lowered his head. His shoulders shook, but Chloe couldn't tell if it was from crying or holding back anger.

Chloe believed him. Mark Wright's reaction lined up with someone who loved his wife and trusted her. His assessment of Joshua Martinson was also spot-on.

Not that they wouldn't check his alibi, as well as phone and credit card records. They'd check every damn thing, but she'd put money on Mark Wright being innocent. She hadn't forgotten about his outburst at the sheriff's office, though. Extreme behavior was something to pay attention to, even if it was borne out of grief.

Wright lifted his head. "I'm sorry, I didn't mean to…it's just…it's all been so hard."

"I understand. Just a few more questions…"

Chloe was glad when Wright readily agreed to provide copies of bank and credit card records. He also provided the password to access their cell phone account, but he didn't know his wife's password to her cloud storage. It was a good start.

After confirming that he had indeed taken his daughters to a movie the evening of his wife's disappearance, they had checked off most of the boxes of what they needed to know from Mark Wright.

Hagen nudged Chloe and tilted his head toward the door before standing. He was right. They had enough for now.

She stuck out a hand. "Thank you for your time, and,

again, we're sorry for your loss. We'll be in touch if we have any more questions." She placed her card on the table.

Wright led them out and closed the door without a goodbye.

Once they climbed into the Durango, Hagen scrubbed his face with his hands. "What do you think?"

She gave herself time to consider the question. "I'm not sure. At one point today, I wondered if our unsub was targeting victims who lived with horrible people. Joshua Martinson is one of the most unpleasant human beings I've ever met. The Marshes are close seconds. Mark Wright was an asshole earlier but seems to be the opposite now."

Hagen leaned closer to the AC vent. "Just because Mark Wright was friendly and kind doesn't make him innocent."

"Hmm." Chloe chewed the inside of her cheek. A kind killer. The idea rang true. And chilled her more than expected.

As they drove back to the sheriff's office, neither spoke. Chloe's thoughts were with Tiffany and Darlene. The two women had built a friendship, trusted each other, and enjoyed each other's company. And some man had found their closeness objectionable.

Same old story. The angry knot in her gut expanded.

To be fair, Chloe didn't know whether Tiffany and Darlene were in love. It was possible. But…she didn't think so. Did it matter to the case? That was the question.

The women's friendship reminded Chloe of her relationship with Bridget. She knew what it was like to love a woman and be loved back, whether out of pure friendship or as a married couple. And she also knew how some people would always consider that love wrong. Evil, even.

Shaking off that depressing thought, her mind wandered to a very different kind of evil casting a shadow over this town.

A kind killer.

A thoughtful killer.

An artistic killer who left flowers to cover his victims' mutilations.

Chloe shivered.

She was once told that the devil had two faces, and the face she needed to be most concerned with was the one that smiled.

10

Stella was sweating by the time she and Ander returned to the Morville County Sheriff's Department. They were the last to arrive, but barely since Hagen and Chloe were just finding their seats. Slade and Sheriff Lansing were already at the front of the room, waiting to begin.

Sheriff Lansing took the lead. "Now that we're all here, let's see what we've got. Forensics has taken the flowers that were found on the bodies and various locations. They're running tests. They're examining for fingerprints on the leaves and stems as well. But, as we heard, these daisies are everywhere round here this time of year."

Ander reached into his briefcase and pulled out a small evidence bag. "You should send these off too."

Sheriff Lansing took the bag and examined its contents. The flowers were crumpled, the edges of the white petals already starting to brown. "Where's this from?"

Ander hooked a thumb toward Stella. "She spotted them outside the bar where Darlene and Tiffany were last seen."

Sheriff Lansing smoothed the outside of the bag with his thumb. "You're sure this is the same kind of flower?"

"They're shriveled and brown from being outside for a week, but I think so. The lab will be able to tell with certainty."

The sheriff studied the petals, turning the bag over in his hand and shaking it twice to free contents that had stuck together. Eventually, he gave a short grunt and laid the bag on the table behind him.

What the hell? The flowers were the connection between the cases. The sheriff shouldn't be so quick to dismiss their lead.

Still looking unimpressed, Lansing folded his arms across his chest. "What else did we get at the bar?"

Stella flipped to her notes. "We spoke to Becky Long, the server on duty the night Darlene and Tiffany went missing. According to Ms. Long, they were drinking, eating, having a good time. They—"

"Yeah, we know they were there that night."

"Right." Stella swallowed, keeping her cool. The sheriff didn't have to be an asshole. "But at a table near them was an older gentleman. He was by himself, just doing a crossword puzzle and drinking coffee."

"And?"

"And...he was charming." Stella mentally groaned at how lame that sounded. "The server took a liking to him and ended up giving him free food."

Slade frowned. "I don't understand. You got suspicious because a guy in a bar got free food? There's a big gap between sponging a snack and dismembering two women."

Words...please come to me.

"Yeah. Of course. What I meant was that this guy was friendly, unassuming, and charming enough for a busy server to want to make him feel wanted and comfortable. And that's *exactly* the sort of person who would have knocked Kati Marsh off her guard at Morville Pond Park. There were no signs of a struggle there, so it had to be someone she knew or someone who looked harmless enough not to arouse suspicion."

Ander nodded. "Like a lonely old man who gets free nachos from a barroom waitress on a Saturday night."

Stella appreciated Ander's support, but she needed to be the one who connected the dots for the team. "At the same time Tiffany and Darlene were there, we've got a charming, unassuming man and a small pile of Shasta daisies stuck in a crack near the doorway."

Sheriff Lansing held his gaze on Stella.

She stared back.

"Okay." His eyes narrowed. "That's a *possibility*."

It was the best she could ask for, considering how weak her theory was.

Sheriff Lansing grabbed the pile of sticky notes from the shelf at the bottom of the murder board. He scrawled the words *old man*, *lonely*, *friendly*, and *charming* in thick, black letters and added them to the edges of the board. He stepped back to admire his work.

"Though I gotta say there are a lot of lonely, friendly, charming, old men in this town. Was hoping I'd achieve the last three of those descriptors myself one day."

Ander chuckled.

Stella only gave half a smile. "Old" and "lonely" seemed to dominate the board. She had a long way to go before she was old, but being alone was already a part of her, and, as far as she could see, it would stay a part of her for a while.

In the end, we're all alone.

Chloe broke her thoughts. "What about the dog? A friendly old man could charm Kati, and he could probably charm a dog, too, but once the attack started? Charm wouldn't cut it."

Ander cast his eyes toward Stella. "It was your idea. You found it."

The image of what they had found in the bushes filled her vision, turning her stomach, so she forced it away. "Yeah, we were wondering about the dog too. We couldn't understand why it didn't attack when the assault began. We think we found the answer."

The entire group leaned forward in interest, but Hagen was the first to speak. "What did you find?"

"A...finger. It appeared to have been gnawed on, and the bone was exposed, but it was definitely a finger and definitely human. Forensics has it. The pictures are on their way over."

"Jesus." Sheriff Lansing ran a hand down his left cheek. "Do they know whose it is?"

Stella shook her head. "Not yet, but they believe enough of the tip is intact to try for a match with Darlene or Tiffany. If it matches one of the women, I believe we've found what the unsub used to distract the Rottweiler while he snatched Kati."

Hagen pushed his chair away from the table. "Why throw a damn finger, though? Shit. Isn't a dog biscuit good enough?"

Ander laid a hand on his shoulder. "I don't think you've got anything to worry about. Bubbles is more likely to lick your hand off than chew down one of your digits."

Stella raised both eyebrows. "Bubbles?"

Ander grinned. "You didn't know that Hagen has a male dog called Bubbles?"

Stella tried to imagine Hagen standing in a park, hair neatly coiffed, shirtsleeves perfectly rolled, yelling his dog's name. For a second, the day's tension fell away.

"His name's Bubs," Hagen declared, laying a hand flat on the table. "Now, can we get back to finding our killer?"

"Yes, please." Sheriff Lansing finished writing *finger* on a sticky note. He stuck it to the board next to the picture of Kati Marsh's car.

Slade brought the agents' focus back to the room. "Hagen. Chloe. What did you get?"

Hagen's expression changed at the question. The redness that had risen to his cheeks when Ander had mentioned his dog's name faded. He was back, his attention fully on the case.

"Chloe and I first visited with Kati Marsh's parents and ended up in a subsequent meeting with her boyfriend, but I'd like to circle back to that later."

Slade nodded. "Go ahead."

"After the Marsh's, we talked to Darlene's husband, Joshua Martinson. He wasn't nice. Angry, blamed Tiffany for his failing marriage. Even thought the women might have been lovers."

Slade lifted an eyebrow. "Were they?"

"Probably not. Mark Wright, Tiffany's husband, thought that Martinson's idea was ridiculous. But then Martinson also thought that Wright might've lost his shit and killed both women."

"And Mark Wright said pretty much the same of Joshua Martinson." Chloe's voice was low and even, as if she were equally unimpressed by both claims. "He sometimes worried about Tiffany visiting Darlene when Joshua was there."

"Both are possibilities." Hagen pointed to the board. "We should mark them up, but I'm not convinced. Martinson is too much of a hothead. I just can't see him playing with flowers. And Wright? He's a nice guy, but he's also got a solid alibi."

Sheriff Lansing wrote their names on notes. "Not sure about nice guys. Appearances can be deceiving. We've had all sorts in here and for all sorts of things you'd never expect."

Stella agreed. She'd seen the same thing during her time in uniform. The most sadistic violence handed out by the gentlest of men. Loving mothers who found a reason to look the other way when someone else's child was bruised and sullen. Gang leaders who gave weekly stipends to old ladies who lived on their blocks. People had a way of surprising.

But Hagen was right about the flowers. Arranging those white petals required a certain sensitivity. An eye for the aesthetic. A level of care.

"I think you've got a point, Hagen." Stella reached for her gold stud and twisted it slowly, one of her nervous ticks. "The way those flowers were arranged on the bodies? Maybe the killer is trying to say something. I mean, if he just wanted to hide the wounds or cover the women's modesty, he could have done anything. Even wrapping the bodies in a blanket would have been enough. This was deliberate. He wanted to make an ugly scene as beautiful as he could. He was trying to be artistic."

"Yes, that's it." Hagen nudged Chloe. "What was it Kati's father said? Kati was working as an accountant, but she had wanted to study history of art."

Slade scoffed. "That's a pretty weak link."

Hagen lowered his head in a semblance of a nod. "Yeah, but is it a coincidence? An art lover and an artistic killer?"

Chloe pushed back her chair and stood. She leaned against the wall, her hands buried in the small of her back. "Darlene and Tiffany weren't artists, and neither was Kati Marsh in the end. And if Hu Zhao is connected to this case, he's a writer, not a painter."

Hagen's face fell. "Yeah, maybe."

"Big maybe." Slade pointed his chin toward Hagen. "What did you two get from Kati's parents?"

"They hate her boyfriend and weren't afraid to tell us

why. The boyfriend actually turned up while we were there. Seemed like a decent guy. Clearly cares a lot about her."

"What's their problem?"

Hagen shot Ander a *you're not going to believe this* look. "Brodie's Black."

"Seriously?" Ander's nostrils flared. "That's still a problem?"

Hagen shrugged. "Kinda interesting, though. We've got a racial issue with Kati's parents and a murderer who doesn't hit the same skin tone twice."

"Interesting, yeah. But where does it get us?" Slade surveyed the room. When no one replied, he lifted a pile of papers from the table next to him. "All right. Good effort, everyone. Even if the results aren't great. I'll just add that we've had some initial reports from the M.E. following the autopsy on Darlene and Tiffany, though we're still waiting for toxicology reports. That could take a while, of course, but in the meantime, the M.E. thinks a hacksaw was used to remove their limbs."

"Nice." Chloe picked at the label on her water bottle. "Who'd own a hacksaw?"

"I do." Slade raised a hand. "Used it to build the girls their treehouse when they were small."

Ander's hand went up next. "I make my own shelves, fix my deck. Man should know his way around a hacksaw."

"Okay. So, we're talking carpenters and anyone who does their own home improvements." Chloe's mouth twisted. "Unless we want to question everyone with a receipt from Home Depot, we need to narrow the options down."

"You can add in farmers too," Hagen suggested. "Must be plenty of farms just outside town here. That might explain his focus on flowers. He's close to the seasons, sees them coming up when he's outside all day."

"The flowers are a strange touch." Stella was speaking

before she thought everything through but plowed on anyway. "On the one hand, he does this terrible thing with arms and legs and fingers and toes. And on the other, he gets all floral and pretty. It's like he's brutal when he takes and keeps the women, but kind when he gives them back. You'd think he was apologizing for what he's done."

"And yet he keeps going. Not much of an apology."

Stella released a long breath. Slade was right. "Maybe. Didn't you mention something about loneliness? Maybe we're talking about someone who lost a loved one suddenly. That could have caused some type of psychological rupture."

Sheriff Lansing held up a hand. "You guys are tossing theories around like you're practicing passes on the basketball court. Let me remind you that we've got a missing person, maybe two, and the clock is ticking. How can we find Kati Marsh before our killer reaches for his hacksaw again?"

Slade lowered his chin. "You're right. Let's get Hu Zhao's daughter in here. Maybe there's something about her father that will connect all the victims and point to someone they all have in common. Maybe he hangs out in an art colony or something. Don't writers and artists commune with each other?"

"It's worth a shot. I'll—"

A knock sounded on the briefing room door. Sheriff Lansing frowned at the interruption. "Yes?"

The door opened just wide enough for a young deputy to poke his head through the gap. "Sir, we've got a Min Zhao here. Says she wants to speak with the federal agents. She still hasn't heard from her father, and she's sure something's wrong."

"She's got good timing." Slade addressed his agents. "Takers?"

Stella was the first on her feet. "I'll do it."

"Okay. Hagen, you go with her."

Heading toward the door, Stella cursed herself for the impulsiveness. Was she even the best agent to speak with the young woman? What could she even say?

Your father is probably just lost. Or maybe he just forgot to tell you he needed a break from his life? Adults do that sometimes.

But, as Stella reached the door, she glanced at the murder board again.

There, next to the photo of Hu Zhao, was the image of the white flower on his kitchen counter, and she knew deep in her gut that the older man wasn't lost, and he hadn't run away.

Not of his own volition.

And Stella was deeply afraid that not all of him would be coming back.

11

The young deputy led Stella and Hagen to the front desk.

Min Zhao stood at the entrance to the Morville County Sheriff's Department, scratching nervously at the wood on the reception counter. No taller than Stella, her hair bent toward her neck in a sharp bob.

"Min Zhao?" Stella pulled out her ID. Hagen did the same.

"Yes. Yes, thank you." Desperation vibrated through her words. "Please, you must help me."

Stella addressed the young deputy, "Is there an interview room we can use?"

"Sure. You can take the first room on the left."

Stella and Hagen led Min to the gray-walled room with no windows and little air. A mirror stretched across much of one side. Any interview could be observed and recorded from behind that wall.

Stella's jaw tightened while Hagen's eyes narrowed. There was something about spaces like this that could change a mood in an instant.

A table stood in the middle with two chairs on each side.

Min sat with her back to the mirror. As soon as Stella sat down opposite her, Min grabbed her forearm with both hands.

"Please. Help me. Something's wrong with my dad. I know it is."

Min's grasp was almost strong enough to hurt, but Stella didn't shake her off. In that grip was a daughter's deep concern for her father. It was a concern that Stella herself had lived with every day when she had been young. She placed a hand over Min's.

"When's the last time you saw or heard from your father?"

Min lowered her head, as if deeply ashamed. "Thursday night. We talked on the phone. He'd gone to the cabin and was letting me know he'd arrived. I don't like him driving at dark and was worried."

"Okay, good. During that conversation, did he seem different in any way? Did he mention if he had any plans for later that night or Friday?"

Min's fingers relaxed a little. "He was going to write. That's all. He goes to the cabin when he wants to focus. He planned to stay there for a long weekend, then come home."

"If he wanted to focus, couldn't he have gone somewhere else without telling you?"

Min shook her head at Hagen's question. "We talk almost every night. Even when he's at the cabin. He knows I worry about him. He has severe arthritis, and he's not in great health. He doesn't look it, but he's quite frail. He always answers his phone. And if he misses my call, he always calls me back. Always."

Stella squeezed Min's hand tighter. "But you didn't hear from him on Friday, right?"

A lone tear trailed down her cheek. "No. I thought he'd just gotten submerged in his writing."

"When you didn't hear from him today, what did you do?"

Min finally met Stella's gaze. "I called several times, and when he didn't answer, I drove up to the cabin. When I found it empty, I called the police." She licked her lips. "I know it hasn't been that long, but you have to understand this is really unlike him. He's always very reliable. And when I saw his car there, but he wasn't, well, I…"

Min pulled her hand out from under Stella's and buried her face behind her fingers.

"I understand." Stella stroked the woman's soft hair. "What about his phone? Did you see it at the cabin?"

Min lowered her hands and took a deep breath. Her eyes were red, her cheeks puffy. "No. I couldn't find it. I tried calling when I was there but didn't hear anything ring. Maybe I missed it, or I guess it's possible the battery was dead. But I couldn't find it, no."

"Can you write his phone number down for me? We might be able to track it." Stella pulled a small notebook and pen from her pocket, flipped to a fresh page, and slid the items across the table.

Hagen tapped a finger on the top of the table. "You said that your father's health isn't good. What about his mental health? Is it possible that he could have wandered off? Has he ever done that before?"

"No." Min shook her head firmly as she finished writing her father's phone number. "His body might give him trouble, but his mind is sharp."

"What about the flower?" Stella took the notebook back. "Does that mean anything to you?"

"I don't know. Like I told the police, my dad loves flowers, and you can find those daisies everywhere now."

Hagen seemed thoughtful. "Would you say a Shasta daisy is one of his favorites?"

Stella heard his doubt in the question. Was the flower relevant here? A strange coincidence?

"Not a favorite, no. But even if it were, I don't think he would have picked just one and left it on the counter like that. He'd take a bouquet and put it in a vase." Min brushed her straight, black hair away from her face, revealing puffy eyes. Stella saw Hu's features in Min's face, thin and gentle. But her gaze was intense. "Look, I know it doesn't sound like much, but it's just not how my dad behaves. He doesn't just take off. He doesn't not answer his phone. And he doesn't pick single flowers and just leave them on the counter to die."

Hagen's eyes were filled with compassion. "Fair enough."

Stella's stomach churned. Min was right. There was too much wrong here. Too much was out of place. "Excuse us for a minute, Min."

Stella stood and motioned for Hagen to follow. They stepped into the hallway, Hagen closing the door behind them.

His face was lowered, his jaw set. "You feeling it too?"

Stella nodded. "Yeah. We need to take a look."

"Yup. I'll square it with Slade. We don't have enough for a warrant, so you'll need to ask Min if it's okay."

Hagen touched her elbow and took off down the corridor, his long stride taking him halfway back to the briefing room before Stella had finished opening the door. She poked her head into the room.

"Min, do you mind if we take a look around the cabin? Maybe we can see something that you missed."

The young woman practically leapt to her feet. "Of course, please do. Here." She reached into her pocket and pulled out a small silver key. Stella took it and paused. Hanging from the end was the keychain made up of a small red cloth embroidered in gold thread with a Chinese character.

Min closed Stella's hand around it. "It's *fu*. It means 'good luck.' Please take it."

STELLA GRIPPED THE KEY TIGHTLY, her knuckles whitening, as Hagen drove Chloe's Durango the fifteen minutes to Hu Zhao's cabin.

She couldn't stop thinking about Min sitting in the station waiting for news about her father. If the luck on the key didn't hold out, Min would soon go through everything Stella had gone through. The news would land like a baseball bat to the chest. The pain would fade with time but never completely. It would always be there, a dull ache reminding her of all she'd lost.

Enough. Let's just get there.

For a guy whose normal ride was a red Corvette, Hagen was driving like a grandpa down the rural road.

Hagen glanced at her. "You okay? You're quiet."

"Hmm. Yeah. Just, you know, thoughts. And memories. Brings it all back a bit, stuff like this."

Hagen's fingers tightened on the steering wheel. "Yeah. Know what you mean."

"I've never been able to make peace with my father's death. I just can't. Cases like these...you know."

"Yeah. Same."

Stella bit her lip. She had such an urge to tell Hagen about her father's murder. She wanted to tell him about the police car pulling up outside her house that day, about her mother collapsing on the floor when she looked out the window, and about the deep hole opening in her chest when she finally understood.

She wanted to let it all out, but she wanted Hagen to go first. His father had been murdered too. He must feel the same hurt she did and carry the same scars.

They continued in grim silence until they pulled onto a muddy track that set the SUV shaking and rocking on its suspension. A small cabin stood between the trees, its gray roof melting into the sky above the leafy canopy. A veranda ran the length of the house, a perfect spot for a writer to lie in a hammock with a pen and notebook.

After they parked under a poplar tree, Stella was the first out of the vehicle. She took two steps toward the cabin before stopping short. "Oh my god."

The driver's door snapped shut. "What?"

Stella didn't have the words to answer as she raced to the veranda.

There, on the deck, was the corpse of a small and frail, old man. He was naked. His left arm and leg were missing. And his wounds and genitals were covered in white-petalled Shasta daisies.

12

Kati Marsh pulled at the ropes binding her to the chair, but they still wouldn't give. Her tears soaked the gag that was covering her mouth and chafing her cheeks.

She couldn't take much more of this. She knew she couldn't. This lunatic was going to kill her and hack her into pieces for some art project, and there was nothing she could do. She wanted to scream.

Do it already.

Just get it over with.

Enough with this chair, with this room, with that awful bucket he held her over three times a day. Enough with his constant prattling about that evil work of his.

Just...do it already.

She inhaled deeply, trying to slow her breathing. The other man had done it. The Asian guy who'd been here earlier had been so calm in the face of this terror. She could do it too.

In. Out. In. Out.

Kati's muscles relaxed. Her heart slowed. She was alive.

There was still hope. She breathed in and out again, settling her back into the chair.

Thank you for showing me that.

She and Hu Zhao—the name the monster had called him —had been unable to speak with the gags in their mouths. But Hu had tapped the floor with his foot to get her attention, then demonstrated the breathing exercises to help chase away the rising panic.

He was gone now. The monster had come down the stairs, pulled down Hu Zhao's gag, and placed a cloth over his face.

Kati had screamed through her gag. Hu kicked and groaned and tried to pull his head away, but what chance did he have? He was small and thin, bound to a chair. It was over in minutes.

Hu's face as his eyes teared up, the blood vessels breaking before closing forever, was burned permanently into her brain.

She'd sobbed as the monster untied Hu, lifted him over his shoulder like a sack of potatoes, and carried him up the stairs.

Why him? Why now?

Hu had only arrived the previous evening. Already he was gone.

Why not her?

She was now approaching her third night. At least that's what she thought. The room had no windows. There was no sound but her own breathing. Time had its own rhythm here.

Why Hu and not her? She didn't understand.

In. Out. In. Out.

Kati pulled at her ropes again. Whatever else that madman knew, he knew how to tie a knot. There was no give in the bindings at all. Her fingers tingled as circulation returned, then they went numb again.

Maybe Juno could have chewed through the knots. Wherever she was. Kati hoped she was okay, that the old lunatic hadn't caught her, and…

Tears came again. Her breathing became faster. If only Brodie were here.

Kati closed her eyes. She imagined Brodie racing down the stairs, untying her knots, kissing her, and helping her out of the chair. He'd meet the old man on the steps. With one solid punch to the face, he would spread the monster's nose across his cheeks, render him unconscious, and he'd clatter to the floor. Brodie would carry her off. They'd marry and move somewhere far away from all this and—

Creeeak.

Kati's eyes snapped open.

The monster closed the door behind him and came down the stairs, one careful step at a time.

Was this it? Was this the moment? Kati sucked in air around her gag. She would not cry. She refused.

"Ah, there you are." He pulled the empty chair closer to Kati, sat down, and stretched his legs. "I can't tell you what a day I've had."

Kati swallowed. Her body trembled.

In. Out. In. Out.

"I must say, I'm quite exhausted. But I thought I'd spend a little time with you because, as much as I love the glow of your skin, Kati, I cherish the sound of your voice even more. Why don't we just have a little chat?"

He leaned forward and pulled the gag from her mouth.

Kati gasped. The edges of her lips were raw. Her tongue was as dry as old leather.

"Good evening, my dear. That's better, isn't it?"

Better? Kati didn't understand and didn't bother to erase the question from her expression.

He patted the air, looking for all the world like a placating grandfather. "I know you're probably still sad about dear Hu Zhao. Such a lovely man. But he looked so scared, don't you think? He made me quite sad, and I can't have that negativity in my project. You know what I mean, don't you? I'm sure someone with your appreciation of art understands entirely. He is now forever immortalized in my great work."

A sob escaped Kati's throat and giant, salty tears rolled down her cheeks, stinging the burn marks left by the gag.

The monster leaned back in the chair as his gray eyebrows furrowed. "Now, that's quite enough. I'm afraid I cannot handle tears right now. Not after a day like today. There is no room for tears in my work. I must ask you to please stop that dreadful crying. Now."

Kati shook with the effort to control her emotions. She swallowed hard, remembering to do what Hu Zhao had taught her.

In. Out. In. Out.

When the monster smiled, she nearly started crying all over again, but managed to keep her feelings in check.

In. Out. In. Out.

She needed to please him. Talk with him. Understand him.

It was the only reason she was still alive.

"So…" Her voice cracked, and she willed saliva to come save her. When she had enough moisture in her mouth, she returned the monster's smile. "How was your day?"

She hated herself more and more with each word.

But she had no choice.

She didn't want to die.

13

Kati was so beautiful, like my Diana. That black hair was shiny and dark, almost obsidian. Her smooth neck was as unblemished as Bernini's Proserpina. Was that an exaggeration? Perhaps. But only a slight one. Some people were simply blessed with more beauty than others, more perfection.

There was little that was attractive about me. My arms ached from my exertions. When I lowered myself into the chair across from her, my muscles knotted. But I didn't tell her that. I didn't want her to worry about me, as I'm sure she would, sweet creature. But my fingers were half-cramped, and my shoulders desperately needed a massage.

I pulled the chair closer to Kati. The movement hurt. Removing dear Hu Zhao's arm and leg had been much harder than I'd expected. Perhaps the saw was becoming blunt. I had to pull and push like some muscle-bound contractor building a house.

When I'd first removed her gag, Kati had looked so unhappy. There was no reason for it. None. If she knew how much her sacrifice would contribute to the world, how much peace it would bring, those tears would be of joy and gratitude.

Then, like an angel, she smiled.

Oh, how perfect she was.

"How was your day?"

My heart threatened to burst from my chest in response to her caring words. My day? I very much wanted to share how perfectly dear Hu's limbs had contrasted with the others, but I'd known women long enough to read their moods. Now wasn't the best time. Maybe later.

"How about you tell me all about you, Kati? I want to know everything. You're just so beautiful."

She didn't smile. Perhaps that was too much to expect so soon, but she seemed to calm a little more.

"What did you do with him?"

A sigh drained the oxygen from my lungs. So, we're back to that? Fine. "As I said, I've immortalized him."

The process of immortalization had been so exhausting that I even considered not taking one of his legs, but I'd come too far to abide such waste. I finished as quickly as I could, not wanting his family to grow too concerned. As a result, the cuts weren't as neat as I'd wished.

The flowers, though. The daisies would make up for the raggedness of the skin. Show how very special Hu Zhao was to me. Of course, I could have used a power tool. That would have saved a great deal of time and effort.

But I was making a work of art. A *work*. Without effort and sweat and sacrifice, where would the work's authenticity be? Its power? Its emotional impact?

No, no. It was better for the cut marks to be less than perfect than to compromise on the material or the tools being used. I would trim up the rough edges before adding Hu to the work.

"Tell me, my dear Kati, why on earth didn't you study

history of art as you'd wanted? I can't imagine someone swapping life with the Old Masters for carried interest and tax deductions." I was genuinely curious.

She licked her lips, and I realized I'd quite forgotten to bring some water.

"I...my parents. I told you. They wanted me to study accounting."

"But, my dear, could you not have told them that your heart lay elsewhere? That you saw a future in art, not double-entry bookkeeping?"

"They're...they're not the kind of people you argue with. They have their opinions and...and they don't listen. Not to me or to anyone else."

I wanted Kati to continue talking. She had such a melodious voice. Not too low or too high, and with such a delicate timbre, it even eased the aching muscles in my poor shoulders. Her voice reminded me of my sweet Diana.

Before she passed on, I would sometimes ask my dear lost wife to read to me. A little Wordsworth or Hopkins or some Whitman on a winter's afternoon in that gorgeous voice of hers. It was my very own slice of heaven. I could have listened to her all night.

I missed her. Did I really have to miss Kati too?

Could I keep her, take care of her, listen to her? I could. But then that beautiful skin wouldn't grace my project?

I was torn.

But, first, a rest. First, I wanted to talk to my dear, beautiful Kati.

"You're not close to your parents?"

She swallowed hard. I knew she only conversed with me because she was scared. But didn't courage grow from fear? Couldn't beauty defeat cowardice?

"They're difficult."

"In what way, my dear? How do they make life hard for

you? You're a grown woman. Surely you're beyond their influence now."

"Brodie." Her bottom lip trembled. "My…boyfriend."

Tears gathered in her eyes again. This was not what I wanted. Not at all. I lifted a finger. "Now, now. There's no need for tears. Deep breaths now. How long have you and… Brodie, did you say? How long have you been together?"

She breathed slowly.

In and out. In and out. That was the way.

Kati lifted her chin and looked directly into my eyes. My heart jumped a little. Such fire in those dark depths. I was grateful that I had tied her knots so tightly.

"Three years. We've been together for three years."

"And why don't your parents approve? I can't imagine that you would bring home anyone you shouldn't. What could he possibly have done that would set them so against you?"

"He…" She glared at me. The look alone pushed me back into the chair. "Nothing. Except be born with the wrong skin color."

How perplexing.

Who would have thought, in this day and age, such ugliness could still exist? I could see her standing beside her dark-skinned beau. Such a lovely couple they would make. This proved my work was relevant and necessary.

"Oh, that's awful. My poor dear. I'm sure you make the most attractive pair. You simply must be together."

Her eyes narrowed. Her breathing quickened. Was it something I said?

I would have chuckled at the misunderstanding had she not been so distraught.

I patted her knee. "Don't worry, my dear. I won't incorporate your Brodie into my piece. Though, you're right, of course. He sounds like he would make a wonderful addition, but you're making a big enough sacrifice for both of you."

Another tear fell, but only the one. "Th-thank you."

Her gratitude warmed my sagging spirits.

I checked my watch. The evening was dragging on, and that blood-soaked floor wasn't going to wipe itself. And I had to dispose of the plastic I'd used to wrap Hu Zhao's body.

The cutting made such a mess, even when the heart no longer beat. But I was always careful not to leave behind any evidence. There would be no cigarette butts slavered with DNA at the crime scene from me.

My dear Diana had taught me well. She always made sure I cleaned everything, including myself, before I came to bed. Such a good habit. It was time to get back to work.

My knees popped when I pushed up from the chair. "I have much to do, my dear."

Panic sent her eyes wide. "No…please…don't go. Please don't—"

The gag consumed the rest of her sentence. She struggled and twisted her long, elegant neck, but I forced the cloth between her teeth.

"Can't be too careful, my dear Kati. I'll come back and check on you before bedtime."

Closing my ears to the sounds of her crying, I climbed the basement stairs, my knees groaning in protest. As I locked the door behind me, I realized I was very close to crying too.

I already missed the sound of her voice.

14

Red and blue lights flashed through the branches of the ash and poplar trees surrounding Hu Zhao's one-story cabin. The sun was low behind the canopy of woods, but the building bustled with activity.

One deputy wound yellow and black tape around the veranda. Bright bursts of halogen flared as the photographer documented the scene. Forensic technicians in their crinkly, white suits and booties padded around the front of the house, bagging potential evidence.

Hagen had called in the teams as soon as he and Stella had gone through the grisly steps to determine that Hu Zhao was indeed dead. A quick scout of the house confirmed that whoever had dumped the corpse was long gone. The perpetrator left no obvious clues behind. Now, it was up to forensics and the medical examiner to look for the invisible clues, the ones that only a microscope in a laboratory could reveal.

Tired to his core, Hagen pushed his hands deep inside his pockets, rested his lower back against a tree, and watched the buzz of activity around Hu Zhao's family cabin.

The door eased open, and Slade and Sheriff Lansing

emerged. They ducked under the tape and peeled off their protective equipment, bagging it in case the team needed it later.

Slade waved Hagen and Stella over to the perimeter. "There's nothing there. No signs of a struggle, nothing left behind. You saw the daisy on the kitchen counter?"

Hagen gave a short nod. "Looks the same."

He glanced over to where Hu Zhao still lay on his back, his unseeing eyes fixed on the fading sky. The stumps that remained of his left arm and left leg were covered with white petals, as were what remained of his right hand and foot. More flowers covered his lower belly in a neat strip that extended from his navel to the tops of his thighs. He might have been on a massage table at an expensive spa, just waiting to begin his aromatherapy shiatsu treatment.

Slade gave a small grunt. "No doubt now."

"They should weigh the flowers too." Stella's skin was still as pale as milk. "Looks like there's a lot more on him than were on the two women."

"Think that means something?" Slade didn't look so sure, but he was a good leader and didn't normally dismiss an agent's theories outright.

"No idea." Stella tugged at her earring. "But I think it's worth checking."

Hagen's gut agreed with Stella. "Could mean that Hu Zhao meant more to the killer than the other two did. Maybe he knew him."

"Fair point." Slade wiped his forehead with the back of his hand. "It's work for tomorrow." He gestured to the forensic teams. "These guys are going to be here for a while, so go get some rest tonight. Dani's booked rooms for us all. Here are the keycards. Address is on the back. Your bags are in my car. Meet back at the station at nine o'clock tomorrow."

He handed each of them a cardboard folder containing a

plastic card, their room numbers scrawled on the cover. Stella had the second floor, Hagen the first.

"The others are there already. We'll need to talk to Min Zhao and find out her dad's known associates. But, again, that's for tomorrow."

Hagen's stomach sank as he thought of the distraught young woman. "Does she know yet?"

Sheriff Lansing joined them at the car, catching Hagen's question. He rubbed his cheek, one of his tells when he was uncomfortable. "Nope. I'm going to head back and tell her now. Better I do it in person."

"Yeah." Hagen exhaled a long stale breath. "Good luck with that." He didn't envy the sheriff's job.

Sheriff Lansing gave a small nod, looking as if the weight of the world was on his shoulders. It probably was.

"Sheriff." Stella stretched out a hand and opened her palm, revealing the small, silver key attached to the red, embroidered keychain. "You can give this back to her. The key worked. The good luck? Not so much."

Sheriff Lansing took the key and walked toward his car that was parked, lights still flashing, at the entrance to the road. Hagen felt sorry for the man. This was his county. His people. His responsibility. It was a heavy load to carry.

Hagen nudged Stella, drawing her attention away from the retreating sheriff. "Come on. Let's head to the motel. I think we could both do with some rest."

They retrieved their bags from Slade's car, and Hagen drove slowly down the narrow, winding street, following the sheriff toward the highway. Stella said nothing all the way. She was still silent as they pulled out into traffic heading to Tennyson.

Hagen glanced at her. "You okay? Want to talk about it?"

Stella took a deep breath and released it. "Not really. I just keep picturing Min Zhao's face when Sheriff Lansing tells her. How do you think she'll react? Scream? Collapse? Sob quietly?"

"Maybe all of the above. You can never tell, can you? Everyone reacts in their own way."

His mother, for example, had shown no emotion at the news of his father's death. Hagen had been outside, practicing his free throw. He remembered his forearm being sore and thinking he needed to stop and take a break.

As he was taking one last shot, a black and white pulled up along the front walk. Two officers, one male and one female, whose names he would never remember, glanced at him as they headed to the front door. This in and of itself wasn't strange. His father was an attorney. Cops stopping by were par for the course.

This visit felt different, though. His father was in court. *Officers shouldn't be here.* That thought crossed his mind. The air, bright and crisp just a moment ago, turned heavy. Everything moved in slow motion, but his senses became fine-tuned. Even outside, Hagen heard the doorbell ring.

He reached the front porch, standing behind the officers, when his mother opened the door. He could still remember the exact words the officers used. The woman cop stepped toward his mother. "Mrs. Yates? May we speak inside?"

Nicole Yates stood framed in the doorway. Her deep brown hair was pulled into a ponytail. She wore her "messy" shirt. It was a paint-splattered, cotton button-down that might have once been a light blue. The kindergartners she taught had been doing a painting project that day.

Something in her face told Hagen she knew whatever these officers had to say was not something she wanted to hear.

"No. We can speak out here. Hagen, you go inside."

He wanted to protest, but this was one argument he knew he would immediately lose. He stepped past the officers and his mother. When the door closed behind him, instead of leaving, he pressed his ear to the wood.

"Mrs. Yates, I'm sorry to tell you that your husband, Seth Yates, was shot multiple times upon exiting the courthouse this afternoon."

Hagen's mother was silent, but he had to cover his mouth to keep from screaming. The basketball he held dropped and bounced over and over on the wooden floor.

After a moment, Nicole Yates asked, "Is he at the hospital?"

"Yes, ma'am," the male officer said. "Unfortunately, Mr. Yates died en route. There was too much damage."

"Is there anyone who can come be with you?" That was the woman again. She sounded so patient, so sympathetic. Hagen hated her a little bit.

"I'll call someone." Hagen strained to hear his mother's words. "Thank you."

"Ma'am—"

"Thank you."

The front door opened, and Hagen's mother found him curled up on the foyer floor. She said nothing. There were no tears, not from her. She sat beside him and wrapped her arms around his shoulders while he cried into a collar that smelled of stale paint.

Now, driving to the hotel, his back suddenly itched, right where his "Vindicta" tattoo pressed against the seat.

Stella stared out the window, watching the world drift by. "And then there's tomorrow. And the day after. How do you get over something like this?"

"You don't, do you? We both know these kinds of things leave wounds that never heal." Hagen swerved sharply as a pickup cut in front of him. Traffic was building.

"Hmm." Stella fell silent again.

When his phone rang, Hagen's stomach lurched. Was that

Slade? Had they found Kati Marsh? He really didn't want to see another dismembered corpse. Not now. Not today. He took a deep breath and answered the call.

"Hey, Hagen." The voice that echoed through the car's speakerphone was female, young. Brianna.

A load dropped from Hagen's chest. He grinned and glanced at Stella. "My sister. The younger one. Hey, Brianna. Listen, you're on speaker, and I've got someone from work in the car, so watch that sailor mouth of yours, okay?"

"Screw you, Hagen. Is that better? Cranked that down nicely, right?"

God, he loved his sister. "Yeah. Good effort. What's up?"

"You spoken to Amanda recently?"

Hagen's smile faded, and he wished he hadn't paired his phone with the Durango. It was going to be one of *those* conversations. Another spat between the sisters they wanted him to settle. This would be awkward with Stella there, and yet…bring it on. Anything that took him away from thoughts of his mother and Min Zhao's loss.

"No, not since the weekend. What's she—"

"Oh, man, they are driving me crazy. Her *and* Clint. You know what she just told me? She said that one day I'll get married and realize that life isn't all about college degrees and my self-centered med school problems. Fu…*screw* her! I told her that at least I have goals. I was never going to get married. She said I was being ridiculous. One day I'll get married and have kids, and then I'll understand. Please. We don't all want to run after a man like she follows Clint around. I'm telling you, she's been like a lost puppy since she met him and moved out to that ranch. All that horsesh… horse*stuff*…has gone to her head. I miss the old Amanda, Hagen. The one we had before Clint Horse*stuff* Brason turned up."

When a spot opened up in the middle lane, Hagen cut

into it. He was feeling more lively listening to his sister prattle on. "Listen, Clint's not going anywhere, at least not any time soon. He's family now. Cut Amanda some slack. She's probably still on some newlywed high. You might hate the idea of the ranch, but you don't have to live there."

"I do hate the idea of it. Sucks. But you're probably right. She'll calm down, especially once she sees how much muck horses can drop each day." Her tone lightened. "How's Bubbles?"

Stella bit back a laugh, making a strange choking sound, but she had a grin that stretched from one ear to the other.

Hagen was going to strangle his sister. "Fine. Listen, we're almost there. I'll speak to you later. Be nice to Amanda."

He disconnected the call and flicked the turn signal. Stella was still looking at him, still grinning.

"Bubbles. You still haven't told me the story."

Hagen pulled the SUV into the exit lane, speeding up the ramp. "Yeah, yeah. My sister's stupid idea. I lost a bet, and she got to name my dog. Bubs. His name is Bubs." He shot through a yellow light. "Except when Amanda's around."

Stella laughed. "Yeah, Ander mentioned something. So, who's looking after Bubbles tonight?"

"Bubs." He practically growled the word. "It's *Bubs*. And I asked a neighbor to take him in. He's a mean-looking monster but a big softie once you get to know him. The dog, that is, not the neighbor."

"Aww. That's so sweet." Stella still wore that big smile, which suddenly fell away. She slapped a hand over her face. "Oh shit! Scoot!"

"I am scooting?" Hagen was confused. Was scoot some kind of slang for driving?

From the corner of his eye, he watched her yank out her phone and frantically text someone.

"Scoot?"

But Stella didn't offer clarification until she finished her text. "My goldfish. When I can't make it home, I have my neighbor's kid, Emily, feed him."

Was she serious? Okay, he'd play.

"You're giving me grief about Bubs, and you have a gold-fish named *Scoot*?"

It was too funny. Too ridiculous. He couldn't have stopped laughing if a bowling ball had been stuffed in his mouth. When Stella joined in and snorted, Hagen thought he'd have to pull to the side of the road until they recovered.

Hagen wasn't used to seeing her so relaxed. So, this was what she looked like off duty, when the day's troubles had been forgotten, if only for a few minutes. It suited her.

He was still smiling when he pulled into a parking space under the red and blue motel sign. A line of windows spread in front of the vehicle, some lit, most dark and empty and lonely. A set of cold, concrete stairs wound up to a second floor.

This wasn't home. It was nothing like home. Any lingering humor died.

In the silence after Hagen turned off the engine, the walls of the vehicle seemed to close in around him.

Stella broke the lonely moment. "Your sister sounded nice. Are you as close to Amanda as you are to Brianna?"

And the walls fell away. *Thank you, Stella.*

"Yeah, kinda. I'm close to both but in different ways. Amanda's more settled now. I just felt responsible for them after our dad died."

"That's very good of you. I'm sure they appreciate you more than you know. I wish my brother had been there after our father died. He would have made everything so much easier."

Hagen couldn't remember the last time he'd spoken to anyone about his relationship with his sisters. Even when

Ander came over, six-pack in hand, they usually spent the evening talking sports or work. Ander would discuss his boy, Murphy, but Hagen always shied away from bringing up his own family. That was his, and his alone.

And now, here he was, talking openly with Stella as though they'd known each other for years.

His palms were sweating. His cheeks grew warmer. And he was sure that his face must have been glowing so red that Sheriff Lansing could have used his head as a police light.

"Let's…let's head in."

Hagen reached for the door handle and pulled. It slipped out of his sweaty fingers with a loud snap.

Stella pushed her door open and peered over her shoulder. "Having trouble there?"

Hagen gripped the lever again, held it this time, and stepped out.

Stella grinned at him from beside the SUV. "Doors are hard, right? Think you'll be okay with the one for your room? Just remember…hold, twist, push, release."

"Twist, release, push, hold." He mimed the actions. "Got it."

Laughing, they took their bags and walked toward the motel.

Hagen reached his ground-level room first. "Hey…watch this!"

Stella peered down over the stair railing. "Are you going to dazzle me?"

He inserted the card into the lock, gripped the door handle, and pulled it down hard. With one sweep of his arm, he pushed. The door swung open. He punched the air. "Yes! See? I have mastered doors." It promptly snapped shut in his face. "Nuts."

Stella's laughter rang into the night as she headed up the remaining stairs. "Keep practicing. If you need any help with the mini-fridge or the microwave or the closet, just shout. I'm right here."

Hagen could still hear her laughing as she entered her room, presumably managing her door just fine.

He entered his room and tossed his bag on the luggage rack. He, too, was still laughing.

Which wasn't how he usually ended his days.

15

Stella was still chuckling as she tossed her bag on the bed and collapsed alongside it, her arms stretched over her head. She couldn't remember the last time she'd talked so openly and laughed so freely.

Hagen was funny. She hadn't expected that.

He always looked so serious, that square jaw as solid and unmoving as a cliff. But he could take a joke, and he wasn't afraid to laugh at himself either. How many men had she met who were willing to do that? Not many, that was for sure, especially men who looked like Hagen.

Bubbles the dog.

Really?

Before she could head down a new path of giggles, she gave herself a mental shake.

Hagen Yates was a distraction, and until she found her father's killer, she couldn't afford to be distracted. They were just two people who worked together. They were two people bonded by the violent loss of fathers. Hagen was a colleague. Even if he was attractive and funny, he was not a relationship consideration.

Focus.

Stella's stomach rumbled. She hadn't eaten since the questionable nachos at lunch. She found a pile of takeout menus in the drawer next to the bed and ordered Chinese. The spices might be a bit strong for the tiny space, but it sounded delicious.

After about fifteen minutes, she missed her apartment. The motel room couldn't have been more basic. The brown wallpaper peeled in the corners. The *No Smoking* signs on the window and the table had failed to prevent the cigarette burns on the carpet. The walls were thin enough to give the room a constant symphony of bubbling pipes, rapid footsteps, and flushing toilets.

But one night wouldn't hurt. She didn't want to think about staying here beyond that, but not because of the bad décor and thin walls.

What would happen to Kati Marsh if they didn't land a break tomorrow?

Stella's stomach tightened again. This time, the pain wasn't from hunger.

The food arrived in no time. Stella placed the two boxes on the table and pulled out her notes from the day's interviews and site visits. She reviewed them as she ate.

This puzzle seemed to have so many parts.

Shasta daisies. Missing limbs. Three victims. A fourth missing.

Two of the victims knew each other, but the third? There was no obvious connection between Hu Zhao, Darlene, and Tiffany. Nor between those three and Kati Marsh.

Stella made a note to ask Min Zhao if her father knew any of the three women.

Min Zhao. That poor woman.

She dug the chopsticks into her noodles and pushed her notebook away.

The first night would be the worst. At least that's what Min would think. But she'd be wrong. Tonight, Min Zhao would be numb, disbelieving. She'd go to bed knowing only that her life had changed, that someone had torn a giant hole in it, one that could never be repaired. Only as the days and the weeks passed would she really understand what that gaping wound meant.

Min would pick up her phone, dial her father's number, and then realize he would never answer. Or she'd find a picture of the two of them and break down. Or she'd have a happy moment, maybe a promotion at work, and realize she'd never be able to share it with him.

His face would appear as she chose a melon in the grocery store the way he'd shown her. She would hear a faint chuckle when she tipped more than necessary because that's what he'd always done. Those were the worst moments, the ones that just snuck up on you.

Enough.

The case. Think about the case.

Forcing herself to focus, Stella pulled her notebook closer.

The perpetrator's choice of Hu Zhao was strange. The victim profile was so different. Three young women she could understand. Weren't they usually the first choice when a psychopath started shopping for victims? But a frail, old man? That didn't fit.

Stella circled his name. Pieces that didn't seem to fit often proved to be the linchpins. Would he be the key to cracking this case? That character on Min Zhao's keychain might not have brought her or her father any luck, but it might bring the team some.

She tapped the notebook with the end of her pen. The taps landed faster. She was starting to get excited about talking with Min Zhao tomorrow.

Stella finished the meal, picking the last traces of noodles out of the bottom of the box with her chopsticks. Time for dessert. She unwrapped her fortune cookie. Before she broke the stale treat open, she closed her eyes, hoping, maybe, the universe had an extra clue for her.

She snapped the cookie in half and pulled out the small slip of white paper.

A truly rich life contains love and art in abundance.

"What does *that* mean?"

Stella crunched down on one half of her dessert as she considered the cryptic message. She crumpled the fortune and tossed it onto the table. Frowning, she popped the other half into her mouth.

"Wait a second."

Feeling a little ridiculous, she picked up the crumpled fortune again. She smoothed it out and read it out loud to the grubby room. "*A truly rich life contains love and art in abundance.* Love and art. Love and *art.*"

She'd initially had the impression of an artistic sensibility after seeing the photographs of Tiffany and Darlene.

The flowers. What else? Those missing limbs and digits?

The arrangement of the bodies was so unusual and so deliberate. The flowers were almost like an apology, an attempt by the killer to make up for what he had taken from his victims. The covering of their genitalia? Was that an attempt to give the victims back some of their dignity?

Stella sighed. It was all so clumsy.

Flowers, of all things. If the killer was trying to be artistic, creative, to send some kind of message, they really weren't doing a great job.

And what was the unsub doing with the arms and legs and fingers and toes they stole? None of the limbs fit together. Maybe the killer was creating some kind of mosaic? They were mixing and matching limbs. Did the different skin tones matter? Were they the correct shade and tone for their composition? Did that make sense?

"That, ladies and gentlemen, is the problem with following clues from fortune cookies."

Stella yawned and checked her watch. It was getting late, and she was exhausted. She'd been staring at her notes for almost two hours. Tossing her pen onto her notebook, she showered and brushed her teeth before climbing into bed.

Sleep didn't come.

All her unanswered questions brought her nothing but frustration that bustled around in her brain. Stella tossed and turned between the sheets, her eyes refusing to stay shut.

One thing was clear. Whoever was responsible for these murders wasn't done. And whoever was able to remove human body parts, return the leftovers, and decorate the corpses was a special kind of wacko. If the team didn't catch the unsub soon, they would find more bodies scattered across the regions. Kati Marsh would be next, but she certainly wouldn't be the last.

Stella rolled onto her side. The sign at the entrance to the parking lot threw a blue light through a gap in the curtains. In the distance, the low but constant roar from the highway competed with the hum of the air conditioner. Someone a few doors down used the bathroom.

As the sleepless night wore on, Stella's anxious mind drifted from flowers to Hu Zhao's body to Min Zhao's sorrow to her own father's death and, finally, to Uncle Joel.

She flipped onto her other side.

No, he wasn't Uncle Joel. He was Matthew Johnson of Atlanta, Georgia. Matthew Johnson didn't have a death certificate.

Had her father known Uncle Joel's real name?

Stella let the idea bounce around her head. Had her father

lied to her and her brother and her mother when he talked about Uncle Joel? The thought made her want to throw up.

Surely not.

If her father had known his partner was undercover, wouldn't he have kept Uncle Joel at a distance, treating the relationship as entirely professional? But Dad had brought him into their lives. He'd practically made him a part of their little family.

And Uncle Joel had never let on, never dropped even the smallest of clues.

Who could do something like that? Who could manage that kind of double life and still develop meaningful relationships?

Stella rolled back into the blue light. She was more awake now than ever.

A psychopath could do that.

But Uncle Joel wasn't a psychopath. He was a good man. He'd always been kind to her and a friend to her father. He was family.

Right?

Okay, to be fair, that's what undercover cops were paid to do...seamlessly blend in while establishing deep levels of trust in order to collect information from their target.

Had Stella's family been his target? Or had Uncle Joel been drawn into the Knox Family vortex while working undercover on an unrelated mission?

Did he love them like she'd always believed he did? Or was it all a lie?

The questions were like knives in her soul.

He'd certainly acted like he cared the night he'd turned up drunk, tears flowing as he told her he was certain that dirty cops had killed her father.

Why would he tell a fourteen-year-old girl such a horrible thing? What would ever make him think she could handle such a burden? What did he think she would do with that knowledge?

He was in law enforcement. *He* was supposed to track those dirty cops down and make them pay. If he didn't really die that next day, if he did fake his death and return to his real family, why hadn't he sought vengeance and justice for her father all these years? Surely, if he had, Stella would have heard about it.

Stella rolled onto her back and stared at the ceiling. Even in the dim light from the motel sign, she could make out the black smudges left by mosquitoes squashed by previous guests.

The questions buzzing in her head were as annoying as the blood sucking insects.

What's the truth?

How can I find it?

What's real and what's pretend?

As Stella covered her face with her hands, she only knew one thing for certain.

There were too many questions and far too few answers.

16

_____

Stella took her seat in the briefing room of the Morville County Sheriff's Department and laid her head on the table. She'd finally fallen asleep around three but had managed less than four hours of undisturbed rest before the *beep-beep-beep* of a truck backing into a parking space beneath her room jolted her straight up in bed.

The sight of Hagen, who had knocked on her door at eight with his hair neatly combed, tie knotted to perfection, and navy blue suit looking fresh off the rack from the dry cleaners, didn't make her feel any better. He'd even been for a run. She hated him a little.

His expression, though, was serious. Whatever humor he had shown the previous night had melted away. This was the old Hagen: craggy, straightlaced, and ready to beat down the day. They barely exchanged a word during the short drive to the station.

At least Sheriff Lansing seemed to match Stella's mood. His face was paler than it had been the previous day. A thin, red line on his cheekbone suggested he'd struggled to focus while shaving. Breaking the news to Min Zhao the previous evening must have weighed on the poor man.

Chloe placed a hand on Stella's shoulder. "Rough night, rookie?"

Stella pushed herself up, hoping she hadn't drooled on the table.

Chloe, too, looked as bad as Stella felt. Her short, black hair, which was usually gelled flat, was dry and uneven, and her face was puffy.

"Yeah. Same for all of us, I think." She glanced at a yawning Ander. He was unshaven, and his hands were pushed deep inside the pockets of his slacks to prevent him from slouching even more in his chair.

Chloe shook Stella's shoulder. "Well, we'd better wake up and get our asses in gear."

"Right." Stella shot her a little salute. "We've got to find Kati Marsh today. And alive. Otherwise…"

"Yeah, all that." Chloe snagged her keys from in front of where Hagen sat. He didn't even seem to notice. "Also, boss is here."

The door creaked open, and Slade strode in. Whatever a day of interviews, dismembered bodies, and a night in a cheap motel had done to the rest of the team, Slade seemed to be impervious to it all. Straight-backed as ever, his six-foot frame overshadowed the room as though the burden of the investigation placed no weight on his shoulders at all.

"Good morning." Slade didn't look impressed with his agents. "Good to see you all looking so bright and sharp first thing on a Sunday morning."

Ander dragged a hand from his pocket to cover another yawn. "Sorry. Not exactly luxury, that hotel."

Slade shot him a disapproving look. "No, but it's all we got. In case any of us need a reminder, Stella and Hagen found Hu Zhao's body at his cabin last night. Left arm and left leg were missing, as were his fingers and toes. Like the two women, the body was naked, stumps and genitals covered with Shasta daisies."

"Lots of flowers." Stella sat taller, her fatigue knocked out by a renewed focus on the case. "The killer used a lot more on Hu Zhao than on the previous two victims."

"Right." Slade nodded. "We don't know yet if that's relevant, but it's possible that Hu Zhao has a connection to the killer that Darlene and Tiffany didn't. That link might be a way in. If we can find it. The sooner we do, the greater the chance Kati Marsh will survive the day."

Ander seemed more awake now too. "Did you find anything at the cabin that could help?"

"Not yet. Forensics was there, but now that there's light, I want you and Chloe to go look around. Check the woods. See if there are any neighbors with cameras that might have caught something. Forensics will find the small stuff, but I want some fresh eyes on the scene. You might spot something they missed."

"What about us?" Hagen glanced at Stella.

"Hagen, I want you to go to the morgue. Talk to the M.E. See if there's anything about the wounds or the cause of death that could help us."

Slade focused on Stella. "You spoke to Min Zhao yesterday. Talk to her again today. Find out who her father's friends were and whether he had any enemies, family secrets, mystery lovers. Who knows? If you're right about those flowers, somewhere in those contacts will be a link that will take us to his killer. But Stella…" Slade lowered his chin, his gaze boring into her from under his graying eyebrows. "Go easy. She just lost her father."

What the hell? Did he think she'd do anything else but go easy?

Slightly offended, she gave him a short nod. "Yes, sir."

"When you're done, join Ander and Chloe at the cabin." He picked up a key fob from the table and tossed it her way. "Rental's out front."

She snatched it. "Will do, sir."

He tossed another one to Hagen.

"In the meantime, I'll have Dani and Mac compile a list of artists, horticulturists, and florists in the area who fit the rough description of the man at the bar the night Darlene and Tiffany went missing. We might just get lucky. Go."

Stella stood and stretched her back. Chloe patted her arm as she sidled past. "I don't envy your job, rookie."

17

Hagen pulled into the parking lot outside the Morville County Tri-City Community Morgue and turned off the engine. He stayed in the rented Explorer, hands on the steering wheel, and steeled himself for what he was about to do.

How had he ended up with the bodies? Slade couldn't pick Ander for this job? Or Chloe? No, they got to take a walk in the woods while he "ogled" the remains of half-frozen corpses.

Going to the medical examiner's was the worst. The deceased really had a way of sucking the joy out of everything like a black hole. Every one of them was a permanent weight dragging on those they left behind. On Min Zhao, on Joshua Martinson, on Mark Wright, and, of course, on Mark and Tiffany's kids. No matter how much time passed, that weight would slow them down and pull them back.

Only finding the scumbag who killed their loved ones would give them a morsel of relief, but even then, how much would it help?

Hagen didn't have the answer to that question…yet. He'd circle back to it once he found his father's killer.

And he needed to do that soon.

He had a vague idea of what he wanted to do with the rest of his life once he delivered the vengeance his father deserved. He'd have love and happiness and all that stuff, just like everyone else.

A brief image of Stella smiling and laughing in his car surfaced in his mind.

Was that possible?

He pushed the thought out of his head. She was attractive. He had no doubt about that. That long, brown hair always pulled back into a no-nonsense ponytail. Those dark eyes so hard to read. That sharp head of hers, always seeing things that others missed. And she understood, of course. She knew what it meant to focus on a hunt.

That was why he had been so cold that morning, so quiet. He had a job to do first.

After he'd found his father's killer, and after *she* had tracked down the man known as Joel Ramirez, then maybe he would see if there was something worth pursuing.

Then, maybe, he'd have that normal life. Then, maybe, he'd be able to build deep connections and a loving relationship.

Something to look forward to.

He left the vehicle and rang the morgue's bell. A woman with narrow eyes opened the door. Her straight, brown hair formed sharp, little arrows on the shoulders of her white coat. Her wide smile seemed entirely out of place amid the entrance's stainless-steel finish and the cloying odor of formaldehyde.

"You must be Hagen Yates." She extended a hand. "I'm Juanita Burroughs, the M.E."

Hagen shook her hand and followed her into the building. The door snapped shut behind him. The smell of cleaning fluid and preservatives seemed to double in strength.

Dr. Burroughs led him down a brightly lit corridor and through a pair of swinging double doors that opened into the autopsy suite.

"It's just you and me here today. And our guests, of course. Not that this lot is much company." She waved an arm over the two tables in the middle of the room. "They just lie around all day."

Hagen tried but failed to produce a little smile at her joke.

Each stainless-steel table was covered by a white sheet that bulged in the middle. Hagen took a deep breath, received a lungful of chemical-laden air, and regretted it. *In the end, this is what it all comes down to.*

After waiting for him to slip into protective gear, Dr. Burroughs pulled on a pair of latex gloves and gripped the top of one of the sheets. "Want to see what we've got?"

Hagen groaned. "Not really."

The M.E. chuckled. "Well, it's all I've got, Agent. If you were hoping I'd show you my stamp collection, I'm afraid that's long gone." Dr. Burroughs grabbed the sheet and pulled it straight down before turning to do the same from the other table.

Hagen's throat tightened as though he'd stuck a couple of fingers down it and was just waiting for his breakfast to surface.

He stood over the corpse of Tiffany Wright. The pictures on the murder board really didn't do the body justice. Tiffany's red curls had lost the luster he would have expected if he'd met her in a bar or at a diner or a PTA meeting. Her face was gray, lips pale. With the flowers removed, her breasts lay almost flat on a chest scarred by a long, Y-shaped incision. The stumps at the end of her left arm and leg were pale, pink knots of fat and muscle with a ring of white bone like a bullseye in the middle.

Darlene looked no better. Her darker complexion had faded, so the two women now lay together in tones of gray. Only the bloodless stumps at the end of Darlene's right arm and leg and on her remaining hand and foot matched her friend's coloring.

Hagen pulled his eyes away from the women and faced Dr. Burroughs. The bodies faded into the background. Hagen's stomach settled slightly. "So, what have we got?"

"Time of death is tricky. Kinda interesting. The bodies were cold when we got them, which usually means they've been lying around for a while, long enough for body temperature to match the surrounding environment. But look."

Dr. Burroughs picked up Darlene's remaining wrist and bent the arm at the elbow. The dead woman's hand rose to give a fingerless wave. A small, quiet creak resounded from her bicep.

"Hear that?" Dr. Burroughs lowered Darlene's arm back into its former position.

Cree-ak.

Hagen didn't even want to guess, but he also needed to say something. "Tendons?"

"That's cold shortening. Ever visited a slaughterhouse, Agent?"

No way in hell. Slaughterhouses were out of sight, out of mind. He dealt with enough killing when he went to the office each day.

Dr. Burroughs wagged a playful finger in his direction. "You meat-eaters. Never think about where your food comes from, huh?"

Nope. He preferred total oblivion. "You're a vegetarian?"

"Twenty-three years. Since the day I started here." Dr. Burroughs patted Darlene's arm, the eyes above her mask growing solemn. The medical examiner might have a wacky sense of humor, but she clearly respected those placed under her care. "So, here's a lesson for you. What do you think happens after a cow meets its end in an abattoir?"

Shit. Did they really need to have this discussion?

"The cuts go straight into the freezer, I guess. Keep them fresh."

"Wrong. If you put meat into a freezer directly after slaughter, the muscles contract. Calcium molecules bind the proteins, and the enzymes that normally loosen muscle fibers don't get a chance to do their work. You end up with tough meat. At slaughterhouses, they electrocute the carcasses before they freeze them so you can grill your juicy steak. These two," Dr. Burroughs laid a hand on the stumps of each woman's leg, "were not electrocuted."

"But they were frozen?"

"Looks like it. Immediately after death." The M.E. held up a finger. "Now, look at this." She snapped on the light of a large magnifier attached to Darlene's table.

Her gray skin brightened, and the mottling on the surface grew clearer. The M.E. lifted Darlene's hand, bent it back at the wrist, and brought the magnifier over the stumps of the fingers. "What do you see?"

Hagen hesitated before stepping closer and peering over the top of the glass. The skin around the stumps was thin and ragged. The white bone dominated the wound, leaving just a small circle of pink tissue that was dotted with tiny, yellowish oblongs, like broken bits of rice.

"What am I looking at?"

"Blowfly eggs."

Hagen managed not to jump away from the body, but he did close his eyes as he sought to calm his churning stomach. When he opened them again, the corpses and their gaping fly-infested stumps were still there.

Dr. Burroughs turned off the magnifier's light. "They're freshly laid, so the bodies couldn't have been there for long. Time of death will be pretty vague. I'd put it at some time between Tuesday evening and Wednesday morning."

"The…the skin around the finger. It looks pretty uneven."

Dr. Burroughs's eyes creased at the corner, giving away a smile under her mask. "Well spotted, Agent. Yes, we can see the same on all the other cuts." She reached for the magnifier. "Want to look?"

"No." The word came out of his mouth like a bullet, and Hagen forced himself to slow down. "Thank you. I'll take your word for it. What do those cuts tell you?"

"They tell me the limbs and digits were sawed off using a hacksaw or something like it. Usually, dismembered corpses have neat cuts with burn marks on the bone, sure signs of a power tool. A chainsaw, usually. These cuts are much more uneven. The bones even show signs of splintering. Whoever did this wasn't afraid of a bit of elbow grease. In fact, I'd go further and say that he *wanted* to put in the effort. A chainsaw would have done this in minutes. A handsaw? You need plenty of time. And a strong stomach. Here, look at this one."

He followed Dr. Burroughs to a bank of square doors lining the back wall.

"Excuse me." Dr. Burroughs reached past Hagen's hip. He moved aside, giving her space to pull out a long drawer. The body that appeared was also covered with a white sheet.

She peeled back the cover to reveal the face and stitched torso of Hu Zhao. His ribs were visible beneath his skin. His eyes were closed as though he was ignoring them, refusing to speak to the FBI or the medical examiner as punishment for letting him reach this state.

Pulling the stump of his left arm out from under the

sheet, Dr. Burroughs gripped a flap of skin about three inches wide that hung beneath it. "Look at this."

The underside of the flap was gray and dotted with wiry, black hairs. The top was as pink as a slice of fresh salmon. "This is shoddy workmanship. You can see the multiple cuts on the bone where he took the saw out, then put it back in again. This is definitely a hacksaw, but either the cuts were made by a different person, or the killer was in a bigger hurry this time. He was certainly less careful."

Hagen swallowed down a curse. "Cause of death?"

"Not sure." Dr. Burroughs placed Hu Zhao's arm back under the sheet, resting her hand on his shoulder, another sign of respect. "It wasn't the sawing. That was postmortem. And there are no other signs of violence on the body. No stab wounds or head trauma. There aren't even any signs of a struggle. I'd put my money on poisoning or an overdose. We'll know more when the toxicology report comes through."

"When will that be?"

Dr. Burroughs's eyes were apologetic. "Ah, I'm afraid that won't be for a good three-to-five weeks."

Hagen swallowed another curse. "That long?"

"Yes, I know, Agent. If you're looking for miracles, you're in the wrong department. All I can tell you is that there was nothing out of the ordinary in the victims' stomach contents. If the killer used poison, I don't think it was ingested."

"Thanks." He was ready to get out of there. "If anything else comes up, let me know. Enjoy the rest of your Sunday." Hagen didn't know why he said that. It must've been reflex.

After handing the M.E. his business card, he strode away from Hu Zhao's corpse and passed between the bodies of Darlene Medina-Martinson and Tiffany Wright while trying not to look at them. When he reached the door, Dr. Burroughs called him back.

"Agent Yates."

"Yeah?" Hagen turned and waited for her to continue, one latex glove halfway off.

"Any news on the missing woman?"

"No. Nothing yet."

The M.E. nodded. "I hope you find her. I don't want any more guests."

18

Min Zhao opened her front door, leaning a shoulder on the doorpost as though she barely had the strength to hold herself up. The intensity that had burned in her eyes when Stella talked to her at the Morville County Sheriff's Department was gone now. The light was out. The darkness had settled in.

Stella didn't need to ask how the poor woman was doing. She knew. Even if she hadn't experienced grief so personally, years of volunteering at the children's hospital had shown her the impact that loss made. The constancy of death gave the doctors and the nurses a thick skin and some a dark sense of humor. But the effect of long-term mourning was carved deepest on the faces of parents who had lost their kids.

They'd turn up for events and fundraisers, some with a warm hug and an easy smile for the volunteers, even though they seemed infinitely tired. Other parents were cold and brittle. Some parents remained forever fragile. One mother, at the rededication of one of the wards, had turned to Stella, tears flowing down her face. "My child died. Am I still a mother?"

Was Min now asking if she was still a daughter?

Stella swatted the question away, refusing to go down that dark path.

"I'm so sorry for your loss."

Min stared blankly, the beginning of grief holding her trapped in denial and shock.

"Do you mind if I come in? I just have a few questions. They might help us to find the person who…" Stella paused. The words were on the tip of her tongue, but their arrival reminded her that she—the team—had failed. Yesterday, Min's father was alive. Today, he wasn't. His death wasn't her fault, but the words dug the responsibility deep into her bones. "The person who took your father."

Min shrugged and turned back into the house. Stella followed, closing the door behind her and heading into the kitchen. Min sat on a barstool, folding her arms on the cold surface of the island.

The kitchen was a mess. The sink contained three days' worth of dirty dishes. The dishwasher was both half-open and half-full of clean plates. A mug of coffee stood undrunk in front of Min's arms, the milk having already developed a light crescent on the surface. It must have been left there, untouched, for days. A vase stood next to it. The red phloxes and white geraniums it contained were wilted and dried.

Stella pulled down the door of the dishwasher. "You sit. I'll do this."

She opened the kitchen cupboards and found where Min stored her plates. Her host didn't move, didn't protest. Stella pulled a clean plate out and stacked it in the cupboard with the others. "Min, did your father have a lot of friends?"

"Hmm?"

"Your father. Was he popular? Sociable?"

Min pulled a tissue from her pocket. "No, not really. He was friendly. And people always liked him. Whenever he did a book reading, people always wanted to stay and chat. The bookstore would have to kick them out. But he liked being alone. If someone invited him to an event, he would usually try to find an excuse not to go. I think he was always happiest in the cabin by himself, with nature and his writing."

Stella hung a pair of mugs on a stand next to a crumb-coated toaster. "What about Darlene Medina-Martinson? Or Tiffany Wright? Did he know them?"

Min shrugged. "No. I don't think so."

Stella moved on to the sink, rinsing the hardened food off the plates and dropping them into the empty dishwasher. This was what she and her brother had done after her father had died, taking on extra chores when her mother was frozen in grief. The food in the fridge had dwindled. The takeout had overflowed from the garbage until they could no longer bear it. Almost three months passed before any kind of routine returned.

How long before Min would find some order in her life again? Stella had no idea. Everyone healed in their own time. They had to find their own way to live again.

"What about a woman called Kati Marsh?"

"Kati Marsh?" Min shook her head. "I don't know. Is she a writer too?"

"No. She's an accountant."

"Then I don't think he knew her. He did his own accounts."

Stella took the coffee from the counter, tipping its contents into the sink. "Where's the detergent for the dishwasher?"

Min stared at her, taking nearly half a minute to decipher the question.

Stella waited patiently until the young woman pointed to the cupboard next to Stella's legs. She primed the machine and turned it on.

"So, your father didn't have any friends at all?"

Min lifted her eyes. "He had me."

"Of course, he did." Stella rushed to reassure her. "Anyone else?"

"The city sometimes asked him to appear at events, and he did signings and readings, but I think he always found company an irritation. You'd never know when you spoke to him, though. He could go for a week without talking to anyone but me and be perfectly happy."

Stella reached for the flowers. Three dry, red petals dropped onto the granite.

Min's head jerked up. "My father collected those."

Stella stopped. The water in the vase was cloudy. The cut stems were so soggy, and the petals were brown and crisp. "They're gone, Min."

Min shuddered and made a small nod.

Stella removed the flowers from the vase and found a plastic baggie. After plucking off several of the better petals and placing them in the small storage container, she set the rest on top of the garbage and tied the bag. She sighed. This was hard, really hard. And the conversation wasn't going anywhere. There had to be a connection. Someone the victims had in common.

"What about interior design? Who designed the cabin?"

"I don't know. It was like that when he bought it. He didn't change anything. He liked the feng shui. That was why he chose that house."

So, no accounting link. No interior design.

Stella twisted her ear stud. "What about art? Was your father interested in art?"

"I don't know. What's the…" Min dropped her head onto

her arms. "Look, he was a writer. He was creative. He made nice drawings of cats for me to color in when I was a kid. But I don't think he was more interested in art than in nature or music or anything else. He liked everything equally."

"Okay. Fair enough." Stella washed her hands and leaned against the kitchen counter and hung her head. Was there any more she could get out of Min? If so, she couldn't see it.

With a sigh, she reached for her card. "If there's anything else that comes to mind—"

"Really?" Min's head jerked up. Her cheeks were red, and there were tears in her eyes. Anger too. "I told you everything yesterday. And what good did it do, huh? I told you he was missing. I told you there was something wrong. What did you do? Nothing. And now, my father turns up on the doorstep of his own house, dumped like some…some damn package."

Stella braced herself for the verbal attack, forcing her expression not to reveal how much she felt she'd let this young woman down. "I'm sorry. Really, I'm very sorry. We are doing everything we can."

"*Now* you're doing everything you can?" Disgust and contempt laced the words in equal measure. "A bit late, isn't it? Will doing everything you can bring back my father?"

Stella was silent. What could she say to that? Nothing could bring back a dead father. Nothing. When she spoke, her voice was little more than a whisper. "No. We can't do that."

"Then I have nothing more to say."

Though she wanted to throw her arms around the young woman and sob with her, Stella picked up the garbage bag and carried it out of the house. There was little point in pushing further. Min would need to pass through the anger step of grief before she'd be open enough to talk freely, to offer up the kind of detailed information that might reveal a clue to push the investigation forward.

Nothing seemed to connect these people. As she dropped the bag into the can at the side of the house, the dead flowers with their greens and reds and grays visible through the plastic, she mentally turned over the profiles of the victims.

A Chinese American man pushing seventy who wrote books about wellness. Two married women, friends with nothing more in common than their pasts. One had kids, while the other was childless. One had been in a happy marriage while the other had been barely hanging on.

They looked different. Tiffany had bright, red hair. Darlene was a brunette. Tiffany was so pale she was almost transparent. Darlene was bronzed, almost Mediterranean. And Kati looked like neither of them. They all had different ages, different ethnicities, different upbringings. Different lives. Nothing connected them. There was no victim profile, no obvious plan. Every victim was unique.

Stella slammed the garbage lid closed and swore out loud. "It's like he's putting together a bouquet."

She froze. Her jaw dropped. That was it.

They weren't looking for a connection. They were looking for a collection.

She snatched her phone from her pocket and called Slade.

He answered with a serious, "What did she tell you?"

"Nothing. That is, nothing useful. But I think I've found the common factor, the thing that ties all the victims together."

"Go on."

Walking away from the house so that Min couldn't accidentally overhear, Stella forced her voice to be steady. "Usually, when we analyze victims, we look for what they have in common, right?"

"Uh-huh."

"But these victims have nothing in common, and *that's* the point. He never picks the same type twice. He wants variety, like a florist trying to pack in every blossom they can find to create the most magical arrangement."

Silence.

More silence.

Stella glanced at her screen to make sure the call hadn't disconnected. It hadn't, and she tried to imagine what her boss was thinking. The same thing she was?

"Yeah, that makes sense, but Stella," his voice lowered to a growl, "if you're right, and let's hope to heaven you're not, then preventing the next kidnapping will be nearly impossible. Who the hell do we protect?"

It was exactly what she'd been thinking. Random crimes were the most difficult to solve.

Stella started to speak but found she had nothing to say. Slade was right. Everyone was unique. The killer could go for anyone next.

19

I almost bounced down the stairs to the basement that morning. I was so excited, so thrilled at how my project was coming along. The limbs intertwined, bending and flexing as if they were made to be together. The skin tones complemented each other perfectly.

When the world saw my great work, they would be awed.

When I reached the last step, I paused to catch my breath. The courage. The conviction. The message of unity and beauty embedded in the material itself. Who could stand in the face of such commitment?

Oh, there would be criticism, of course. There always was.

I could hear them already, decrying the cost of the material, asking if the price was too high.

"Who does he think he is?" they would say. "Is the message really worth the price?"

Of course it was!

But I still had more work to do, and until my project was complete, I could tell no one about it. At the moment, there was a striking hole, a gap in the piece that needed to be filled.

My dear Kati.

She understood. She loved art. She told me so. And how could someone that beautiful not appreciate the aesthetics, the colors, the tones I was incorporating? How could she not long to be part of it?

She was human, though, and the human brain was wired to protect its owner. Her limbic system would urge her to fight to her last breath, even when the rest of her mind understood the necessity of her sacrifice.

When I entered the basement, Kati's eyes widened. She shook in her chair, thrusting her head from side to side.

Her limbic system was alive and well, it seemed.

"I know, I know." I rushed to reassure her. "You want me to take off your gag. I am so sorry I have to leave it on when I'm not here. I just can't trust the soundproofing, you see. Here." I pulled her gag down. "Now, I'll be able to hear your beautiful voice again."

She took a deep breath. "You evil sonofabitch! You murderer. Scum. Get out. Get out. Let me go!"

The vitriol didn't stop there.

Oh, it was awful. The noise. The screaming. Her mouth was dry from the gag, making her voice hoarse and ragged.

And the names she called me. Who would have thought a woman of such beauty could be so coarse, so vulgar? And so false. Did she really believe what she was saying?

"Quiet!" Before I even knew what I was doing, I'd raised my hand, ready to strike.

No! What was I doing?

Her eyes widened even more. "Go on, you evil, little monster. Go on, hit me."

Taking a deep breath, I lowered my arm. No, I was a peaceful man, a man of beauty and love and art. I would never hit anyone, let alone a woman.

But I could shut her up.

I dragged the gag over her mouth. She struggled, but I would not give way. She mumbled as I tied the cloth tight, but as long as I couldn't hear those ugly curses, I could put up with her noises. The sacrifices an artist had to make.

Pulling the other chair closer, I sat in front of her, folding my arms and crossing my legs. "If you cannot act in a civilized, cultured way, then you will have to wear that gag. And you will not interrupt me while I speak. Now, I have already told you about the project I'm creating. What I have not told you is why I am creating it. Would you like to know that? Would you like to hear the inspiration from the artist himself?"

She quieted, as I was sure she would.

"Very well. It all comes down to my darling Diana. Such a beautiful woman, with such smooth skin the color of, well, I used to think of it as a kind of sandy loam." I leaned over and brushed my fingers along Kati's forearm. Goose bumps raised along her perfect skin. She tried to twist away but couldn't.

"Rich and earthy. And how it would shine in firelight. We lived in Chicago, just the two of us. I'm afraid we couldn't have children, so we devoted our lives to each other. And to art. I was an artist and a curator, and she was my model. My muse, perhaps I should say. She was such an inspiration."

Kati wasn't mumbling or complaining anymore. She was breathing heavily but listening intently. I knew she would. She was such a caring, sympathetic soul.

"We were so happy together. And then one night, two years ago exactly, my darling Diana went out to pick up our takeout. She didn't want to wait for the delivery boy, said she fancied a walk. I…I thought nothing of it. I…why should I have? Who would have…?"

A lump formed at the back of my throat. Kati's beautiful

brown eyes fixed on my face. I knew she was feeling my pain. Of course she was.

I swallowed hard and continued. "She was killed. Murdered. Stabbed. Because of her skin color. Just one more number in that year's hate crime statistics. They never caught the people who did it. Did they even look? I doubt it. There were so many such crimes that year."

Closing my eyes, I waited until I recovered my composure.

When I opened them, I folded my hands neatly on my lap. This was so difficult, so painful.

"Diana's loss hit me very hard, as you can imagine. I had a complete breakdown. I stopped working, stopped painting. Eventually, I decided to stop altogether. How could I work without Diana? What was the use of even trying?"

I rolled my sleeve away from my wrists, letting Kati see the scars. She had to know why she was making her sacrifice, why her contribution was so important.

"I took the portrait of her that I had been working on, and I set it on the floor of my studio. Then I took my palette knife and set it down next to her. And I cut my wrist. I waited to die."

Kati was silent. She sat in that chair without moving, utterly transfixed. I could tell she was shocked. Who would have thought that I, someone who had so much to live for, had once tried to take my own life? But the same could be said of Mark Rothko, of Constance Mayer, even of van Gogh himself.

Artists were a sensitive lot.

"But as the blood spilled from my wrist, it flowed onto the portrait. It ran through the cracks in the paint, pooled in the swipes, and soaked into the canvas. Such a beautiful color! No red was ever that red. No paint had ever brought such life to a portrait. I decided to live. I called an ambulance.

It arrived just in time to save me. Once I was well enough, I sold my house, moved here to Tennessee, and devoted my life to my new collection. Humanity as Art. Humans make up part of every masterpiece I create."

I smiled. I was sure she was impressed, but with the gag in her mouth, her expression was difficult to read. But how could she not be impressed?

"The collection has been a huge success so far. Landscapes and abstracts and figurative art, all with a touch of humanity. Some hair mixed into the base. A little saliva to soften the paint. Some blood to darken the reds. The critics love it."

I stroked the scars on my wrist.

"If only they knew just how much of myself I put into each work. But for the anniversary of my dear Diana's death, I must stretch myself. I want my art to have an impact, to change the world. To create peace on Earth. And the rest, of course, you know."

Leaning back, I lifted my hands, ready to accept her apologies now that she understood the importance of my work.

"I will showcase the whole of human beauty, love, and unity. Of course, I can't do that by myself. I need contributors who represent the diverse human experience. With generous lovers of art, like you, my dear Kati, I am making the classic peace symbol out of different shades of human limbs."

She was quite calm when I finished. Speechless.

"I've been prattling on for far too long. What would you like to talk about? You know how much I adore hearing your voice. You can tell me anything."

Eager to hear her sweet voice, I stood and pulled down her gag. She didn't scream. She just moved her jaw from side to side and pursed her lips.

Just as I was growing frustrated by the delay, Kati looked me in the eye. "I think you've experienced a deep loss, and I'm sorry for you. I think you need help dealing with your grief. And you need it now before you harm anyone else. From what you've just told me, I don't think Diana would want you to do this. I think she'd want you to get help now. I can help, if you'd let me."

Hearing my darling Diana's name on her lips had such a strange effect. Feeling dizzy, I sat back down, and closed my eyes.

Beyond my closed lids, I saw my beautiful wife on the slab. Where was that color she once had? All of it was gone. She was so gray, so colorless. All her beauty, her color, had leaked out of those slashes and punctures covering her body. I saw her face, the green eyes that had lost their vibrance looking up at me, pleading with me to go on without her.

The room spun, twisted, dropped beneath me. I was entirely lost. My new world had floated away, leaving me with nothing but the remnants of my old one.

For the first time, I noticed that Hu's blood had splattered across my shirt, and I was appalled at myself. "Forgive my bad manners. I should have changed before I came down. But my work isn't done for the day. I have a new piece to add to my project, and I should start while it's still fresh."

The room steadied, growing still. There was Kati. So beautiful. So wonderful.

"Please listen to me. I can—"

Smiling, I resisted her efforts and pulled up her gag. Shaking my head, I took her lovely face between my hands to calm and assure her that her words hadn't angered me one bit.

"No, no. I mustn't. I can't stop. Not now." I pressed my lips to her forehead. "I'm almost there."

20

Special Agent Chloe Foster pushed the door to the Morville County Sheriff's Department open and let the cool air waft over her. The ten-minute drive from the Zhao family cabin had been too short to cool the effects of a sweltering day spent trawling the woods and the grounds around the house. Her t-shirt stuck to her back. Sweat still dripped down her temples.

The search had been a waste of time. Ander had found Hu Zhao's phone in the first hour. It had been tossed into the woods and landed in a mound of fallen branches. The device had delivered few clues. Forensics quickly confirmed the lack of fingerprints. The only messages were a long line of missed calls from Min. Geo-tracking had shown that the phone hadn't moved from the site. The killer must have dumped it as soon as they'd kidnapped the elderly man.

Smart move.

The rest of the day had been a bust too. Hours of tramping through woods had turned up nothing but bugs and dead branches. Surely, there were better ways to spend a Sunday afternoon.

Ignoring the stare of the deputy sitting at the reception desk, she lifted her face to the air-conditioning unit and peeled her shirt away from her back. She shivered. The cold air felt *so* good.

Chloe groaned when her phone rang, but she pulled it out of the back pocket of her cargo pants and checked the caller.

Tanya Tomm.

Odd. Tanya was an old college friend of Chloe's wife. She and her boyfriend, Daniel, came to Chloe's kickboxing matches. And sometimes, she and Bridget would listen to Daniel play his guitar at a local bar. But when Tanya called or texted, the call would usually go to Bridget. Chloe would always get their news secondhand.

She hit the green button.

"Hey, Tanya. What's up?"

"Chloe, you have to help." Tanya's voice was higher pitched than usual, the tone urgent. "I'm really worried."

Chloe stepped back outside for privacy. The afternoon heat hit her like a hot, wet towel.

"Slow down, Tanya. Take a breath. What happened?"

There was a pause at the end of the line. A brief one. "It's Daniel. He went out this morning, and he hasn't come back."

That was it? Tanya's boyfriend had gone out all day? Seriously?

Chloe had been in law enforcement long enough to not completely dismiss a person's worry, though. "What time did he leave?"

"About ten. He said he had a surprise for me. It's my birthday in a couple of days. I figured he was going to pick up a present or something, but he didn't come back. He hasn't called, and he's not answering his phone. It's really weird, Chloe. He's not like this at all."

"Have you tried his friends?"

"Yeah, I've called his friends and some of his family. No

one's seen him, and he hasn't been in touch with anyone. I know it's early to be freaking out, but I'm scared."

Chloe chewed her bottom lip. She wanted to tell Tanya to sit tight and prepare to give her boyfriend a tongue-lashing when he crawled home sunburned and half-drunk. He hadn't even been gone half a day. But something was gnawing at her insides.

Tanya's tone and demeanor were so similar to Min Zhao's. Her insistence that something was wrong felt identical. She wondered if the case was getting to her.

Chloe had been skeptical yesterday, convinced Hu Zhao was too different from Darlene and Tiffany and Kati Marsh to fit the victim profile. But she'd been wrong. She needed to be cautious now.

"Daniel probably ran into an old friend or went for a walk, and his phone's out of juice. He'll probably come home in a minute, wondering what all the fuss is about. I'll look into it, though. What do you want for your birthday? Where might he have gone?"

"Um, there was an antique necklace I mentioned last week when we were wandering in the art district. There's also a painting I really liked at the Peace of Art Gallery—"

Chloe recognized the name right away. "The Darwin Rhodell place? I've got one of his pieces in my office. Expensive."

"Yeah, that one feels like a long shot."

Chloe pulled out a small notebook and pen from one of her leg pockets. "What was the name of the antique store?"

"The Time Capsule, but he might also be digging through vinyl stores. It's just weird he's not picking up his phone."

"Well, in the meantime, just think of all the different ways he'll have to make it up to you when he gets back."

"Thank you, Chloe." Relief was clear in Tanya's tone. "I really appreciate it."

Chloe disconnected the call, sweat dripping down the back of her neck. She wasn't one for instincts and emotion. Facts. Clues. Data. The look in a suspect's eye. All of that was a lot more accurate than a burning in your belly telling you something was wrong.

She'd rather leave that approach Stella. The rookie seemed to have a pretty sharp intuition.

Chloe wasn't Stella, but her radar was beeping wildly now. Tanya and Daniel lived in East Nashville. It wasn't terribly far from Morville, not much farther than Hu Zhao's cabin.

As Chloe considered everything she knew about Daniel, the burning in her gut grew warmer. He had always been reliable, straightforward, and dependable. Tanya was right. Disappearing for hours wasn't like him at all.

She shoved open the door and strode back into the sheriff's department.

———————

21

S tella scooted her chair forward in the briefing room to
let Chloe pass. Her colleague's brow was furrowed, her
face drawn. "You okay?"

"Hm?" Chloe took the chair next to her, dragged her
notebook out of her canvas backpack, and wiped the sweat
from her brow. "Yeah. Just…I'm not sure. Maybe nothing.
Slade not here yet?"

"He was still in Lansing's office when I came in. I think he
was giving him a pep talk."

Sheriff Lansing entered first. His face was pale, and his
unshaven cheeks had developed a five o'clock shadow that
was merging with his mustache. Even his skin seemed to be
weighing him down. As he had done that morning, he
pushed his chair into the corner and said nothing.

Slade soon followed with a folder tucked under his arm.
"Ander, what have you got?"

Ander pushed away a curl that sweat had glued to his
forehead. "Chloe and I had a fun day in the woods."

Hagen nudged Ander with his elbow. "Hey, Stella and I
were there too."

"Yeah, eventually. We were the ones sweating out there all day. And the only find was discovered in the morning. We picked up Hu Zhao's phone. The cyber team is going over it now, but I just spoke to them again. They say they've got nothing. The phone hasn't been anywhere unusual, there are no prints, and his contact list is shorter than mine."

Slade sighed. "Shame. That might have been useful. Hagen, what did you get at the morgue?"

"Mostly the heebie-jeebies."

Slade fixed him with an iron gaze. "Apart from that?"

"Apart from that, a few details. The M.E. thinks Tiffany and Darlene were missing for at least three days before they were killed, and their bodies weren't lying around for long." He turned to Ander. "You can tell that by the state of the blowfly eggs in the open wounds."

Ander wrinkled his nose. "Nice."

"Yeah, they were. Like the little fish eggs you get on the top of that sushi you like so much." Hagen swiveled back to Slade. "Hu Zhao's story is pretty similar. There was minimal decomp, so the unsub either held them for a couple of days before death or…"

Slade rolled a hand, telling him to get on with it. "Or what?"

"Or they were frozen. The M.E. said the bodies showed evidence that they had been frozen for a period of time after they were killed."

Slade frowned. "Do we have a cause of death?"

"No. Dr. Burroughs says the kill came before the dismemberment. There are no obvious signs of trauma to the body. Other than the chopping, of course. She's sent off samples to check for toxicity and thinks it'll be about five weeks before we get those results."

The SSA wrote the information on the board. "Right. Not

much we can do about that." Slade turned his attention on Stella.

Hagen held up a hand. "There was one more thing. Dr. Burroughs was sure the killer used a hacksaw or something like it to remove the arms, legs, and fingers. But when the unsub cut up Hu Zhao, they seemed to have rushed." He turned to Ander again. "You could see the cut marks on the bones, and there was this big flap of skin hanging off the bottom of Hu Zhao's arm. It was this big." He indicated several inches with his thumb and forefinger. "Looked like the killer just wanted to take his bits and get the body the hell out of there."

Ander's face was the picture of disgust. "Nice. I saw a spider in the woods. It was gross, man. Like the size of my thumb."

Stella pushed down a smile. Although she appreciated the banter, her mind was on the timer that was ticking down for a beautiful, young woman…unless she was already in someone's freezer.

She shivered. "But we don't know what made the unsub rush. If he's holding his victims for different amounts of time, Kati Marsh might still be alive, and we've no idea how long she's got."

Slade tapped his pen on the note that said *freezer*, apparently thinking the same thing Stella had. "Freezing the bodies changes our assumptions, but I want us to work under the belief that Kati Marsh is alive and waiting for us to save her." He turned back to the team. "Let's get our asses in gear and figure this thing out. Otherwise, we're not going to keep her in one piece. Stella, you had a theory."

Stella swallowed. She had a theory, but it really wasn't much more than that. And as Slade had pointed out, the idea wasn't that helpful either.

"I might have figured out something that ties the victims together."

Chloe's head snapped in her direction. "Really? You kept that quiet."

"It's not…don't get too excited." Should she even say it out loud yet? Even in her head it sounded crazy. "It's just that every victim is completely different. Usually, when we analyze victims, we look for similarities, right? We expect the same age, same sex, same hair color maybe. Killers have types. But these victims are all different. If you stood them all side by side, you have a range of different skin tones, ages, and sexes."

Chloe folded her arms. "If you're right, Stella, predicting the next victim will be damn difficult."

"True, but that variety also creates a kind of visual appeal. Look at how he leaves the bodies. The victims' physical differences might be the killer's main focus. Call it a hunch, but I'm thinking we're looking for maybe a designer or an artist? Only someone with an eye for that kind of aesthetic would be that fixated on appearance."

Hagen leaned back in his chair. "Sounds like a long shot."

"Stella might have pitched a long shot, but it's shorter than anything the rest of you have thrown." Slade opened his folder. He pulled out two sheets of paper and handed one each to Ander and Stella. "I've had the team at Nashville draw up a list of local artists who also fit the description of the old man at the bar."

Hagen lifted an eyebrow. "Damn. Well done, Nashville team. How'd they get on?"

"They did good. The description Ander got out of that waitress was a big help. Sex and age cut the options down a lot, and once they started looking for gray hair with a bit of frizz, they got down to a handful."

Ander pulled the sheet closer. "He might not always look like that."

"Sure. But we've got to start somewhere. Caleb sent the pictures to the waitress. She ID'd four possibilities, and two that come closest. Hagen, Ander, you've got a guy called Gary Glenderson. Chloe, Stella, you've got a Darwin Rhodell."

Chloe reached for the drawing. "Darwin Rhodell?"

Ander scowled at the name and address on the sheet. "Gary Glenderson? Anyone heard of these guys?"

"I have." Chloe seemed distracted as she gazed at the picture. "Bridget's into art. We go to galleries and art fairs sometimes. It's kinda cool. You should try it."

Ander pushed his chair back and stood. "Think I'll pass, but if you see a picture of dogs playing poker, grab one for me, okay?"

Slade lifted his hand. "Okay, enough. Get moving. Let's start with these two and see what we get."

Stella stuffed the drawing with the name and address of the artist's studio into her pocket and stood. She froze when Chloe knocked twice on the table.

"There's one more thing." Everyone's attention swung to Chloe. "It might be nothing, but I just got a call from a friend in East Nashville. Her boyfriend is missing."

Stella's stomach twisted. Another one?

Slade rested his fists on the table. "How long?"

"About six hours. He doesn't look anything like the previous victims. A dark-complected Black man. And he may have been in the art district, shopping for a birthday present. Darwin Rhodell's gallery specifically. It's the second time Rhodell's name has come up in thirty minutes."

"We'll go check him out." Stella dropped a hand on Chloe's shoulder. "But don't worry yet. I bet everyone who lives in or near the Nashville metro area is scared to death now. Whenever someone breaks their routine, you can be sure that everyone in law enforcement, from parking attendants to the attorney general, are getting calls."

"Stella's right." Slade held the door open for Ander and Hagen. "Keep an eye on it and let me know if he doesn't turn up soon. For now, focus on those artists' studios. You've got a girl to find. Go."

22

Just after Hagen had arrived at his previous assignment in San Francisco, he'd dated a very interesting woman. Jane had been something of a hippie, all tantric healing and chanting before breakfast. She'd shared an apartment out near Haight-Ashbury with two yoga teachers. Every time he'd gone over, the place stunk of incense.

The smell had been one of the reasons he called off the relationship after one month. There was only so much smoke a man could take between drinking wine and deciphering karma sutra drawings.

And here, ten yards outside Gary Glenderson's white-timbered house, that same scent polluted the air.

Hagen waved his hand in front of his nose. "Certainly smells like we're in the right place."

Ander's eyes had started to water. "Artists, man. They can't use Old Spice like normal people?" He walked up to the door and knocked hard. "Let's get this over with."

Hagen joined him just as the door opened, sending an even thicker layer of sandalwood ballooning into the front yard. He could almost feel the aroma's tentacles swimming his way and wanted to run before they could permeate his suit.

"Hello!" Gary Glenderson beamed a broad, warm smile.

Hagen put him in his late sixties. Old age was close. Yet Gary seemed to be trying to fend off the years by tying his gray hair back in a ponytail.

The move didn't work. The hair that remained at the sides curled uncontrollably while his bald scalp reflected the afternoon sun. Behind him, a stack of canvasses and frames leaned against the foyer's wall, blocking much of the entrance. At least Gary's smile was welcoming.

When Ander sneezed, Gary's expression morphed to concern. "I'm sorry. It's the incense, isn't it? I can overdo it, I'm afraid. My wife did love it. She's passed now, but I like to keep some sandalwood going as much as I can. The house doesn't seem the same without it."

"That's no problem, sir." Hagen told his first lie and pulled out his ID. "It's a lovely smell. I should get some. I'm Special Agent Hagen Yates of the FBI." And there went his second and third.

Ander sneezed again.

"I'll get some for my colleague too." Hagen slipped his badge back into his pocket. "We'd just like to ask you a few questions in relation to an ongoing investigation. Hope that's okay?"

Gary's eyes widened. "Is it about those murders? How can I help?" He started to wave them inside the house, but when Ander sneezed for the third time, he closed the door behind him. "Let's talk in the backyard. It's less, um, fragrant. Come, come."

Ander was right on the man's heels. "That's perfect."

Gary plucked a flower from a bush and pressed the petals to his nose. "I often work outside. The fresh air is so good for you. Fresh oxygen. Clears the senses, improves creativity."

No Shasta daisies, Hagen noticed. Damn.

They followed as Gary practically skipped around the house. The artist seemed to have boundless energy, despite his age. His ponytail bounced with every step, like a bushy squirrel's tail.

Once they entered the backyard, any amusement they felt toward the man disappeared.

Bones littered the rear lawn. An ox skull hung from the low branch of a black walnut tree. Stacks of what looked like femurs were piled beneath it. Other bones, which would require an orthopedic specialist to identify, were laid out in odd design shapes.

Ander froze on the spot. "What the…"

"What the what?" Gary inspected their obviously surprised faces. Then he laughed. "Oh! These. I'm doing a piece on how our interiority reflects our exteriority. It's coming across quite nicely."

"None of these are human, are they?" Ander stepped toward the ox skull, his face grim.

"Human?" As Gary looked from Hagen to Ander and back again, his friendly smile faded. "Wait. You don't think I…" His mouth opened and closed like a fish. "Now, just one minute. If you think…I'm a peace-loving man, I'll have you know. I'm an animal rights activist. Always have been. I demonstrate against vivisection and veal, and I…I run a website promoting the protection of bees. I wouldn't hurt a fly."

"Just an ox? Or deer? Or—"

Gary waved away Hagen's question with an angry chop of his arm. "I wouldn't hurt anyone. The idea is ridiculous. You must be *insane*."

"Sir, you have bones in your backyard."

The artist stepped forward, pointing an index finger at Hagen's chest. "For a project." He took a deep breath, and

Hagen half-expected him to make an *om* sound. The breathing didn't work. When Gary spoke again, his face turned redder with every word. "I don't know who put you up to this, but if someone told you that I'm involved in these terrible crimes, they're lying."

Hagen was tempted to break the finger still pointed at him but simply held up one of his own. "Sir, no one has—"

"You should arrest them for..." Gary's eyes bounced inside his skull as he searched for the right words. "For wasting police time. And making false accusations. I suppose you'll need an alibi, won't you? Well, I'm afraid I don't have one. So there."

Hagen let the finger drop as he absorbed the outpouring of words, studying the artist's face closely. Was that real indignation at the thought that someone might think he was a murderer? Or was he protesting too much?

If Gary were their unsub, he'd know that someone would knock on his door one day. And he'd know that he'd need to convince them that he was too nice to have done anything like chop up a bunch of random people. He'd be ready to show them a shocking bone collection and prepared to show shock and outrage.

Hagen tapped into his gut. Which was it? Indignant animal lover? Or desperate killer?

His gut told him nothing. Not yet.

Gary strode over to Ander, the scent of sandalwood following the artist like a poisonous mist. "I used to have a store in Morville where I sold art supplies and whatnot, but these days, I rarely leave the house, except for the odd grocery run. No. If you're looking for someone who can vouch for me, you can...you can talk to my four cats and my three dogs. Or maybe you'd prefer the chickens out back?"

Ander lifted a hand to stop the man from getting any closer. "Sir...*achoo*." He ran a hand under his nose and tried again. "Sir, I can assure you that you're not…*aah…aah…* you're not…*achoo*…an official suspect in the investigation."

Hagen would've helped Ander out, but this was just too funny. Plus, stepping back gave him a better opportunity to watch the artist's body language.

"An *official…?*" Gary slammed his fists onto his hips. "So, you think I'm an *unofficial* suspect, do you? Well, let me ask you this. Do you have an *official* search warrant?"

Hagen took a deep breath. What the hell was the matter with this guy? Did the water in this town cause people to morph between Jekyll and Hyde? "No, sir, we don't. We just—"

"Then you two can take an official hike. Go on, get the hell out." Gary stomped toward his back door. Not finished yet, he turned on his heel, waving a finger. "I've never been so insulted in my life. I'm just glad my wife isn't alive to see this. She'd tell you I wouldn't hurt a damn fly. Now go on, get lost."

Hagen glanced at Ander, who was busy trying to stop another sneeze with the palm of his hand. When Hagen returned his attention to Gary, the door slammed shut behind him.

Ander dragged an already used tissue out of his pocket and blew his nose. "He was nice."

"A bit extreme. We'd barely even started."

"Artists, man. Drama queens, the lot of them."

Hagen gave a short laugh and took out his phone to take some covert pictures of the yard. The bones might be enough for a search warrant. Maybe. "Yeah, and quite a temper for an aging hippy. You'd think they'd be all peace, love, and instant cooperation."

When he took the last image, the pair headed back to the front.

"Yeah, though maybe it's not surprising." Ander propped

an arm on the hood of the Explorer. "I mean, we did just practically accuse him of killing and dismembering three people. I'm not sure how I'd react to being accused of something like that if I hadn't done it."

"And if you had done it?"

Ander shrugged. "Even harder to know how I'd react."

"Exactly. I don't know how to read that reaction. And that incense. What was he burning in there? A forest?"

"I don't know how he can breathe." Ander waved a hand in front of his face. "I can still smell it from here."

How could anyone live like that?

A thought occurred to him. "Think it's strong enough to hide the smell of a body?"

Ander's eyes widened. "Shit. I was so busy trying to breathe, I didn't even think of that. Think we should bring him in?"

"Because of incense? No judge will sign off on an arrest warrant for that. Not based on the variety of the victims, a waitress's vague description, and bad taste in aromatherapy."

Ander pulled open the door. "Let's hope Stella and Chloe are doing better."

Hagen eased into the driver's seat. He shared Ander's hope, but a thought was sneaking into the back of his mind. What if they were wrong about the artist theory? They could be chasing their own tails while the unsub was changing his hacksaw blade.

He shivered and gunned the engine.

―――――――

23

S tella didn't say a word as Chloe backed into the parking space, slamming the brake an inch from the sedan behind her. She dragged the wheel around, hit the gas, and straightened the front, ending the parallel parking maneuver with a violent jolt.

Chloe did everything in her life the same way…at Mach speed and with no apologies.

Glad to have survived the drive over, Stella unclicked the seat belt and reached for the door handle before Chloe attempted another maneuver.

The street was broad and mostly empty at the tail end of a Sunday afternoon. The Hollyoaks Café next door seemed to be doing good business, but the antique store on the other side of the street had already closed for the day, as had the vinyl record store next to it.

Chloe threw up her hands. "Great. Guess we can't check for Daniel down here. That'll have to wait."

"We can ask Rhodell at least." Stella squinted into the late-day sun. "Which way are we headed?"

Chloe pointed down the block where a wooden sign

painted in rainbow colors announced the Peace of Art Gallery. "That's the one."

Stella examined the logo. "Nice colors. Wonder what his art's like."

"It's not for everyone. He has a pretty unique style. Big on bold colors." Chloe flushed. "Bridget really likes him."

Stella grinned. Chloe, the art lover. Should that have surprised her? Maybe not. Stella was convinced there was a lot under that prickly coating Chloe didn't want others to see.

At the entrance, a sign instructed visitors to ring the doorbell for entry while a camera peered down at them from above. She pressed her thumb to the doorbell and lifted her ID to the lens.

When the door buzzed and clicked, Chloe pushed it open, and entered into a grand gallery lit by spotlights bright enough to make her squint. Gray walls softened their intensity, and Stella wondered if the muted color helped the works stand out. Most of the pieces were landscapes, but the artist had avoided realistic representations, using interesting textural pieces and opening his color palette.

Skies were never pale blue. They were a wash of purples and lilacs and crimsons. Trees, embedded with tufts of fur and real bark, became mottled shades of brown topped by every imaginable variety of green. Seascapes became excuses to play with tones of blue and white, with rainbow-tinted fish scales flashing in the display lights. A rolling wave said less about the movement of water and more about the different varieties of shade and shells hidden in a line of surf.

These bold colors weren't for everyone. But Stella could see why Chloe's wife liked the pictures so much and why Chloe admired them too.

A man emerged from a door at the end of the gallery, wiping his hands on a rag. No taller than Stella, his button-down shirt might once have been yellow, but it was now smeared with every color she could imagine. Splashes of vermilion and white were scattered across the front of it. His sleeves and collar blazed in splotches of orange, purple, and a deep, deep red.

Above it all, gray hair stood out on the side of his head, giving him a slightly bewildered appearance that belied the bright smile of welcome stretching across his face.

"Welcome to my gallery. Darwin Rhodell." He shoved the rag into the back of his waistband and extended his hand. "Was that an FBI badge I saw on the screen? Don't see that too often in here. How can I help you? I'm sure that in work like yours, a little art could be good for the soul."

Stella shook his hand and returned the smile. "I wish we were just here to see some art. It's all very…striking. Are these all yours?"

"Most of them, yes." Arms wide, he turned in a circle. "There are a few pieces made by other artists in the area. I do like to support the local community. There is so much talent here in East Nashville. Can you tell which ones aren't mine? A little investigative challenge for you."

Stella surveyed the room. She'd always wanted to learn to tell the difference between this art movement and that one, to understand what an artist was trying to say and how they were saying it. But criminal justice degrees left little time for art history or visits to museums.

Standing in that gallery, comparing one painting to another, her heart ached a little. She couldn't tell these paintings apart at all. They were all colorful and abstract, even when they tried to depict a landscape or still life. She liked some more than others but couldn't really put her finger on why.

Chloe walked up to a canvas depicting a road snaking through a pasture. Trees in fall tones of scarlet and auburn cast long shadows over the grassland, stretching the dark lines of their trunks across the ground. The scene darkened as the eye followed the road to the corner, suggesting the arrival of winter and the shortening of days.

"This one's not yours. If I had to guess, I'd say it was Sofia Benson."

Darwin clapped his hands. "Very good. Well done, Agent…?"

"Foster. Chloe Foster."

"Well done, Agent Foster. I see you have an eye for art. And you know your local artists. Good for you."

Chloe's face reddened a little. "Your works are never this dark. I don't think you'd use so much shade. Unless it was a silhouette. Sofia Benson has a thing for shadows, though."

"Yes, exactly! Sofia is a lovely lady. Have you met her?"

Chloe shook her head. "I've not had the honor, no."

"Oh, she's very nice. You'd like her. Everyone does. But she does have a dark streak that comes out in her work. A little pessimistic touch that I think mars her *oeuvre*, although lots of people like it. And you're right. I like to keep that touch of darkness out of my own paintings. Far better to lift people up than drag them down. Now, can you spot any others?"

Stella scanned the room again. At the end of the gallery, a picture hung vertically. While the colors on most of the other works were bold and primal, this painting was muted. The grays and deep black of the background overpowered the burgundy dress of the woman it framed.

Darwin followed Stella's gaze. He took a deep breath and headed in the portrait's direction. "Ah. This *is* one of mine." He turned back to Chloe, who had followed him down the gallery. "You wouldn't expect it to be one of mine, would you? Because of the dark colors and the subject, of course. This is the only portrait in the gallery."

"Your wife," Chloe murmured.

Darwin inclined his head. "Yes. I finished it from memory shortly after she died. Which is why I hope you will excuse the indulgence of the painting's melancholy. It was a difficult period."

Moving closer, Stella admired the painting. The image was almost full size, the subject beautiful. Darwin's wife had a narrow chin and high cheekbones. Her eyebrows were painted in charcoal smudges that narrowed into sharp, little needles. The burgundy dress seemed striped with deeper reds. Her black hair fell in waves, revealing only the slightest glints of light before disappearing into the background. Her dark skin faded with the shadows.

The picture sent a chill down Stella's spine. In a room full of wild colors, this painting was too powerful, dug too deep. "I'm sorry for your loss."

Darwin lifted a hand to his heart. "Thank you. Now, how can I help you?"

Stella glanced again at the painting and couldn't help but see Kati Marsh's face in the portrait. Would Kati, also dark-haired and green-eyed, end up in a painting like that, disappearing into the darkness? She swallowed the rush of emotion the thought induced. "We're investigating a case involving multiple homicides and are interviewing locals for any clues."

"Oh, lord." Darwin lifted his hand to his mouth. "I'm afraid I don't follow the news very closely, but I did learn of Hu Zhao from his lovely daughter. Hu and I, we often attended the same events. He was a writer, you know. Very talented. There are other disappearances?"

"Homicides." Stella watched his face closely. "Not disappearances."

His expression remained constant, depicting a gentle

sadness. "I don't know how I can help, but if there's anything I can do…"

"Can you tell me where you were on the night of Saturday, June fifth?"

Darwin's eyes widened at Stella's question. "Where…? What? Why?"

Chloe smiled.

For a moment, Stella wondered if her partner was going to place a reassuring hand on Darwin's arm. She didn't go that far. "We believe our subject may circulate within the art circles. It's just a line of inquiry, but if you can answer my colleague's question, that would be a big help."

"Of course, of course. I understand. Let me see…Saturday night." Darwin reached behind him and retrieved his rag. He wiped his hands again as he thought. "Oh, yes, of course. The fifth was this *last* Saturday. Yes, yes, I had some friends over for drinks. My apartment is right above the gallery. We had wine and cheese and whatnot. I can give you their names and numbers if you need them."

A bell exploded within the silence of the gallery, causing both Stella and Chloe to spin around. On the other side of the glass door entrance stood two men, hands in their pockets, sandals matching their khaki shorts.

Darwin lifted his hand to his heart. "Made me jump too. It never ends here. It really doesn't. Barely have time to paint." He chuckled. "Still, shouldn't grumble, should I? The alternative would be far worse. Do excuse me a moment."

Stella shot him a reassuring smile. "Of course."

He headed toward the door and let the pair in. "I'll be with you gentlemen in just a second."

The men could have been brothers with their graying beards and matching shaved heads. Their vibe, however, indicated a different type of closeness as they moved in unison toward the first painting.

Darwin returned to the agents and lowered his voice. "Now, those numbers." He went to the counter and found a scrap sheet of paper. When he'd finished, he handed the paper to Chloe.

"Thank you. One more thing." Chloe stopped Darwin before he could turn away. "There may have been a young man in the gallery earlier, looking for a birthday present. His name is Daniel. He's about five foot nine, skinny. Black. Big smile. Probably wearing a t-shirt with a band of some kind on it?"

Darwin's eyelids fluttered as he considered her question. "I'm afraid I haven't seen anyone of that name or description here today." He indicated the two men admiring a multi-hued rendering of a sunset over a waterfall. "Thank you very much for stopping in, but I must attend to my visitors."

Stella smiled. "We understand. Please call us if you think of anything that could be helpful to our investigation." She and Chloe dropped their cards on the counter before showing themselves out.

"Almost Sunday evening and the guy's still doing business. Wouldn't have thought an artist would be so busy."

Chloe shrugged. "You'd be surprised. He's a big name in the area. But would someone that busy have the time to drive to Morville to stalk a young woman enough times to know her running schedule?"

Would he? Possibly. "I suppose he could make time. He's his own boss, after all."

"Is that what your Spider-Sense tells you?"

Stella almost laughed. "My Spider-Sense? Cop's Instinct, maybe. Did you notice the eye flutter when you asked him about Daniel? It deviated from his baseline."

Chloe nodded. "I did, but it only tells us that he was processing information. I didn't notice any other indicators to point toward a cluster of deception. Did you?"

"No." Stella's spirits sagged. "He fits the waitress's description, though. He needed a haircut, and he was nice. Didn't we say the unsub had to be nice enough to put someone off their guard? We can't rule him out."

Chloe looked to the heavens. "Jeez, Stella. We can't rule him out, and we can't rule him in. Not getting far, are we?"

"No." It was a depressing thought. "No, we're not."

Stella pulled open the car door, hoping Ander and Hagen had done better.

They were reaching the end of another day, and they were still no closer to finding Kati Marsh.

24

Stella sat in the Morville County Sheriff's Department briefing room for the third morning, knowing little more than she had on the first.

Here we go again.

What should have been a single night in a motel had turned into two sleepless nights. She rubbed her eyes, knowing she couldn't complain.

It was also another night in captivity for Kati Marsh.

Or another night in a freezer.

Chloe scrabbled with her phone and charger in the corner, cursing the "useless motel outlets." Her phone was dead, and she practically vibrated with annoyance as she waited for it to charge enough to get a signal.

Ander's curls didn't have their usual spring. "I think we should bring in Gary Glenderson. He fits Becky Long's description of the man at Patty's Pub & Grill. He's an artist, so he chimes with Stella's theory. And he was mean as hell and plays with bones. Get him in here. DNA. Fingerprints. And we lean on him. See if he cracks."

Slade studied the murder board. "That's all pretty thin.

We won't get an arrest warrant based on a description, an idea, and a bad attitude."

Stella rolled her stiff neck. "I don't think we're getting anywhere with either of them. We need to take another look at Nashville's list and broaden the search."

"I think Stella's right." Hagen agreed without looking at her.

In fact, he didn't appear to have noticed her at all. Whatever connection might have clicked between them on their way back from Hu Zhao's cabin seemed to have unclicked.

Better that way. No point in getting distracted.

"Becky could have gotten her ID wrong when she examined the photos that Caleb sent," Hagen continued. "She wouldn't be the first witness to misidentify someone."

"And if she got the ID wrong, maybe she got the description wrong too." Anger, borne of frustration and impatience, burned in Stella's gut. "That bar was pretty dark, even at midday. We might have narrowed the field down too far, too fast. And that's about the only thing we're doing too fast. We're going to have to pick up the damn pace and cover a lot more ground. We need to find Kati now."

Slade nodded. "Right. There were no bodies found overnight, so—"

The door to the briefing room swung open, and Sheriff Lansing strode in, a sheet of paper in his hand. His face was like granite. He stopped next to Slade and addressed the room.

"We've got another body."

Stella's stomach turned in on itself. *We lost Kati. Shit.*

She took a deep breath and braced herself for the news.

Lansing lifted the sheet of paper, shook the creases out of it, and read out the details. "Tanya Tomm of East Nashville has discovered the body of her boyfriend, Daniel Swanson."

The gasp that followed was short and quickly stifled.

Everyone shot a glance at Chloe, whose face had paled. Her hand now covered her mouth.

In the silence immediately following Lansing's announcement, Chloe's phone beeped. A series of notification dings sounded. Chloe read her messages, her face growing paler by the second. Stella's heart went out to the other agent.

Lansing continued, unaware of the undercurrent in the room. "The body was found in an alleyway behind their apartment building as Tanya Tomm was taking out the garbage." He tossed the paper on the table. "The body was naked and missing a right arm. The wounds and genital area were covered with Shasta daisies."

Chloe darted from the room. Stella placed both hands on the table, ready to launch after her, but Slade stopped her in her tracks. "Give her a few minutes."

Stella wanted to ignore the order but sank back in her seat. She could only imagine how Chloe was feeling and wanted to reassure her that Daniel's death wasn't her fault. Of course, she'd done what she could with the tiny pieces of information Tanya had given her.

Slade picked up the paper Lansing had tossed down. "East Nashville, huh? Guess our hunting grounds just got bigger."

25

Yellow police tape flapped in the morning breeze. Daniel's body had been removed, but the tape remained, sealing off the end of the alley where garbage cans stood in a tidy row, waiting to be filled. The fence behind the cans had recently received a fresh coat of creosote. The wood looked too brown and clean for the crime it had witnessed.

The words "hate crime" had been mentioned multiple times by the forensic team. But, at the bottom of the alley, where the fence planks met the concrete, several petals from a daisy had worked their way into the cracks.

It wasn't your fault. There was nothing you could have done.

The thought had become Chloe's mantra since she had rushed out of the briefing room and into the parking lot. Once outside, she could breathe again before releasing a long, silent scream that would have shattered windows had she given it a voice.

It wasn't your fault. There was nothing you could have done.

She knew, intellectually, that Daniel's death wasn't her fault. They just weren't close enough to cracking this thing. And the killer was too damn careful to leave clues. He was too cautious. Too smart. And they were moving too damn slow.

It wasn't your fault. There was—

I should have tried, dammit! I should have done more than question one art gallery owner. I shouldn't have assumed Daniel would come rolling through the front door again, all apologetic and stinking of beer.

Chloe squeezed her eyes closed. She wasn't going to cry. She wasn't.

Stella stood next to her behind Daniel and Tanya's building, probably worried that Chloe wouldn't be able to get her shit together after this.

Surely, the new girl blamed her. Why wouldn't she? And she must be able to sense Chloe's self-loathing.

"It wasn't your fault, Chloe." Stella's hand was gentle on her shoulder. "There was nothing you could do."

For a moment, the tension melted away. Hearing someone else say out loud what she'd been thinking had a powerful effect. But the sensation didn't last. Anger and guilt came flooding back. Chloe clenched her fists, her short nails digging into her palms to block the scream of rage that wanted to burst out.

I'm going to find that sonofabitch. I'm going to find him now.

Stella's fingers gripped her shoulder. "Hey, there was nothing you could have done about Daniel. And there's nothing we can do that will help him now. But Kati Marsh hasn't turned up yet, which means she might still be alive. We *can* do something to keep her that way. Let's focus on her. That's how we bring justice for Daniel and Hu and Darlene and Tiffany. We save Kati. Okay?"

Chloe gave a short nod and pushed down hard on her anger. That rage wasn't going anywhere, which was fine, but she needed a clear head to think.

They climbed the few stairs to the first-floor apartment

and rang the doorbell. At the sight of Tanya, all puffy faced, with her russet hair disheveled and its party-girl purple streak out of place, Chloe just wanted to turn and run. She waited for Tanya to hit her, to yell, *"You did this. You should have found him. Look what you've done."*

Instead of yelling, Tanya burst into tears. She threw her arms around Chloe and sobbed into her shirt.

Wrapping her arms around Tanya, she rested a cheek on her friend's shoulder. From the corner of her eye, she saw Stella take two steps back and walk to the end of the corridor. The stairwell window seemed to give her a view of something interesting in the parking lot.

Chloe held Tanya tight. She didn't want to let go, but after a long moment, Tanya pulled back and wiped her eyes. "Come on in."

The last time she'd visited, they'd been drinking red wine and eating some strange Gruyère Bridget had found in a fancy East Nasty cheese shop. Every time a new song poured out of the speakers, talk had drifted back to the playlist Daniel had put together. Now there was no music, and the two guitars hanging on the wall above the sofa looked mournful.

Tanya curled herself into the corner of the sofa, her legs tucked beneath her. Chloe took the other end while Stella perched on the edge of the armchair opposite. They could have been three friends talking about love and celebrities and the state of the nation. But they weren't.

Tanya wiped her nose and pulled her legs in tighter. "How could anyone do this to him? Why? He was…he was such a nice guy. He was so harmless. He could make a friend out of anyone." She reached forward and touched Chloe on the knee. "Do you remember that time we went to that Vietnamese place on Fatherland, and he got to chatting with the couple at the next table? He made us push our tables together so that we'd be one party. That was what he was like. He was so friendly. How can someone talk to him and…and do that?"

Chloe gripped her friend's hand. She remembered that evening. And she also remembered how she sometimes found Daniel's friendliness a bit too much. Chloe had envied his amiability, but on more than one occasion, she'd worried Daniel would trust someone he shouldn't.

Is that what happened? Had he stopped to talk to someone who was looking for a victim instead of a friendly conversation?

Stella leaned forward. "Was there anything unusual about Daniel recently? Had he mentioned a new place he liked to visit or talked about a new friend?"

Tanya pulled some fresh tissues from a box. "No, I don't think so. He was the same. Busy, fun, just himself, you know. He said he was going out to get a surprise for me, but I don't know what it was. I don't know…" She broke into sobs again.

Chloe moved until she sat next to her friend and pulled Tanya into her chest. As tears soaked her t-shirt, Chloe thought of all the hundreds of shops in East Nashville that Daniel might have visited. Would he have gone for flowers? Fancy chocolates? She could see him spotting some rare piece of music in an online catalog and rushing out to pick it up.

The possibilities were endless.

"Do you have an app like *Find My Friends* or *Life 360*?" Stella asked.

Tanya nodded but didn't move from her position. "Yes, but Daniel had turned his location finder off because he didn't want me to know where he was going."

Damn.

Even if they restricted the choice to shops within walking distance, there were still far too many possibilities. Daniel was lean and fit. He could have walked one block or twenty. And maybe he hadn't gone to a store at all. East Nashville was filled with local artists who worked from home or sold out of their garages—Gary Glenderson, for one. Darwin Rhodell, for another.

The East Nashville police had officers out canvassing the area and gathering camera footage. They'd share their findings with the Morville County Sheriff's Department, the place that was running point. Going through all that video footage, even with three law enforcement groups, could take days. And they didn't have days. Kati Marsh might not even have hours.

Ping.

Chloe's phone alerted her to a message.

Ping.

Stella's phone did the same.

Chloe let her colleague check the message. Her arms were busy.

"It's Slade." Stella pocketed her phone. "He wants us back at the resident office as soon as we're done."

Chloe nodded and let go of her friend. "We need to get going. The sooner we catch this bastard, the better. If you think of anything, if you remember anything that might help us, you call me right away. Bridget's on her way over. I don't want you to be alone, okay?"

Tanya wiped an eye and gave a small nod.

As they made their way back down through the parking lot and past the alley with its yellow tape, Stella placed her hand on Chloe's back. "We *will* get him, Chloe. We will."

Chloe didn't reply. She knew they would.

She just didn't know how many mutilated bodies would be found before they did.

26

I n honor of Daniel and to fulfill my promise to the young
man, I'd finished the piece he'd commissioned before
deciding to add him to my great work. It was a shame
neither he nor Tanya would ever see it. I carried it into the
storage room and rested it against the wall. Satisfied, I sat
among the empty easels and canvases on the floor to take
one last look at it.

I'd taken the photo Daniel had provided and used it to
create four panels, each with a different background color.
Less photo booth, more Andy Warhol. But, of course, I'd
added a little extra human touch. For Tanya's hair, I used
some of Kati's, dying each of her dark locks a different
color.

Daniel and I had met in a sandwich shop off Gallatin
Avenue. I was ahead of him in line but struggling with the
purple chalk and the little cheese drawing someone had
made in the corner of the chalkboard menu. The cheese
color was sickly, and the perspective was all wrong.

"Try the Italian sausage. Best thing they've got here."

That was what Daniel had said, distracting me from the

sketch. I took his recommendation, and we ended up chatting about food and music and art while we waited.

Such a friendly young man. And he'd been so excited when he learned I was an artist. He brought out his phone and showed me a picture of him with his girlfriend, Tanya. They were sitting by a lake. The sun cast silver lines on the water behind them. Their lips touched but their eyes were open, gazing into each other's souls.

The composition really was the simplest expression of love, almost kitsch. But it had such colors. His rich, brown eyes and his black, curly hair spiraled out, reflecting the setting sun like an angel's halo. Her green eyes and russet hair with that single purple swoosh flowing past her ear really completed the image.

"Could you make this into a painting?"

My instinct was to say no. That wasn't how I worked. Turn a photograph into a painting? I wasn't a translator. I was an artist. I created, not transformed.

But there was something about him and about that photograph. He had such a naïve charm. The depth of his eyes. The emerald glints in hers. His rich, earth-toned hands holding hers. And their love. Was there anything purer than deep, young love?

A simple commission to celebrate the devotion of a beautiful, young couple. Why not?

But Daniel was destined for greater things.

I sighed and pushed the painting back against the wall.

When Daniel had walked into the studio yesterday, he'd worn a loose t-shirt, revealing long, thin arms so smooth and even-toned from elbow to fingertip.

That color juxtaposed against Tiffany's freckled paleness. That arrangement!

And the love that beat in Daniel's heart. It would flow through my art too.

Don't take a local. It's too dangerous.

But he'd been so perfect. Seeing him at the door, I'd been struck by such an urge, one that flowed through me like electricity, tingling the tips of my fingers.

The sun outside had been merciless, so I offered him a drink, knowing he wouldn't refuse. As he admired the work on my walls, it had been so simple to slip a little Rohypnol into his cup. A few seconds later, I handed him his refreshment and waited.

I remembered how off guard he'd taken me by dropping so quickly. Too quickly. As he prattled on about how my gallery was his last stop after a day full of birthday shopping for his lovely Tanya, he staggered, collided with a wall, and collapsed to the floor like a drunk student at a party.

I hadn't known what to do, so frozen in indecision as I'd been.

The gallery was open. A patron could ring the bell at any moment. I had no idea whether Daniel had told someone where he was going. The phone in his pocket had likely pinged that he'd stopped at this address.

My stomach was in knots. What if Tanya was *right at that moment* sitting in a car outside the gallery checking her watch? Any minute now, she could knock on the door to see what was keeping him.

If she did, I'd decided to take care of her too.

When no knock came, I forced myself to move…to do *something*…and dragged him into the cutting room, away from prying eyes. Finding his phone, I powered it off before hoisting his lanky frame onto the worktable and pushed a chloroform-coated rag over his face, holding it there.

My heart had been beating like a sparrow's as I waited for the drug to work. It was quite different from the way it was depicted on TV shows and movies. People didn't simply go to sleep a few seconds after their mouth was covered. It could take up to five minutes, even more, before the drug went into effect.

Movies also didn't share how dangerous the chemical could be. If too much was applied or for too long, death was the result.

Good thing for me, that was exactly what I'd wanted. A peaceful death that left no marks to flaw such beautiful skin or to leave any evidence behind. Another benefit of chloroform was that it left a body quickly.

Daniel's heart was still when I pressed my fingers against his throat.

His chest no longer rose and fell.

He was gone.

Normally, I would have taken time to appreciate the subject's sacrifice to the arts, and I regretted I had no time to do such honors. I removed his clothes and immediately applied the hacksaw to his right arm.

Back the saw went, then forward. Back and forward. Sweat beaded on my forehead, but I refused to stop. Back and forward. Back, and…a jarring pain reverberated up my arm. The blade was stuck.

Damnation!

With more effort than I would have preferred, I dislodged the blade and frowned.

I'd cut no more than a quarter of the way through the bone. Changing the angle, I tried once more, not stopping as sweat dripped down my neck and back.

Almost there. Just a little more…

Skrick, skrick went the steel against the bone. There was no more than a centimeter left to cut…and that's when the blade snapped.

I fought the impulse to throw the saw at the wall. Of all the times for my tool to let me down.

Calming myself, I pulled a new blade from the drawer.

When my doorbell rang, I'd spun around. On the security screen in the corner of the room, three young women stood at the door.

I froze. What did I do now?

Ring.

The doorbell rang again. Still, I ignored it. The women stood there until one spoke to the other, and they turned and left. I exhaled in relief.

Changing the blade as quickly as I could, I finished the job with shaking hands until Daniel's arm lay next to him on the table.

Such shoddy work. The cut was ragged, and, in my haste, the blade had left thin scratches on his forearm.

This was not how an artist should work. Creation was a process that required sacrifice and patience and time. For a moment, as I stared down at Daniel's unmoving form, blood dripping onto the cold floor. I shouldn't have given in to the impulse.

Yet…when my gaze shifted to that beautiful arm beside him, the tension faded. What gorgeous patterning he would bring to my work. His love for Tanya would infuse the creation. Love could fade, but I was immortalizing this couple's devotion in my masterpiece.

In the storage room, I gazed at Daniel's commission again. That I had spent more time painting this insignificant work than collecting Daniel's contribution made my heart ache.

Perhaps I should visit Tanya and explain to her the splendor of Daniel's sacrifice?

But no. When my piece was unveiled, she'd know. Maybe she'd even collaborate with me one day, her love and grief spilling into my future pieces.

At least she had him back now. And I had arranged him so nicely.

But don't do that again. No more local contributors. Or more impulsive actions. Your work is not complete.

If only all my collections had been as easy as Darlene and Tiffany. I had driven to that pub in Berthar Lake, hoping to find only one source for my project. I'd found two. So beautiful they both were, and happy, filled with the simple joy of being alive.

When I noticed the nice waitress grab a pack of cigarettes and head down a back hallway, I made my move. Approaching the pair, I mentioned that I was stepping outside to have a certain *special* smoke and invited them to join me.

Tipsy as they were, they agreed. "We just need to pay our bill first." Darlene's voice was just as lovely as her face. Truly perfect.

"Allow me." I tossed a hundred onto their table, and being a gentleman, I even carried their drinks.

A drop in each one. Easy. Smooth. Not like the sloppy job with poor Daniel.

Sighing, I stood and pushed Daniel's painting behind the other canvases.

I'd do better next time.

27

T he familiar walls of the FBI's Nashville Resident Agency CID office reduced the strain and tension that had settled on Hagen since the start of the case. The office did feel a little like home, especially after two nights in a motel and briefings in someone else's station.

When he spotted Chloe, her face pale and drawn, all that tension surged back. A jolt of pain spread across his shoulders. Her downcast gaze and ashen cheeks displayed her grief. She blamed herself, of course, though there was nothing the agent could have done.

It was the curse of their line of work. Deep down each of them believed they should be able to control outcomes. Hagen certainly believed if he'd just thought faster, moved quicker, spotted the connections sooner, he could have saved every victim.

Self-loathing? Self-blame? Those emotions came with the badge and the gun.

Chloe's quiet expression reminded him why he was there. To stop the next killing. To find Kati Marsh. To dig the murderer out of his hole and blast him with justice.

Slade stood at the front of the room. He waited for Chloe and Stella to take their seats before clearing his throat. "Chloe, Stella. Did you get anything useful from Tanya?"

Chloe shook her head. "She doesn't know anything. Daniel was going to get her a surprise, so he'd turned his location tracking off. She had no idea what it was or where he was getting it from. Bridget's with her now. If Tanya finds something or remembers anything, we'll know."

"Right. So, we're on new ground here. An East Nasty victim brings us right back home."

He crossed to the corner of the room where the murder board had been set up. He added a pin to Daniel and Tanya's apartment and stuck a picture of Daniel to the side of the board.

The victim's brown eyes looked straight out at the room. To Hagen, Daniel seemed to be accusing him of letting him die.

I know what you mean, Chloe. I feel it too.

Slade stepped back. "The new victim is Daniel Swanson. He was found behind his apartment complex missing his right arm and covered in part by Shasta daisies. He was unmarried and lived with his girlfriend, Tanya..." Slade paused and reached for his notebook.

"Tomm." Chloe's voice was flat. "Tanya Tomm."

"Right. Thanks, Chloe." Slade's expression filled with sympathy for a moment before snapping back to the briefing. "He was also an assistant manager at a sushi restaurant and played acoustic guitar on weekends. Chloe, anything you want to add?"

Chloe lowered her eyes. "No."

The room fell silent. Hagen took a deep breath. "Was he good?"

Chloe frowned but didn't look up. "Good at what?"

"Guitar. How was he?"

A smile lifted one side of Chloe's mouth. "Yeah, he was okay. I mean, he wasn't going to be a star or anything. But he could riff, and he had a good voice."

Stella squeezed Chloe's arm. "Are you sure you want to be in here for this?"

Chloe's head snapped up, and Hagen could almost see her give herself a mental shake. "Yeah…sorry." Pushing herself up straighter in the chair, she focused on the front of the room. "I'm good."

Stella lowered her arm back on the table, her fingers twisting together. "So, we've got another victim who's completely different from the others. A Black male a little younger than Tiffany and Darlene and much younger than Hu Zhao. They all have unique looks. He fits the non-pattern pattern."

Hagen realized she was missing one aspect of the differences. "There is a pattern Daniel doesn't seem to fit. The unsub has brought each of the victims back. He took Darlene and Tiffany back to the place he took them from. Same with Hu Zhao. But Daniel was left outside his own apartment."

Ander shot Hagen a quizzical look. "He may have taken him from the apartment, though."

Hagen considered that option. "That's true, but he does make sure that the victims are found. He even cares how they look when they're found. He doesn't want their loved ones to suffer."

Chloe's nostrils flared. "They're going to suffer anyway."

"But that does give us a chance." Stella toyed with the stud in her ear. "If he always brings back his victims, then we can say more definitively that Kati Marsh is alive."

If she wasn't in a freezer.

Slade cleared his throat. "Lansing has deputies staking out the park where Kati went running. He's also got cops outside her apartment and her parents' house. I think you're right.

We can assume that she's still alive. And not to sound cold, but if the killer turns up at any of the sites with her body, he's ours. Our job is to find him before then, to keep her alive. What else? Anyone?"

"Why only one arm?" Ander scratched the top of his head. "I'm sorry, Chloe. But we need to be able to…you know. We need to be able to talk about what happened."

Chloe shot Ander a look hard enough to break rocks. "I know. Talk about it. Don't let me stop you."

Ander swallowed. "Why only one arm, huh? Why didn't he take a leg as well? Or any of the fingers and toes?"

"Maybe he was in a rush?" Stella's offer sounded more like a question than a suggestion.

"Then that's bad news, isn't it? If he couldn't finish what he started, he'll need another victim."

Slade tapped a knuckle on the table. "There's something we're missing. There has to be. This lunatic has a method. He has habits. Unusual habits, sure, but they're habits, nonetheless. There's a weakness there that we can exploit. What is it?"

"I think Hagen's right." Stella's ear was turning red from all the twisting. "About the victims' families, that is. Why should the unsub care about them? He doesn't care about the victims themselves. Maybe there's something about their loved ones that play a role in his choices. Maybe he's picking his victims from the edges of his social circle. If we can map the social circles of the victims' families, maybe we can find someone they all have in common."

Slade chewed his bottom lip. "Okay, that's worth a try. But let's invite them here, outside their comfort zones. Stella, call the Marshes and Brodie Stanley in for a second interview. Hagen, you've got another shot at Joshua Martinson and Mark Wright. Ander, you're with Hagen."

Chloe raised a hand. "What about me?"

Slade ignored her question. "I'll have everyone else work on a new suspect list from the waitress's description." He tacked the sketch artist's rendering on the board. "Mac, start tracing contacts…social media, geographic locations for work and home. Look for overlaps. I don't want one more body. Go."

Hagen pushed himself up from his seat, ready to do just that—go. He didn't entirely agree with Slade, though. There was one more body he'd like to see. The killer's.

The sooner he was standing over that corpse, the happier he'd be.

———

28

Joshua Martinson, Darlene's widower, sat in a plastic chair too small for his thighs. His forehead rested on his thick forearms. He straightened his back as Hagen and Ander came in.

"What do you guys need?" Martinson's demeanor was very different from the other day. The anger was gone, replaced with an earnestness Hagen struggled to believe. "Whatever you guys need to find this sonofabitch, I'm here for you."

Hagen mentally shrugged. They'd find out soon enough if the man's mellow mood would stick or not.

"Thank you, Mr. Martinson. We appreciate your cooperation." Hagen took a seat across from the man. "Here's the thing. We're still attempting to connect the killer to the victims. We know Darlene and Tiffany were old friends." He paused, waiting for a reaction from Martinson. None came. "We're trying to find a connection between Darlene, Tiffany, and the other victims."

Martinson raised his fingers, displaying his palms. "Like I said, man. Whatever you need."

Ander sat next to Hagen. "Good. Tell us about you and Darlene. What did you guys do when you weren't working?"

Martinson blew out his cheeks. "I dunno. We worked. We came home. Sometimes, I cooked. Sometimes, she did. Depends who came home first. On weekends, we'd do our own thing. Once a month or so, Darlene would usually do something with Tiffany. I'd usually go fishing."

"By yourself?"

"Yeah. Fishing wasn't…Darlene wasn't into the water. We…" He swallowed hard. "Truth is, we didn't do too much together. Not these last years. Only thing we ever did together recently was watch a show on the box before we went to bed. Maybe if…if I'd made more effort…" His face crumbled. "Maybe she wouldn't have gone with Tiffany that night. Maybe she'd still…"

Ander laid a hand on the widower's forearm. "It's not your fault, man. Don't beat yourself up."

Hagen's eyes traveled from Ander's hand to Martinson's tearful face. Grief did do strange things to men.

After his father's death, Hagen's grief had settled into his marrow, lodging deep. And he knew it wasn't going away, not until he claimed vengeance on the person who'd gunned down his father.

Was that what had happened to Stella too? He wasn't sure. If she *had* followed the same path, she did a pretty good job of hiding her rage.

"What about art?" Hagen asked. "Either of you go to art fairs, galleries, that sort of thing?"

Martinson snorted. "Art? Not me. Never could see the point of that stuff. Darlene neither. Least, she never mentioned it to me. Who knows what she did half the time, though? Especially when she was out with Tiffany. Man, that woman could have taken her anywhere. I don't—"

"So, neither of you had any regular hobbies?" Hagen had no intention of letting the man go down that path again.

Martinson lifted a shoulder. "Not really. I don't think Darlene did either. Maybe Tiffany would have known more. Sorry, guys. I haven't been too helpful, have I? Listen, are you going to be able to catch him or not?"

Not if all family members are like you, we won't. He doesn't think *his wife had hobbies? Pathetic.*

Hagen curbed his bias toward this guy and gave him a confident nod instead. "We won't stop looking until we find him." He tapped the folder sitting in front of the man. "Are these the records we asked for?"

Martinson pushed the folder across the table. "Yeah. We only have one credit card and our checking and savings accounts, so that was pretty easy." His mouth pressed into a thin line. "I couldn't find the password to her cloud storage for pictures and whatnot."

Hagen made a note to secure that warrant.

"While we go through these records, I want you to go through them too. Did you keep a set for yourself?"

Martinson nodded. "On my computer."

"Good. Go back through everything. See if any of her purchases might jog your memory. For example, if she bought a new pair of shoes, did she come home and mention where she was hoping to wear them? Stuff like that."

For the first time, Martinson actually appeared to be interested in doing something besides blame his wife or feel sorry for himself. "Yeah...I can do that. Do you think it'll help?"

Hagen pushed his business card across the table just in case the man had tossed the previous one. "Call if anything, big or little, jumps out at you from the records or if you think of anything that might help."

Martinson pushed to his feet. "Sure, man. Like I said, whatever I can do to help."

MARK WRIGHT LEANED in the corner of the interview room adjacent to Joshua Martinson's, his hands deep in his pockets. Before Hagen finished pushing the door fully open, he took two strides toward them.

"What the hell's going on here? I told you everything I know already, and I don't appreciate being dragged all the way down here for nothing."

Hagen stopped, one hand still gripping the door. Wright had been so polite and distraught in his living room. His Jekyll and Hyde was interesting.

He indicated one of the chairs at the table. "Please take a seat, Mr. Wright."

"I don't want to take a damn—"

Ander pulled himself up to his full six-four frame and whipped the chair back from the table. "Sit."

Wright sat. "There. Happy now? Can I go?"

Hagen laid both hands on the back of the chair opposite Wright but didn't sit. He hadn't intended to look down on the man, but if Tiffany's husband was going to be this aggressive, he needed to be reminded who called the shots. Let him feel small, sandwiched between Hagen on one side of the table while Ander stood behind him.

"Mr. Wright, we're trying to get a better idea of any possible connections between the victims. We've got a few questions for you. Is that okay?"

Wright fell back against the chair and shoved a manila envelope across the table. "Those are the records I found, but you ask whatever the hell you want. You're just wasting time, mine and yours."

Hagen ignored the envelope. "We know that Tiffany was an interior designer. What did she like to do in her spare time?"

"Spare time?" Wright snorted. "Tell me, Agent, do you have kids?"

"No."

"Yeah, I can tell. If you had kids and a mortgage, you wouldn't be asking stupid-ass questions about spare time."

Ander came around from behind Wright and took a seat. "I've got a kid. I've also got spare time."

Another snort, louder this time, shot from Wright's nose. "Maybe you should spend that spare time with your kid then."

The muscle in Ander's jaw worked, but he kept his expression neutral. "Maybe I should. But you need to understand, we're asking these questions for a reason. So, what did Tiffany do in her spare time? Did she have hobbies, take workshops? She was a designer. Was she taking more classes?"

"Hobbies? No, she didn't have any damn hobbies or take any classes. She worked. She played with the kids. She met Darlene for drinks, and she fell asleep in front of the TV at the end of a hard day. For chrissakes." He raked his hands through his hair.

Ander ignored Wright's irritation. "What about art? Did she go to art shows and exhibitions? Try to find ideas for her designs?"

"She...christ. No. Furniture was her specialty. But now, she doesn't have a specialty because some asshole killed her and chopped her to bits. And instead of looking for the killer, you've dragged me all the way down here to ask about her favorite artists." Chest heaving, he fell back against the chair.

Ander leaned forward. "Did she *have* a favorite artist? Because if you ask me, that—"

"What the total hell?" Wright leapt to his feet, face contorted by grief and rage. "Isn't there still a girl missing? And you're sitting here asking me about freaking art?"

Hagen thought Wright might punch Ander, though his partner didn't flinch an inch. "Mr. Wright, please—"

"You're crazy." Tears and sweat poured down the man's face. "Her blood is going to be on *your* hands. Yours!" His knees buckled, and he collapsed back into the chair. "Someone else is going to die because of you."

29

S tella's mind swirled in a thousand directions as she waited for Chloe against the wall in the corridor. Flower petals. Severed limbs. Skin tones.

Were they connected, or was she pulling a theory from her ass, desperate for some type of link between the victims?

She just didn't know.

An office door opened, and Chloe stepped out, drawing Stella's attention to a whole new set of concerns. Though Chloe's head was high, her posture straight, her pale complexion and the wounded look in her eyes gave away the depth of her sorrow.

Did Slade order her to go home? Or would she continue on this case?

Stella was about to find out.

Chloe rested her shoulders against the wall and crossed her arms. "Did you get ahold of the Marshes?"

Okay. So, they were going to talk about the case. She could do that.

"Yeah. They're on their way."

"What about Brodie Stanley?"

Stella glanced at her watch. "He should be here any minute. You joining me for his interview?"

Chloe didn't answer. Instead, she gazed at a spot on the floor where the tile met the baseboard. Her mouth was set in a firm line, which made all the muscles in her face seem tense. The emotional toll was showing. Maybe she needed to go home.

Stella touched Chloe's arm. "You okay? What did Slade say?"

Chloe lifted her head but looked straight through Stella. Where had she gone? In her mind, was she home with her wife, perhaps, or still sitting with Tanya, consoling her friend? Or apologizing again for not preventing her boyfriend's murder?

Then Chloe blinked twice, and, as if the motion had hit a reset button in her head, she straightened. "He said the usual. 'Not your fault.' Blah, blah, blah. Like that shit ever helped anyone." She scrubbed her hands over her face. It regained some color by the time she was finished. "What can I say? He tried."

"Are you—?"

"Agents."

Stella glanced at the deputy standing at the end of the hallway. "Yes?"

"Brodie Stanley arrived. I put him in Interview Room Three."

"Thank you." Stella turned her attention back to Chloe. "If you want to sit this out, I can—"

"Come on, let's get on with it." Chloe peeled away from the wall and strode away. Stella took a deep breath and followed.

Jeez, if Chloe had a thicker shell, she'd be a tortoise.

They found Brodie sitting at the table, a mug of coffee in

one hand and his phone in the other. A small, black backpack leaned against the chair leg.

He lowered the device as they came in. "Any news?"

His eyes darted from Chloe to Stella and back again, searching, no doubt, for some piece of information written on their faces.

Stella pulled out the chair opposite him and sat. "Sorry, Mr. Stanley. Not yet. We're hoping you can help. We're looking for a connection between—"

"Between the victims. Yeah, Sheriff Lansing told me. He said you wanted to know about Kati's hobbies and stuff? And call me Brodie, remember?"

Stella smiled. "Of course. And please call me Stella."

Chloe dropped into the remaining seat. "We need to know everything about Kati's life. Any classes she took or shops she visited even once. What she did in her free time, the places she would go."

Chloe's tone was getting a bit too intense, so Stella jumped in. "That type of information will help us determine if there is a link between Kati and the other victims. That link could help us narrow our search."

"Yeah, I get it." Brodie pushed a loose dreadlock away from his forehead, his handsome face a mixture of worry and hopelessness. "I don't know how much I can help there, though. Kati's never been big on hobbies. She prefers running with Juno to going to the gym. She'd rather read a book than go to a ball game. I mean, she's super friendly when you get to know her, but she's not a joiner or anything." He frowned at the table, clearly thinking. "She loves art but doesn't really dabble in her own painting much anymore."

They'd already known that Kati had been pushed into accounting instead of art by her parents, but the reminder sent Stella's heart rate up a notch. "Tell me more about how Kati is able to express her love of art." Stella glanced at Chloe.

Her expression hadn't changed. She displayed no excitement and no anticipation. But she had to be thinking the same thing. She had to be feeling that same little butterfly fluttering in her belly.

"Well, she loves art fairs and museums. Whenever we went into town, we'd always go to East Nashville and check out the galleries. She loves all that."

Stella folded her hands on the table to keep them still. "When was the last time she went to a gallery? Do you remember?"

"I don't have dates or anything, but…" Brodie lifted his bag from the floor and pulled out a handful of flyers, catalogs, and brochures. "When you called and said you wanted to talk about hobbies, I grabbed these."

He pushed them across the table. Each piece of marketing was decorated with pictures of paintings and drawings, the names of artists and galleries. "Wherever we'd go, she'd grab whatever they had. They'd just pile up on the kitchen table." He shrugged. "Should clean up more often, I guess."

Chloe dragged a handful of the flyers toward her.

Stella reached for the rest. "Glad you didn't. Smart thinking bringing us these."

They all looked so similar. Artistic portraits. Landscapes. Still lifes. This art fair taking place here, that new exhibition opening there, all showing the same kind of abstract sculptures and paintings of flowers. She wasn't sure how anyone could spend more than ten minutes in a gallery without feeling that they'd seen it all.

Brodie exhaled and rubbed his hands down his legs. "I just want to do whatever I can to help, you know? She's out there. Alive, somewhere. I know it. You…" Tears pooled in his eyes. "I just...look, I just can't imagine my life without her. She's the sweetest girl I've ever met and..."

Brodie's voice faded away as Stella pulled out one leaflet from the pile in her hand.

The flyer advertised an art crawl in Franklin. The painting at the top of the page was strangely familiar. A gilt frame held a colorful sprawl of a rolling pasture. The sky was a rainbow of pastel shades, the ground every hue of green and brown, as though every possible color imaginable was represented on that one hill. And the single view had provided a chance to raid the color palette.

"I've seen this." Stella scanned the bottom of the flyer where the show listed the artists exhibiting their works.

Chloe leaned over to get a better look. "The painting?"

"Yeah." The butterfly wings that had flapped in Stella's stomach when Brodie mentioned art stretched into those of an eagle.

The first name, the artist at the top of the list whose picture was featured on the flyer, was Darwin Rhodell.

Stella flipped the flyer around and showed it to Brodie. "Did you guys go to this?"

Brodie peered closely at the page, squinting from across the table. "That one? In Franklin? Let me think." He opened his phone and tapped the calendar icon.

A line at the bottom indicated that the fair had taken place last month, three weeks before Kati went missing.

That was it. That had to be the moment. He saw her. Followed her.

He tapped his screen. "Nah, I was helping a friend move that day."

Stella closed her eyes and sighed, deflated. She dropped the flyer onto the table. *Of course, Darwin Rhodell would turn up on these things. He was a famous local artist. Why wouldn't he be there?*

"Kati went to that fair by herself. She said it was nice. Good atmosphere, friendly artists."

Stella's head jerked up. "Friendly artists? Did she talk to anyone?"

He considered the question a long moment. "She never mentioned anyone specific."

Shit.

Was this even the right train of thought, or was her desire to catch the person chopping people up giving her tunnel vision? Stella wasn't sure. She needed to talk it through with Chloe, but not in here.

Popping up from her seat, she gave Brodie a quick smile. "Excuse us for a moment, will you?"

Chloe followed her from the room, pulling the door closed behind her as soon as she reached the corridor. "What are you thinking?"

Stella blew air from her cheeks. "Darwin Rhodell. The dates of his Franklin show match the timeline. He sees Kati at the fair. He follows her from there. Stalks her. How long would it have taken him to figure out her habits?"

"Yeah, it's possible." Chloe leaned a shoulder against the wall. "Or not? All we really know for sure is that Kati and Darwin Rhodell were in the same place at the same time. Could be a coincidence. They might never have even seen each other."

Stella's gut was shouting otherwise. "Or maybe that's where he saw her for the first time. Look, his name keeps coming up. He's artistic. He's suffered an emotional loss. He's friendly and charming. He looks like the man at the bar where Tiffany and Darlene were last seen. Tanya mentioned her love of his art to Daniel. Quite frankly, he's the best lead we've—"

The door to Slade's office creaked open. The SSA emerged, a pile of papers under one arm and his reading glasses held loosely between his fingers. "What's the best lead we've had?"

Stella took the flyer from Chloe's hand and showed it to Slade. "This. It's not much, but it might be something. Three weeks before she went missing, Kati was at the same art fair as Darwin Rhodell. I think we need to talk to him again."

Slade took the flyer and pushed his glasses onto his nose. He released a quiet grunt as he scanned the page, then gave it back. "Yeah. That's at least worth investigating. I'll have Hagen and Ander talk to the Marshes. You two get over to Rhodell now. It might be nothing but ask him about that fair. See how he reacts."

Chloe pulled the car keys from her pocket.

"Hey." Slade removed his glasses and gave them both a hard look. "Anything seems off, don't press. Call it in. He might be nice and friendly, but if it's him, he's killed four people already. Don't underestimate him."

30

The time could have been early morning or late morning. Or even afternoon. The day was…Kati tried to count. Had he turned out the lights three times? Or was it four? Ten? Did he always turn out the lights at night, or did he also shut them off during the day?

Kati couldn't tell.

The basement had no windows to let in the sun and almost no sound to mark the changes in traffic flow. Occasionally, muffled voices seemed to make their way downstairs, but they always sounded so distant and faint. Each time she heard them, she'd shouted for help until her throat was sore and the gag made the edges of her mouth bleed. But thanks to the material and the walls, she hadn't been surprised when no one kicked down the door and carried her out of that basement.

She closed her eyes. When she opened them again, she wasn't sure whether a minute or an hour had passed. Did it even matter? Would knowing how much time she'd been held here change a damn thing?

Kati had always been a bit of a lone wolf. Now, she'd give anything to change that.

She'd had company, briefly—Hu Zhao—and lost that company. Since then, she'd had nothing but the monster who'd brought her here. Nothing but the growing pain spreading from her stiff neck to her shoulders. Now, the ache seemed to have settled permanently in the small of her back.

Hoping to draw her attention from the ache, she gazed around the room and watched dust motes floating through the light. A fly buzzed from one wall to the next. She'd already counted the marks on the chair and the tiles on the floor and even the number of bumps on the black foam he'd glued to the back of the door, walls, and ceiling.

At one point, she'd even tried counting her tears, but she couldn't keep up.

Stop feeling sorry for yourself!

For the thousandth time, she worked her hands in the binds, cursing when the pain forced her to stop. She pushed at the gag with her tongue, thinking maybe this time, she could loosen it just a bit.

Not only was her captor an amazing artist, he was a master at tying knots.

Dammit.

If she could only get loose, she'd make him pay. She kept imagining again and again what she would do to him if she got the chance. How she would stomp on his face and kick him up and down those stairs.

Those fantasies were satisfying, but the anger never lasted long. Neither did her daydreams of Brodie.

When she began to lose all hope, she'd close her eyes and relive her best moments with her boyfriend. The way her hand fit perfectly into his. The way he made her feel beautiful each time he looked at her.

Too often, though, her mind wandered away from the peace she'd found with Brodie and landed in the middle of one of the many arguments she'd had with her parents. She'd flinch at the words they used to describe both him and their relationship. Flinch at how much she hated that she'd been born to two people filled with so much hate.

In her darkest moments, she'd pray for everything to just end.

Maybe she'd be better off being part of the monster's painting. Maybe he was right, and what he was working on would bring peace and love to a world that needed it.

And then she'd think about him holding her over that damn bucket. He would hand-feed her like some sort of baby, then talk to her like a friend. For days now, or possibly weeks, she'd had no one to talk to but *him*, with his blood-stained shirt and saccharine voice.

She dreaded the sight of him. Yet she waited all day for him. He was the only break in this never-ending nothing. She wanted to see him now.

She was hungry. And thirsty.

And she needed to pee, dammit.

What was taking him so damn long?

Maybe he was dead. She hoped he was. She hoped he'd died slowly, impaled by his own paintbrush. But what if he had died, and now no one would ever find her?

What if she died here, in this chair, of starvation or thirst…or loneliness?

She took a deep breath, slowing her breathing.

In and out. In and out.

Surely, someone would find her before then. They'd come to sort through his things and open the door, and she'd be sitting there waiting to blow apart his lovely old-man reputation.

Maybe he wasn't dead, though. Maybe he'd gone on vacation and left her to rot until he got back. Hadn't some maniac in Austria done that once? Raised a family in his basement, then flew off to Thailand for two weeks, leaving them to fend for themselves?

But she couldn't fend for herself. She was tied to a chair.

She needed him.

She wasn't sure what hurt more. Her desire to beat him to death with this chair or her dependency on him.

What if he'd forgotten about her? He was clearly nuts. He could have done anything. Maybe he'd just erased her from his memory, forgotten she even existed.

Oh my god, he's left me here to die! I'm going to die here, alone, in this stinking room.

Calm, Kati. Stay calm.

In and out. In and out. That's it.

The panic eased. The trembling in her fingers settled.

Focus. He's still here. Believe he's still here. Think! How are you going to escape?

What could she do?

He liked her. That was clear. Creepy, but maybe useful?

Maybe she could do better at pretending that she totally got what he was doing. She'd tell him that she understood his vision. She could say that she wanted to help him realize his goal...without being dismembered, of course. If only he would just untie her.

What else?

He was lonely. He missed his wife and wanted companionship. Maybe she could provide that companionship. She could become a friend, a good friend even. She could talk to him. Laugh with him. Let him trust her until, one day, he'd let her out. Just for a few minutes. Just for fresh air.

And then she'd be free.

Even if he didn't let her go but just untied her, that would be all she'd need. He wasn't big or strong. One smack over the head with a chair leg, and she'd be out of there and…

In her imagination, she ran down the road to bang on the door of the nearest house. Her leg jolted at the thought of it.

Wait, what was that? Was the rope loose?

Her ankle had moved more than before. There was some give there, where previously there had been none. She squirmed, twisting her knee first one way then the other. When she looked down, there was at least a centimeter between her ankle and the chair leg.

Just a little more.

She writhed again, pulling and tugging.

C'mon, Kati. You can do this. Pull!

"You're trying to leave me, aren't you?"

Kati froze. She hadn't heard the door open. She had been too focused on her ankle and that little sliver of space between it and the wood.

Standing in front of her, he shook his head, more sad than angry, more disappointed than outraged. Knees popping from the effort, he knelt in front of the chair and took the rope binding her ankle in his hands.

Kati's foot wriggled desperately, fighting against him almost without conscious thought. She shook her head. She tried to say no. The gag and her sore throat stopped everything but the smallest sound.

"I thought you were beginning to understand." His eyes brimmed with tears. "You know you're very special to me. I wanted you to work with me. I thought we could be partners. Now, I see what a foolish dream that was."

He retied the knot and pulled it even tighter than before. The rope bit into her skin, but she didn't even feel it. She didn't feel much of anything anymore.

Rrring.

Kati jumped at the sound, surprised that she could even

hear it. Glancing at the top of the stairs, her heart leapt to see a gray wall past the open door. It was the first time she'd seen anything but the black foam in days.

Her captor sighed. "Customers always come at the very worst moment, don't they?" He wagged a finger at her. "Now, don't you move. I'll deal with them quickly and be right back for you."

31

S tella pushed the doorbell again, keeping the button compressed this time. "Be here, dammit."

"What do you think?" Chloe lifted a hand and beat the wood three times with her fist. "Think he's out?"

"Monday?" Stella kept the button firmly compressed. "Mid-morning? He's probably inside painting, no?"

Chloe cupped her hands around an eye, trying to see through the pane of glass. "If we're right, let's hope not. I don't know. Maybe…" She jerked back with a little yelp. "Shit…he's here."

Darwin Rhodell's face was nearly plastered against the window of the gallery door. He wore the same paint-splattered shirt. His hair was as wild and frizzy as it had been the day before.

"Agents, how lovely to see you both again." He pulled open the door and waved them inside. "Do come in."

As they stepped into the middle of the gallery, a new landscape on the wall behind Chloe's shoulder caught Stella's attention.

It looked familiar, with Darwin's wild colors and use

of bold shapes. But to Stella, it wasn't the style. It was the subject that was familiar. A park. Morville Pond Park. The last known location of Kati Marsh. She'd stood at almost that exact spot with Ander a couple of days ago.

Her stomach tightened.

Darwin followed her gaze and chuckled. "Do you like it, Agent Knox? Can I call you 'Stella'? I'm really not formal at all. Just another of my landscapes. Nothing special."

"It's...it's lovely." She forced a pleasant smile. "We just wanted to follow up on some of the questions we asked yesterday. You've probably heard that another body was discovered last night."

Darwin sighed deeply. "Oh, yes. I did hear. What a dreadful thing. It's all everyone has been talking about. How is the poor boy's girlfriend? I hope it hasn't affected her too badly."

Though Stella doubted Tanya would be okay for a very long time, she softened her answer. "She's...shocked. But she's getting help. She'll need time."

The artist made a sympathetic noise. "Grief is such a difficult, unpredictable thing that affects each of us in different ways. I'm afraid it never goes away."

His sincerity threw her for a moment. If he was the killer, Darwin was certainly the most sympathetic one she'd ever met.

"No. I don't think it does." Stella's own grief had buried itself deep within her. Some of the sorrow had merged with anger after Uncle Joel's revelation, but the sadness was always there, embedded in her marrow.

Darwin slapped his hand to his forehead. "Forgive me. I'm being rude. Let me fetch you something to drink. Tea? Iced water? Soda, perhaps? It's such a hot day already."

Chloe held up a declining hand. "Thanks, but we have a

lot of ground to cover. We just need to ask you a few quick questions, and then we'll be on our way. Stella?"

Stella pulled her notebook out of her bag. A question about the art show and whether he had seen Kati Marsh was on the tip of her tongue, but something struck her. What had Chloe called her gut feeling? Spider senses? She was no Peter Parker, but something was itching at her insides now.

She frowned. "You asked about Daniel Swanson's girl-friend. Did you know him? Or Tanya? Were they customers of yours?"

Distress flashed on his features so quickly that Stella would have missed it if she hadn't been watching him so intently. The smile was back an instant later. "Daniel was a customer. A patron, I should say. He commissioned a portrait from me. But Tanya?" He tapped his lower lip with a finger. "No, I don't know her at all. I've never met her, in fact."

Chloe opened her mouth, but Stella beat her to it. "What portrait?"

"Daniel commissioned a painting for her birthday. I recently finished it, actually. I'll deliver it to her, free of charge, of course. I'd love to hear what she thinks about the finished product…when she's ready, of course." He clasped both hands over his heart. "It will be a wonderful memento, a picture of the two of them together."

Chloe's eyes narrowed. "You were working on a painting for Daniel Swanson? A painting he'd commissioned for Tanya?"

"Oh, yes." Distress flashed again. "That's why this whole thing has been so shocking for me. Who would have thought that I would know someone who…" He made a show of shuddering. "But, then again, I do know a lot of people."

The dots weren't connecting here. "Yesterday, you stated you hadn't seen anyone of that name or description."

Darwin's lip curled.

Was that contempt? Stella wasn't sure.

"His name didn't register with me, is all." He tapped his temple, chuckling. "Age does that to a person, I'm afraid."

Stella wasn't going to let him get away with dodging the question. "How many times did you meet with him about the painting?"

"I only spoke to him twice. Once in a sandwich shop and once here, when he commissioned the piece. He was so insistent, and they were such a beautiful couple. At least as far as I could see from the picture he wanted me to paint. It's not something I usually—"

"Can I see it?" Chloe's eyes were fixed on his face, unblinking and hard.

"The…the painting?" He took a few steps back, holding up his hands as if defending himself from a charging bull. "Oh, no. I couldn't possibly. Not until Daniel's girlfriend has seen it. It wouldn't be right."

"Of course, I understand." Chloe's expression told a different story.

Removing a handkerchief from his pocket, he mopped at his forehead. "I just hope it will be of some consolation to her when she gets it."

Why was he sweating? Stella decided to keep pressing. "Can you tell me when Daniel commissioned the piece?"

"Hmm…let me think. Must have been more than a month ago. He wanted it ready about now. The painting wasn't a difficult job. Quite easy to fit around the thousand-and-one other things there are to do in an artist's life." He offered a *what-can-you-do* chuckle as he tucked the hankie back into his pocket.

"His girlfriend didn't mention anything about a painting."

Darwin flinched away from Chloe's question, either not

liking her tone or body language. "Ah, no. She wouldn't. It was a surprise, you see."

Yes, Stella could see. She could see that something wasn't right about this man.

And her boss said to call if anything felt off. But was what she felt enough to convince a judge to sign off on a search warrant?

She needed to find out.

Stella tapped Chloe's elbow and motioned toward the door. "Thank you for your help, sir." Stella didn't bother to stick out a hand. "I'm sure Tanya will love the painting. We'll be in touch if we have more questions."

To her relief, Chloe followed her from the gallery without question. When they were no more than ten yards from the building, Stella pulled out her phone.

"You calling Slade?"

Stella nodded. "Yeah. Daniel goes out to get a surprise for Tanya and disappears. And our friend Darwin Rhodell is preparing a surprise for Tanya. Slade told us to call in if we got something. Chloe, we've got something."

Chloe didn't look convinced. "Just a second. You're talking about a major East Nashville artist here. And you've seen him. He's not much taller than me and twice my age. Does he look like a killer?"

"You know as well as I do that—"

Chloe held up a hand. "I don't disagree with you. He lied about knowing Daniel. How do you take a commission from a guy and not remember his name? But we're talking Darwin Rhodell here. Arresting him will cause an uproar if we're wrong."

Stella twisted her ear stud. It turned easily between her fingers. "But you saw how flustered he got in there. Maybe he didn't mean to mention Daniel. He just blurted it out. He's nervous. I think there's enough. We owe it to Kati Marsh to try."

Several long moments passed before Chloe nodded at the phone in Stella's hand. "Make the call."

Slade answered on the first ring. "What've you got?"

"Sir, Darwin Rhodell brought up Daniel Swanson's name as we were questioning him, then got nervous when we pressed. Remember that Daniel was going out to fetch a surprise for Tanya's birthday?"

"Yeah."

"Turns out that surprise was a painting of Daniel and Tanya by none other than Darwin Rhodell himself. Is that connection enough for a warrant?"

Stella could almost hear Slade's brain considering the question. "Maybe. Get back in there, the two of you. Look around. See if you can spot anything out of place. Keep him busy and distracted, away from Kati, *if* he has her."

Chloe bounced on her toes, looking as excited as Stella felt.

"Yes, sir."

"If I can get a search warrant, I'll let you know. And Stella…?"

"Sir?"

"Remember…if this is our guy, he's a dangerous man. Any sign of hostility, you call for backup right away."

"Yes, sir." Tucking her phone back into her pocket, she turned to Chloe. "Let's go."

32

"Hagen. Ander. With me."

Slade stood in the doorway of Interview Room Two. His phone was gripped in one hand, his forehead creased with worry. "I need to see you both."

Hagen nodded to his SSA. "Sure."

Shit. What happened now?

"Yeah, sure. Why not?" Mark Wright threw up an arm as his lip curled into a snarl. "Go ahead, Agent. Make yourself a cup of coffee. Put your feet up. Go on. Take all the time you need. I'm here all day, aren't I?"

Hagen ignored the complaint. "Actually, you're free to go. Thanks for your help." He held the door open and waited while the widower stomped out.

He was actually glad to see him go. They'd learned less than nothing since it turned out that Tiffany had been the one to take care of all the family bills. The manila envelope had only held a handful of wrinkled receipts and very little else. When pressed, Wright confessed that he didn't know the passwords to any of their accounts. At least, that's what he'd said.

Hagen had been only seconds away from filing for a warrant for those records when Slade interrupted. He made a note so he wouldn't forget to do that later.

"Man." Ander frowned as the agents followed Slade down the hallway. "You told me he was the nice one. If he's friendly, what's Martinson like?"

Before he could break into a spiel about how people change during times of tragedy, Slade cleared his throat, regaining their attention. "I just spoke to Stella. Daniel was going to buy a surprise for his girlfriend, remember? That surprise was a painting…by Darwin Rhodell."

"Jeez." Hagen rubbed his chin. "That's a break. Not the artist I expected, but still."

"While I work on getting a search warrant, you two talk to Mac and see if you can get some background."

After heading back into the interview room, Ander made the call.

"What can I do for you, Goldilocks?"

Hagen chuckled as Ander turned an interesting state of red. "We need everything you've got on Darwin Rhodell."

The sound of a clacking keyboard came through the speaker. "Here we are. No criminal record, not even a parking ticket. But he does appear on a police report from Chicago. It's a couple of years old. Yikes, his wife was murdered."

Hagen whistled low under his breath. "Murdered? We knew he was a widower, but nothing about his wife's cause of death. What happened to her?"

More clacking. "Just a sec. There. The wife, Diana Rhodell, was stabbed. Cops thought it was a hate crime because she was French Canadian and Latina. There was a lot of that going on in Chicago at the time. Never solved."

"A hate crime." Hagen rubbed his temple, trying to force his brain to connect the dots. "What did Stella say in the briefing? Something about skin tones. Is that why he's taking people of different ethnicities? Is he trying to push out some kind of message with the skin colors?"

Ander didn't appear to be convinced but played along. "In some cracked, artistic lunatic kind of way? Or maybe he's trying to blame the world for losing his wife? Or take revenge? Man, who knows what goes through these people's heads?"

"I don't know, but he ticks a lot of our boxes." Hagen counted off the profile similarities on his fingers. "An older man who's charming, friendly, and lonely. Check. A widower who lost his wife to an abnormally tragic hate crime is definitely someone who has suffered a loss. Check. Took part in an art festival that at least one victim that we know of attended. Check. Ran in similar circles to another victim. Check. Made art for another victim. Check." He waved his fingers. "Checkmarks all around."

"A warrant is on its way." Slade strode into the room. "But now, Stella isn't answering."

Something twisted in Hagen's chest as he pulled his phone from his pocket. "I'll try Chloe."

He jabbed the screen and held the device to his ear, Ander watching him closely.

"Hey, guys, they're not stupid." Mac's voice came through Ander's speaker. "If they know not to engage, then they won't."

Hagen wasn't so sure. "Then they'd answer their phones. Rhodell might not give them a choice."

And if they saw a sign that Kati was in there, they wouldn't have waited. Neither Chloe nor Stella would sit around and wait for orders if they thought someone's life was in danger. None of us would.

Hagen lowered his phone from his ear and shook his head, a cold wave passing down his spine.

Trouble.

33

They came back. Of course, they did. I knew they would.

The moment they left, so suddenly after I so carelessly mentioned Daniel, I knew they'd be knocking on my door again, ready to sniff around some more.

I'd hoped it would take longer than five minutes, though.

Now, they were standing in my gallery, once again, ready to fire questions at me, blowing away all my little fibs.

Even as I offered them a seat and a cup of tea, the voice inside my soul wouldn't give me a moment's peace.

You're too early, Agents! I'm not done yet. Patience, please. Soon, the entire world will know everything. But not yet. I just need a little more time.

Their return was my own fault. I'd said too much. She made me nervous, that…what was her name? Special Agent Knox. Stella. I'd been distracted by those gold-flecked eyes and flawless olive skin. And when she pressed me, I panicked. Oh, I could be such a fool sometimes.

In hindsight, I knew what I should have said when they'd visited with me earlier.

I should have contorted my face into a mixture of worry and confusion. "Daniel?" I would have used my best old-man voice to convey the depth of my concern. "Is that the name of the poor, young man? I'm afraid I don't know him at all."

She might even have believed me.

The other one...Agent Chloe Something-or-other. Would she have taken my word and been content with my denials? She had a friendly smile, which she clearly didn't use enough. And such a pretty face. Hard with just a hint of vulnerability.

She was an art lover, that one. Someone who loved art couldn't possibly harbor ill intent, could they? The very essence of art destroyed ill will. That was why my piece was so important. Why it would change everything.

The beauty of my masterpiece would cleanse the world of hate like a shaft of purifying light.

That was why I must continue. Why I had to finish what I'd started. Whatever the cost.

And I needed to do it soon. Time was running out.

Though the agents had smiled, I'd seen the suspicion behind their eyes. I could tell because an artist had to be observant and see things that others missed. I saw through them both.

"It's a hot day, and your gallery is nicely air-conditioned." That was what Agent Chloe Something-or-other said when they'd reappeared at my door. "You won't mind if we hang around and admire your work?"

She was lying. Of course, she was. Such a disappointment.

I didn't want to hurt her. I didn't want to hurt either of them. I liked them—I would have liked them a lot more under different circumstances. And they would have liked me.

But these weren't those circumstances.

I folded my fingers together on my chest and spoke the truth. "Now, Agent. I think we both know that's not true. A beautiful soul like yours should never have to lie. It's quite beneath you."

The way Agent Chloe Something-or-other's expression changed had been quite amusing to watch. Her hand drifted to her side. I was sure, I *knew*, that soon she would be pulling her gun. Both of them would. Violence was the only language some people understood. The only language they spoke.

Which was exactly why I had to complete my work.

Only my art could overpower the force of that violence and replace their bullets with love.

She thought for a moment before speaking, clearly debating whether to continue with her lies. *Please don't.* We were in a gallery, surrounded by so much beauty and honesty. Any untruth would fill the air like a bad smell.

"You're right." Chloe Something-or-other had the grace to blush while Stella Knox watched my every move. "Actually, we came back because we'd like to take a quick look around the building. You don't mind, do you?"

My building? My gallery? The nerve.

"Well, actually, I—"

"We could get a warrant."

I laughed before I could stop myself.

My mirth didn't stop Chloe from continuing. "But to be honest, that would mean tearing this place apart. I'm not sure you'd really want a bunch of big, burly agents trawling through your art gallery, would you?"

I almost gasped. I didn't expect such a threat from this Agent Chloe at all. She had seemed so friendly, so sensitive beneath that hard exterior. A show of indignation would have pleased her too much, though. She would have enjoyed seeing my anger. I wouldn't give her the pleasure.

Her colleague tried to reassure me. "The search is just a formality, sir. We'll be able to cross you off our list and move on to the next site. We've all got a boss to please, you know?"

What could I say? If all they performed was a quick look, I might be fine. But I needed to keep them out of the basement. And the cold room. If they moved the sheet and saw my great work…

All would be lost.

"Of course. I have nothing to hide." It almost took more effort than I possessed to keep my pleasant smile intact. "Shall I offer a tour?"

Heading toward the portrait of my darling Diana, I stopped at Agent Chloe's sharp voice. "A tour isn't necessary."

Turning on my heel, I offered a gracious bow. "Of course. May I stay in my office until you're finished? I have a great deal of paperwork to complete."

"Of course." Agent Stella's smile wasn't nearly as bright as before.

Agent Chloe moved first and was by my side in an instant. "I'll go with you."

This was an unexpected development. I hadn't counted on them splitting up.

Mind whirling, I fought not to show my alarm. "I'd very much enjoy your company, my dear. Would you like some tea or coffee?"

"I'm fine, but thank you."

Ah. I did so appreciate good manners.

As I stepped into my office, a sharp squeak of the hallway door told me that Agent Stella had opted to go upstairs. That was good, giving me a few extra minutes to think.

"What's behind those doors?"

I waited until I was seated in my chair before turning to answer Agent Chloe. "Storage, my dear. The one to your right is unlocked since I only keep office supplies and canvases and such inside. You will need a key for the left as it houses my safe and other valuables."

It was a lie, but I just needed her to turn her back for a second.

Agent Chloe stared at me for longer than was comfortable, and I began to fear that I might have done or said something to draw her suspicions. "May I have the key?"

"Of course." I nodded toward the right closet door. "You'll find it hidden under the small wicker basket on the top shelf in the back."

Another lie, but it worked.

Turning her back on me, she opened the door and stepped inside the deep closet. As soon as she disappeared, I pulled open the bottom desk drawer.

My little Springfield XD was such an ugly thing. Black and stubby. The barrel too short, the trigger guard too straight. I'd bought the gun after Diana was murdered, then tucked it away. I never wanted to see that awful weapon again. I hadn't even used it when I collected material for my masterpiece. A firearm was for emergencies only.

This was an emergency.

The weight of the pistol was heavy in my hands, though strangely comforting. Just holding the grip gave me a sense of reassurance. The touch of the trigger told me that all would be well, that all was in hand.

What I assumed to be frames rattled from the closet just before something fell with a clatter. I rolled my eyes. "I must ask you to be careful, Agent! Don't break anything."

Neither that closet nor the one next to it worried me. Upstairs didn't worry me either.

It was what would come next that sent a chill down my spine. Once they finished these searches, they'd head down the hall and find the freezer, the cold room where my work was coming together. And there, at the end of the corridor, was the entrance to the basement.

What if Kati heard them? What if she made a noise?

Another frame fell in the storage room. I froze and listened.

Kati had made noises before. But the groans, mumbles, and attempts at a scream were muffled by her gag and the padded walls.

The first time she'd tried to call for help, I'd been in the gallery with a client.

"I have contractors in," I'd told the lovely lady seeking to make a purchase. "Such a distraction. And the mess, so awful. Worth it, though. Soon, my basement will be the perfect studio."

The client had smiled and said that she understood completely. They'd made terrible noises when they'd renovated her bathroom too. We commiserated.

I doubt these agents would accept that excuse as easily as my client had done.

Footsteps clamored down the steps from my apartment. The hallway door opened and closed just as Agent Chloe called, "The key isn't in here."

Feeling as spry as a cat, I moved from my chair to the corner of the room.

They'd given me no choice. None. After all the work I'd done, all the sacrifices I'd made. My message was too important to be lost.

Agent Chloe emerged from the storage closet with her hands empty as I knew they would be. "Did you hear—"

Rrring.

Her phone.

The bell wouldn't be saving her. Not in this instance.

As Agent Stella came through the door an instant later, I swung my weapon up. I didn't think. I barely aimed as I squeezed the trigger.

A bang, a flash, then a red splash struck the cream-painted walls. Crimson dots sprayed a diagonal swoosh across the front of the metal filing cabinet.

Oh, look. I'm Jackson Pollock.

Chloe Something-or-other staggered, but before she had a chance to fall, I'd spun, aiming my weapon at Agent Stella Knox. Her hand had almost reached her holster.

"Now, now, Agent Knox. Let's not do anything silly."

She didn't move.

What should I have done? Shot her there and then? I suppose I should have. That would have been the easiest thing to do, the safest too.

But as Agent Chloe's phone stopped ringing and Agent Stella's started, Knox lifted her hands.

Her sleeves, rolled back to combat the outdoor heat, fell farther up her forearms with her hands held high. Such beautifully smooth, copper-colored skin.

I licked my lips.

Too beautiful to waste.

34

A badge.

Kati blinked, sure she was dreaming. It was still there, though. The person coming down the steps had a badge of some sort clipped to their belt.

Hot tears welled in Kati's eyes and ran down the side of her nose. She was saved. Her rescuers had come at last. All the fear and horror of the previous days seeped out of her like a balloon that developed a sudden leak. Her muscles relaxed as she sagged in the chair.

"Go on. Down you go."

No. That was *his* voice. Kati didn't understand.

Clarity came as a woman appeared, her hands in the air. And behind her...behind her was Darwin Rhodell. He had a gun in each hand, and both were pointed at the woman's back.

Noooo.

Kati screamed, but her shout was muffled through her gag. She bit on the material, willing her teeth to rip it in two. Tears streamed thicker than ever as she pulled on her ropes, twisting, tugging with all her might. She had to get out of there. She had to.

The woman caught her eye, giving her a small nod and wink.

What did that mean? Did the woman have a plan? She didn't look like she had a plan. She looked like she was in the same mess that Kati was in. For days, Kati had hoped that the police would come, that law enforcement would find her in this stinking basement, save her, and drag Darwin to some tiny cell in the bottom of some moldy dungeon for the rest of his days.

And now they'd come. One person. In captivity. Just like her.

Damn them.

Kati couldn't stop sobbing. She just couldn't.

The woman nodded again.

What good is that? I don't need reassurance, dammit. I need to be rescued.

Darwin prodded the women in the back with one of the guns. "Now, now. Behave nicely, Agent Stella, please." They reached the bottom of the stairs, which was when Kati saw the letters…FBI. "We'll have no communicating between the two of you. I don't want you plotting. Go on, in the corner over there."

He pushed the agent again, shoving her toward the corner of the room to the same place he had tied the kind Asian man.

"And no funny business, please. I'd really rather not shoot you, but I think you know perfectly well that I would kill you in an instant if I had to." He lowered his voice until it became almost a growl. "Both of you. Now, Agent Stella. Do, please, sit down."

Stella surveyed the room. She seemed to be sizing it up, taking in each corner, recognizing its emptiness.

Forget it. There's no hope here. None at all.

"Where?"

"Let's not play silly games, shall we? On the floor. Go on, back against the wall. Cross your legs. Crisscross applesauce. That's it."

Stella turned until her back was against the wall. But her eyes remained fixed and unblinking on the monster. In that glare was all the hatred that had filled Kati's heart since the moment she'd been shoved into that car. If looks could kill, that look would have blasted through the monster and turned half of East Nashville into a radioactive crater.

But all Stella could do was glare. The distance between the pair was too far for the agent to do more.

Don't try it. Please don't try it. You won't make it across the room before he gets a shot off.

And he would take that shot. Kati had no doubt about that.

I don't want to see someone die. I don't want to be alone again.

Stella slid down the wall, onto the ground, and folded her legs so that her knees were almost flat against the floor.

Darwin waved one of the guns. "That's it. Hands on your knees where I can see them."

Stella did as she was told, her fingers spread over her kneecaps.

Letting out a sigh of what seemed like exhaustion, the monster sat on the bottom step, both weapons still in his hands. "I'm sorry it had to be this way. I really didn't intend this to happen. I wish you could have just left me alone and let me finish my work in peace. That was all I asked. It wasn't much, was it? All you've done is make my work harder. And now, I have your friend upstairs to deal with as well." He sighed. "Well, waste not, want not. That's what my mother used to say."

Kati watched Stella's face darken. "Darwin, leave Chloe

alone. Don't you touch her, you sonofabitch. Don't go near her."

"Tut. Such language. And from such a lovely looking lady. Isn't she beautiful, Kati? Why, she's almost as beautiful as you. That skin. What would you call that color? Desert Sand, perhaps? Maybe that's a little too light."

He smiled. Of all things, the crazy sonofabitch smiled.

"Oh, I think you two are going to get along like a house on fire. We'll all have such lovely talks before…well, you know. I must do what I really must do when faced with such beautiful material."

"Is that your thing? Skin hues?" Stella's voice was even, her face still. "That was what we figured. What are you? Some kind of racist?"

Darwin gasped, and his smile fell away as he gaped at the agent. "A racist? Me? The very idea. Of course, I'm not a racist. The opposite, my dear. The exact opposite."

What was she doing? Did she intend to keep Darwin talking? What for? He wasn't killing now, but it was only a matter of time. There was no escape from here. None. The only question was who he would kill first.

"But you are collecting skin colors, aren't you?" Stella pressed. "Who does that, if not some sort of white supremacist?"

"An artist, my dear!" The words were a shout. "An artist. That is what I am, not a racist." The murderer had the gall to look offended. "Good lord, you've seen the portrait of my darling Diana. Do you really believe that some white-hood-wearing thug would marry a woman of her race? Can you seriously think that one of those knuckle-dragging troglodytes would have been capable of painting a picture like that? Please."

Stella appraised him, looking him up and down. "Quite right. My mistake. You can't be a racist. Just a common murderer. So, what are you doing then? We figured that you were collecting different skin tones, but we just couldn't understand why."

Darwin grinned and turned his attention to Kati. "Shall we tell her, my lovely? Shall we let her into my secret? I suppose we could share, couldn't we? After all, she won't be able to tell anyone else. But all in good time. First, I want to hear all about you, my dear Stella. What makes a lovely young lady like you join the FBI?"

Stella arched her back and folded her fingers together in her lap.

Kati relaxed for the first time. The FBI agent was stalling, waiting for backup. She had to be.

"Family tradition. My father was a police officer, a sergeant. You'd have liked him. I'm not sure he'd have liked you, not now anyway. But he was a...a very kind man."

"Was? Can I take it that he has passed? Have you also felt the pain of grief?"

Stella's eyes flashed. "He was killed in the line of duty. They never found the person responsible."

"Oh, my dear. I'm so sorry. I know that pain. The injustice of it. The cruelty." Darwin's head wagged side to side. "There are such cruel people in the world."

"There are, aren't there?"

Kati smiled through the gag. Stella was forming a bond with the lunatic, bringing out what they had in common. The monster—Kati refused to call him by his real name—would never understand his own cruelty, but at least Stella could throw in a dig or two.

The monster didn't notice the insult. He set one of the guns next to him on the step and pointed emphatically at Stella. "You see. You understand. *This* is why my work is so important. This irrational hatred is exactly the cruelty I want to counter. I'm really just like you. You work with your guns."

He tapped the pistol next to him. "I have my art. We both hope to build a better world. One without hate or pain. Or grief."

Stella's eyes remained on the gun. Slowly, she lifted her head. "Is that what your work is all about then? Dealing with your grief?"

"Oh, my dear. Of course, it is. You do understand. Clever and beautiful. How wonderful. But not just my grief. I want to end all the grief that the world feels whenever someone is violently taken from them. I want to send a message that will end all this senseless killing."

Kati wanted to leap out of the chair and throttle him. End their grief? By causing more? Was he insane? Of course, he was. Whether he had been a lunatic before he had lost his wife or whether that loss had caused something in him to snap, Kati wasn't sure. But she also didn't care.

"Younnn hnnn."

She tried to speak. She had to tell him what she thought, but that damn gag blocked her words. Stella looked toward her and almost imperceptibly shook her head. Kati fell silent.

What's the point? He's going to kill us. Can't you see?

Stella lifted a hand to her ear and twiddled the gold stud in her lobe. "That's fascinating, Darwin. But what exactly do the different skin tones have to do with your message?"

"What a wonderful question. She is so clever, isn't she, Kati? The skin tones are everything, my dear. You see, we are every one of us beautiful. There are those who might say that we are all God's children, but the way I see it is that each one of us is a unique treasure. Each of us has our own special contribution to the world. By displaying diverse beauty in my art, by giving it a new frame, if you will, I will create a new appreciation for each one of us. The result will be the end of hatred, the end of killing. We will simply love each other as we should. That is what my work will do."

Stella looked impressed. "Wow, what a concept. That is incredible. Tell me about this...this new frame of yours. What exactly are you building?"

Darwin lifted a hand and slapped his thigh, delight oozing from his every pore. "You see, Kati. This is what I was hoping for. A pleasant chat about my new piece. It's so wonderful to be able to talk about it with two beautiful, intelligent women who appreciate what I'm trying to achieve. Let me tell you all about it, my dear Stella. And then I'm afraid I must get back to work. And with you two, I think my work will be complete."

35

Hagen reached for the door handle, his right hand gripping his Glock, one finger stretching along the trigger guard. Ander was by his side, legs apart, shoulders braced. Slade was behind him, back to the wall. Both had their weapons drawn too.

Down both sides of the street, Sheriff Lansing and the deputies he'd been able to scramble up were forming blockades, effectively cutting off this section of the art district. They came in silent and hung back so Darwin Rhodell wouldn't notice.

Hagen licked his lips. His mouth was dry, and his heart thumped in his chest.

On the way to East Nashville, Hagen had tried several times to call Chloe and Stella but had received no reply from either. Mac had confirmed their phones were inside Darwin Rhodell's Peace of Art Gallery.

There were a few good reasons why neither answered their phone. They might have set them to silent. The reception might be poor inside the building. They might be too busy making an arrest to answer right away.

Hagen didn't believe any of them. The bad reasons were more numerous and a lot more likely.

Slade had laid out the plan. "As soon as we get there, we go in hot, weapons drawn but quiet. We have to assume he's got at least one and maybe three hostages and that he won't hesitate to kill. Hagen, you're on point."

Hagen swallowed hard, curling his fingers around the door handle to the gallery.

The bottom half of the door was wood, painted a yellow so bright it hurt his eyes. The top half was made up of four small windows. The glass was thick and frosted, molded into circular waves that refracted the light.

They'd already covered the camera above the door, though Hagen worried it was too little too late. He looked through the window. The room was dark. The spotlights in the ceiling produced long-armed stars on the glass. There was no movement. No sound.

Where are they?

A fire lit in Hagen's chest. He took a deep breath, lowered the door handle, and pushed.

Nothing. He shoved again. The door didn't budge. He shook his head at Ander.

Ander hooked his thumb over his shoulder and peeled away from the wall, his long legs taking him to the corner of the building in a few strides. He disappeared around the side.

Hagen followed to an alley that ran between Darwin Rhodell's studio and the chiropractic office next door. Three brightly striped garbage cans stood in a neat row.

Next to the cans was a side door. The black, steel structure looked more like the entrance to a secret nightclub or an illegal gambling den than an art gallery. Ander had already taken a position next to it with his weapon raised to his shoulder.

Hagen stopped next to the door, one arm brushing the wall. Slade pulled up behind him.

Gripping the door handle, he shoved down and pulled. Pushed.

Locked. Again.

"For chrissakes!" His voice was low, a hiss barely louder than a whisper, though he wanted to bellow a curse loud enough to blow the door off its hinges.

Ander turned and sprinted around the next corner of the building. His head jerked back around the brickwork, sending his blond curls flying. He waved Hagen on.

Racing past him, heart thumping, Hagen found another door that opened into the parking lot behind the property. A gray Volkswagen was parked not too far from it. Hagen paused only long enough for Ander to run to the far side of the door and for Slade to catch up before jamming the door handle down.

Locked. Again.

Where was the damn SWAT team with their damn battering ram?

The fire that had been burning in Hagen's chest since he had imagined what Darwin Rhodell might be doing to Stella and Chloe behind those walls exploded. That psychopath might be sawing off Chloe's leg by now, and all they'd done was run around the building, testing door handles.

Slade gripped his shoulder. "Back to the front. We have no choice. It's going to be loud and hard."

Hagen growled low in his throat. "The harder, the better."

As Slade called for a battering ram over the radio, the three of them ran back the way they'd come, each with their guns held low, barrels following the line of their legs. When they reached the front entrance, a deputy with a breaching device was jogging over. The guy was fast, which Hagen appreciated. "You do the honors, Deputy." He turned to Ander and Slade. "Same plan on breach."

The deputy aimed for the lock, swung back, and shoved the ram forward. The glass above the door handle shattered, but the door didn't quite give way.

Before the deputy could give a second attempt, Hagen held up a hand. "Let me try."

He was still committed to going in as quietly as they could, if that was even possible now.

Jamming his left hand through the hole, Hagen reached for the lock. Pain seared up his arm. Blood ran down a shard of glass still embedded in the window frame.

Nothing serious. Forget it for now.

His fingertips found the lock and twisted.

Nodding at Ander, he swung the door open, and they entered the premises, guns drawn. The gallery was empty. Small spotlights shone onto the paintings lining the wall. A desk stood in the corner next to the steel door that led to the alley. The chair behind it was empty, one drawer open.

Ander's voice sounded in his ear, "Clear."

Slade tapped Hagen's shoulder and pointed to a passage at the end of the gallery. The corridor ended at a closed door. Four other doors lined the walls.

Where the hell are Stella and Chloe?

Hagen moved past Ander to the first door and tried the handle.

Locked.

Does this lunatic lock every freaking door in the building?

He stepped back and sized up the barrier. The wood was cheap, as though Darwin had installed it for privacy rather than security. Hagen lifted a foot and directed a flat kick right at the point where the lock met the doorpost.

The wood splintered.

Hagen kicked again, and the door burst open. A second later, he was inside, clearing the corners.

A large desk filled much of the room. A monitor faced the back wall where a filing cabinet stood with one drawer half-open. A red splash had sprayed over the cabinet and the walls.

"Shit."

Sweat pooled in the palms of Hagen's hands.

Whose blood is that? Stella...

Stepping around the desk, his heart sank when he spotted a black-booted foot.

Chloe!

Hagen raced over to where Chloe lay. Her t-shirt was torn above her shoulder, blood pooling beneath her. Her skin was gray, her eyes closed.

"Chloe." Hagen's voice was hoarse.

No answer.

Hagen placed two fingers on the side of her neck. Was that a pulse? Or was that his own heart beating hard enough to break out of his chest?

Relax. Focus. Find the pulse.

One beat. Two beats. There it was, weak but present.

Hagen breathed out. *Thank God.*

A voice came from the doorway. "How is she?"

"Alive. Just."

Slade's face was pale. He came around the other side of the desk just as Hagen holstered his weapon and began to put pressure on the wound.

Slade triggered his lapel radio. "SSA Paul Slade. Agent down. Ambulance required." He gave the address.

After receiving confirmation, he knelt next to Chloe and pushed Hagen's hands away. "I've got her. You and Ander find Stella. Save Kati. Get the bastard."

Hagen rose on legs that felt like cement. His hands were

wet, palms red. He stared at the gore for a second before wiping his palms down the sides of his pants. Pain shot up his arm. Fresh blood oozed from the cut on his hand. Ignoring it, he pulled his weapon from its holster again.

The weight of the Glock between his fingers eased his tension. His eyes narrowed. Chloe and Slade receded from the corner of his eye until all that was left was the room, the passage, and what might lie behind those doors.

Hagen came out into the corridor just as Ander emerged from the door opposite.

"That room's clear. Just canvases and stuff. What's in there?"

Hagen gritted his teeth. "Chloe. She's down. Slade is with her. An ambulance is on its way."

Ander's mouth opened slightly, then closed into a tight line. He adjusted the grip on his gun. "Let's get him."

Hagen moved to the next door. Somewhere in this building was Stella, and he was going to find her. Rhodell had gotten Chloe, but he wasn't going to let that sick murderer take Stella. He needed her.

A stainless-steel door stood in front of him. Hagen yanked the large metal handle down. There was a click and a rush of air and the door eased open.

A blast of chilly air struck Hagen's face. His breath puffed out ahead of him. It was a freezer. Goose bumps rose on the skin beneath his sleeves.

A white sheet covered the wall at the end of the room. In the middle stood a long, metal table, a pink smear marring the steel floor next to one of the legs. A handsaw rested on the surface, its jagged teeth stained red.

Hagen gripped his gun harder.

This was the room. This was where Rhodell killed and hacked up his victims. That table was his butcher's block.

Into Hagen's ear, Ander said, "It's clear. She's not in here, Hagen. Let's go."

"Wait."

Hagen stepped forward, drawn by the white sheet draped over a large canvas like a ghost in midair. He reached out and pulled, staining the white fabric red with blood from his wrist. But he barely noticed that as the sheet fell to the floor, revealing Darwin Rhodell's masterpiece.

"Oh my god."

Hagen gave the room one last look, then pulled himself away and turned to face Ander. "We need to find this bastard. Now."

They hustled to the two remaining doors. Ander pointed to the opening on the right and lowered his voice. "That leads to the parking lot."

"Hmm." A trickle of sweat dripped into Hagen's eye, and he shouldered it away. "That just leaves one more."

He advanced to the end of the passage. The door's gray surface was smooth and unmarked. Pieces of black foam poked around the edges where the door met the jamb. Hagen glanced at Ander, who stood in the middle of the corridor, weapon lowered.

"Soundproofing." Hagen pointed at the foam.

He gripped the door's gold-colored knob and laid an ear against its surface.

Was that a voice? It sounded like a voice, but it was muffled and low. Hagen couldn't be sure whether it was male or female.

What else?

Sirens. From the street. Distant now but drawing closer. That must be the ambulance for Chloe. Hagen's shoulders relaxed a little. She would be okay. She had to be okay. Now he needed to make sure Stella would be okay.

Darwin would hear the sirens, had most likely heard them rushing around up here.

He needed to move fast.

He gripped the doorknob and turned.

Not locked.

36

"Humanity as art. What a concept. That's such an incredible idea."

Stella sat, elbows resting on her knees, raising her voice in fake excitement, attempting to cover a noise she thought she heard upstairs. Breaking glass? She wasn't sure.

The room was eerily quiet. Darwin had done a good job soundproofing it. How else would he have been able to keep Kati Marsh locked up here for so long without anyone noticing?

But she had definitely heard something. A bang. A tinkle. A muffled shout upstairs, perhaps.

She hoped she'd heard a shout. Maybe Chloe was getting help now.

Christ, if he'd killed Chloe...

The thought made her tremble. She wanted to dive across the room, grab Darwin by his shirt collar, and punch the living daylights out of him. Instead, she interlaced her fingers so tight her knuckles turned white.

Easy there. Calm down. Just keep him talking. Help is on the way.

Insanity glowed behind Darwin's eyes as he smiled. "Why, thank you, Stella. That's such a kind thing to say. I realize that some people might argue the price for my message is rather high. But with such a message, *can* the price be too high? We are, after all, talking about a complete reevaluation of humanity itself, a new appreciation of our own beauty and of each other. I think such a leap in mankind's thinking is worth a little sacrifice. To reach the pinnacle of art itself, to attain what all artists have attempted since the days of…of the caves of Lascaux is surely worth a little lost blood."

Stella forced herself to smile. It wasn't easy. Taking people's limbs to display their beauty? Sacrificing people on the altar of his art?

And she'd let down her guard around him, allowing him to get the upper hand because he was kind.

Stella glanced at Kati. At least she was still alive. Seeing her tied to that chair had been such a relief. A world of weight had lifted from her. There was a chance at least one of Darwin's victims would make it out alive. Not all their efforts over the last few days had been wasted.

"I'm sure your wife would appreciate the idea, Darwin. What do you think she'd make of your work?"

"My darling Diana? Oh, she…" Darwin fell silent. When he spoke again, his voice was filled with emotion. "I'm sorry. I…it's just…we were very close, you see. The day I met her, I knew she was all I needed, everything I could ever want. Think Camille Claudel and Auguste Rodin. Or Dora Maar and Pablo Picasso. Or even Kiki de Montparnasse and Man Ray. She was my muse, my love, my life. She was the sun that rose each morning, the moon that lit my nights. Twenty-six years we were together, and barely a day apart. When she died, when hate, that awful monster, tore her from me, I was devastated. The light went out of my life entirely."

He sniffed away a tear. There was such pain in his face.

Darwin Rhodell was just an older man bereft and heart-broken, driven to insanity by the loss of his greatest love. He sat half-bent on the bottom step, as if his spine couldn't support the weight of his grief any longer.

Stella's heart even ached for him a little. Then she remembered the mutilated bodies of Tiffany Wright and Darlene Medina-Martinson, of Hu Zhao and Chloe's friend Daniel Swanson. She remembered Chloe, the blast of the gun, the blast of blood that sprayed across the wall.

Pain, Darwin? I'm sorry you felt it. But I'm glad you're feeling pain now, and I hope you'll feel a heck of a lot more of it soon.

A thin line of yellow light appeared on the wall of the stairway behind Darwin.

Is someone coming down the stairs?

It had to be. Neither she nor Chloe had answered their phones and hadn't called in. Slade would know that something was wrong. He must have sent help by now. Or maybe someone outside had heard gunshots and had called 9-1-1.

Or did Darwin have an accomplice that they didn't know about? Frankly, they'd known so little during this case that anything was possible.

Stella shot a look at Kati. The young woman peered past Darwin's shoulder toward the top of the stairs. If Darwin noticed, he'd turn to see what she was looking at, and...

"I'm sorry to hear that, Darwin. The death of your wife must have been—"

"Death?" Darwin lifted his chin and straightened his back. "The cold-blooded, hate-filled murder of my wife, you mean?"

"Yes, that. Will you tell me more about her?"

He settled some. "My darling Diana was generous, kind, and loving. She had a heart that was bigger than...bigger than...oh, it could fit the world. She would love the colors, of course, and the textures of my work. She always did. Such a help. You asked me what she'd think of my latest creation? She would be wild about the idea. But I'm afraid she would also be as frustrated as I am about the difficulties of implementing it. This is the problem with big ideas. The bigger they are, the harder they are to bring to life."

Darwin adjusted his grip on the gun. The muzzle still pointed in Stella's direction. The second gun, her Glock, was still on the step next to him. If only that gun were a little closer. If only his finger weren't on the trigger of his own weapon.

The artist shook his head, his wild, wispy hair floating around his face.

The smile and melancholy from before transformed to rage in an instant. "Why couldn't you have just left me alone? I would have finished my work in peace, and the whole world would come to see the art in humanity, the beauty in all of us that I want so much to show you. But you had to interfere. You had to try and stop me. Well, I'm sorry, my dear Stella, my beautiful Kati. But I have no more time to waste, no more time to collect pieces. Now, I'll just have to make do with what I've got. I must add your friend upstairs to my work. And then the two of you, and I'll be done at last."

He rose to his feet and lifted his gun just as a voice shouted from the top of the stairs. "FBI!"

Hagen!

Relief poured into Stella, warm and energizing. She had never been happier to hear her colleague's deep voice.

"Darwin Rhodell. Drop your weapon."

Darwin spun toward the stairwell. In an instant, Stella was on her feet. One step, two, and she was diving through the air. She slammed into the back of his knees, forcing them to buckle. He collapsed, crashing face-first onto the stairs.

Though Darwin's gun clattered from his hand, he had the presence of mind to reach for the Glock pinned under his leg. Stella locked her arm under his armpit and pulled him away. He was heavier than he looked. Stronger too.

Kati was screaming through her gag as footsteps clattered down the stairs.

Stella jammed a foot against the bottom step and pulled Darwin's arm back. He stretched his hand, his fingertips landing an inch from Stella's Glock.

"No!" Stella pulled, her shoulder straining.

A red, leather Oxford shoe connected with the gun and sent the Glock skidding across the floor. It smacked against the wall. Hagen stood over them at the bottom of the stairs.

"Nooo!" Darwin screamed in anguish.

His arm slipped out of Stella's grip, and he was on his hands and knees in a second. "You can't stop me. You mustn't. My work, my beautiful work."

He twisted toward his own gun that had fallen at the foot of the stairs. He was almost there.

Stella was faster.

"Shut up about your work."

She slammed a right hook hard into Darwin's cheek, and a loud crack echoed through the basement as Darwin's head spun. He dropped backward, landing with a groan on the cement floor. Blood trickled from his left nostril.

A swarm of deputies raced down the stairs, containing a screaming Darwin.

"Yours, I think." Hagen picked up Stella's gun and pressed it into her hand. "Some punch you've got there. I think you broke his cheek."

"Thank you." Stella holstered the gun, still pissed at herself for allowing an old man to take it in the first place. "I'd be more than happy to break a lot more."

Ander slipped behind her and knelt at Kati's chair. He pulled down her gag and freed her wrists and ankles from the chaffing ropes.

Seconds later, a sobbing Kati flew into Stella's arms, her tears soaking her shirt. It didn't matter. Stella held on tight as the deputies pulled Darwin to his feet.

"Oh, you are both so beautiful." Blood painted the artist's teeth as he smiled. "You would have made such wonderful additions."

37

"You ever seen anything so…wrong?"

Hagen stood in Darwin Rhodell's freezer room, one gloved hand gripping the white sheet that had covered Darwin Rhodell's "great work."

Ander took a deep breath and grabbed a handful of blond curls. "You know something, man. I really don't think I have."

In front of them, Darwin Rhodell's masterpiece, the work he had been putting together so carefully with chloroform and a hacksaw, leaned against the back wall. A sheet of metal stretched from the floor to just shy of the ceiling. A fringe of dismembered fingers and toes dotted the edges. Arms, grayish and frostbitten from the freezer room, formed three-quarters of a circle in the middle. Fingers entwined, stumps touching bloody stumps. Ashen-colored muscle rubbed against yellowy-white fat and bone.

A line made up of legs, cut just below the knee, divided the circle into two. Two more legs extended from the middle of that line to the edge of the circle, one foot pointing one way, the other foot pointing in the opposite direction.

Ander released a deep breath. In the room's icy air, his

sigh looked like a cloud. "Reminds me of that da Vinci draw-ing. The one of the naked guy."

Hagen raised an eyebrow. *"The Vitruvian Man?"*

"Is that what it's called? When did you become an art expert?"

"It's called 'education,' dude. Some of us paid attention in school, and some of you…learned how to roll joints behind the gym."

"Practical skills, man. That's what learning's really all about. Pretty sure I got more use out of my education than you got out of yours."

Hagen almost smiled. To laugh while facing this horror? That was beyond him.

"Yeah, but I don't think he was going for da Vinci," Stella said from behind them. Hagen turned, surprised. She'd been escorting Darwin Rhodell out a few moments ago.

Stepping closer to the grisly art, Stella referenced the leg that cut through the circle, careful not to touch it. "That's the peace symbol. That was his message. His killer style. Peace and love. Delivered in a package of murder and mutilation."

Ander shook his head. "What the heck was he thinking? Did he really believe that people would overlook the mater-ial? Just ignore what he'd done? What did he think would happen when that thing left the freezer room?"

"I don't think he thought that far." Hagen examined the decomposing body parts. "If he had thought ahead, he'd have known that his beautiful work of art wouldn't stay beautiful for long. That thing's about as durable as peace and love."

Stella somehow managed a smile. "You're such a cynic, Hagen. But take another look. See those gaps where the hands don't meet? And where the fingers and toes don't touch?"

Hagen ran his gaze around the edges of the canvas. The fingers and toes were spaced out. Darwin had been leaving room to fill it in with new digits. The circle of arms and legs was incomplete on one side, the space big enough for at least three more victims.

She indicated that area. "Those spaces are there because we stopped him. If we'd done nothing, he'd have filled them with bodies of other innocent people. We did good today. All of us. Medics say Chloe's gonna make it. Kati Marsh is on her way to the hospital for a checkup. We saved people."

"Hmm." Hagen fell silent.

"I'll go see when the crime scene techs will arrive." She shivered. "It's freezing in here." Stella exited fast, her hands tucked deep in her pockets.

The work, with its arms and legs, dominated the empty room. Whatever else that space might once have contained or would be used for in the future, it would always be where Darwin Rhodell had created his grisly art.

Hagen couldn't take his eyes off the monstrosity. The stiff fingers half-curled. The legs smooth and dark-haired, denoting female and male. There was humanity pinned to that board, but only a man like Darwin Rhodell could find beauty in that composition or in his medium. Hagen certainly couldn't.

"Hagen…" Ander stepped up beside him.

"Hm?"

"Wanna ask you something."

"Shoot."

"Were you worried before we opened that door?"

Hagen snorted. "There was a long list of things I was worried about. Which do you mean?"

Ander exhaled a long breath. "That Stella was dead."

Hagen stared at the artwork, forcing his emotions into a deep compartment inside his heart. "Yeah. I thought she might have been."

Ander nodded. "Yeah, me too. Hurt like shit."

He patted Hagen twice on the shoulder before leaving the room. Hagen remained unmoving, trying to see the peace sign Stella had indicated.

She was so perceptive. It surprised him that Ander was perceptive too.

Had Ander noticed the connection he and Stella seemed to have had in the last few days? Had he seen the way she looked at him, sometimes? The way he sometimes looked at her, supported her, perhaps, more than he did other members of the team?

Hagen hoped he hadn't been that obvious. He hated the idea that anyone—especially Ander—could see the thoughts and feelings that roiled beneath his skin.

Hagen rubbed his cheek. Once, he and Ander would have talked chemistry like that over a couple of beers while watching a ball game on a Saturday afternoon. He didn't want to do that now. Not about Stella. There was too much there he could say, too many emotions he'd prefer not to give a voice to.

He followed Ander out of the room, emerging into the passage just as Slade directed the forensics team toward the freezer room and down into the basement.

This case was done. The time had come to get back to the other one, the unofficial one. His case.

Yeah, Stella had survived the showdown with Darwin Rhodell, and he was glad for a number of reasons. But only one of them mattered…

She would still be able to help him. She would still be able to give him the chance he needed to avenge the murder of his father.

And he would help her do the same.

38

Two days after the arrest of Darwin Rhodell, Stella sat on the ledge of her window in her loft apartment, fingers curled around a mug of cocoa, temple resting against the glass. The sun was still half an hour away from setting, but already, the shadow of her building blanketed the road below in darkness.

Part of yesterday and all of today had been filled with checkups, debriefings, and paperwork of one digital form after another.

"You wouldn't believe the paperwork, Scoot." Behind her, the goldfish chased flecks of fish food, oblivious to the tedious requirements of work life.

Slade and Sheriff Lansing had both given statements to the press, answered reporters' questions, and batted away the most prurient queries, but Stella was sure that she would still be reading and hearing about the case on the news for days, if not years, to come. She wouldn't be leaving the horrors of that basement or the cold room of the Peace of Art Gallery behind her any time soon.

The text Brodie sent to the team thanking them for

bringing Kati back to him had helped, as had the half-dozen enormous boxes of chocolate that Kati's parents had delivered to the office.

Even Caleb and Ander hadn't been able to finish them in one sitting. Though, they'd done their best to try.

Almost losing their daughter appeared to have mellowed Harry and Carolynne Marsh. Maybe they'd even look kindlier now on the man who made her happy. He had, after all, helped them crack the case and find Kati in time.

Stella took a long sip of cocoa.

She pushed open the window. Traffic was building, but the evening breeze had lost the worst of the day's heat and felt soothing. The darkening day had already turned the tan wall of the furniture store on the other side of the road a deep orange.

Or would that be ochre? Wasn't that what Darwin Rhodell would have called it? Amber? Tawny brown, maybe?

Gray. That was the only color he'd be seeing now. Gray walls in his cell and gray stripes on his uniform. And nothing brighter for the rest of his life.

How could someone so friendly, so full of love and compassion, have turned into such a monster? Stella was sure that if she had met Darwin a few years ago, before his wife's tragic death, she would have found him charming and sweet. A little odd maybe—she would never have understood his obsession with art—but nice. She understood how easily his victims were pulled in, how easily she had been pulled in. They hadn't seen the darkness beneath that friendly exterior.

Loss changed him, left him numb, and hollowed out his moral center.

Had grief done the same thing to her?

Stella shuddered.

She didn't think her suffering had affected her like that, but her father's death had certainly changed her. She'd been fourteen when he died, little more than a child. In the immediate aftermath, as she and Jackson helped their mother through her grief, Stella felt she had aged about three years in six months.

Then her brother died.

Each of those deaths had left her numb for a while. There were times when the tide of grief rolled out, taking the whole world with it, leaving her utterly alone. Only, slowly, did life and the point of it all seep back in—though she knew nothing would be the same again.

But while each death had landed the same heavy blow, the scars they left were different.

Jackson's was a gaping wound that nothing could fill. There was just a space where there had once been laughter, teasing, and a shoulder always ready to support her when she needed it.

Her father's death? That was more impactful. It was a cage that held a living thing, constantly scratching and gnawing and crying out for justice to set it free. She would have no peace until she did.

Was that what Darwin Rhodell's art had been about? That agitated space begging for peace?

Peace seemed further away now.

But at least she had a friend helping her on that journey.

While Stella had been trawling Morville and East Nashville for a painter with a handsaw, Mac had been stealing quiet moments to fish in the FBI's databases for information about Matthew Johnson. She found plenty.

There were lots of Matthew Johnsons in the FBI's records. Car thieves and drug dealers. The odd rapist and murderer. Wife beaters and fraudsters. But none were cops from Atlanta who had adopted Joel Ramirez as an undercover alias.

Mac figured there was probably some kind of firewall in

the database preventing her from accessing those records and finding out who, exactly, Matthew Johnson was. But Mac wouldn't let that stop her. Like a true investigator, she hit the phones and reached out to a former instructor from Quantico—now a special agent in charge at the Memphis field office—hoping to find some answers.

"Maybe a higher authority and more years of networking can open some of the doors we need," Mac said, shrugging, as Stella had filed her last form for the day. "Or at least some of the files."

"Oh, Mac. You're brilliant." Stella hugged her, and for a moment, all the tension and horror of the last few days melted away, replaced by all the possibilities that hope, friendship, and teamwork could create.

But a friend, a database, and a connection weren't the only tools that could bring Stella back to her former Uncle Joel, whoever he was. Atlanta was a big city. There were plenty of people in it called Johnson. Stella would knock on the door of every one of them if she had to. She'd track him down if he was alive and squeeze out all the information he had. And if he really was dead, she'd find his family and discover what they knew.

And if he moved?

Then she'd just work harder to find him.

If her work had taught her anything, it was that no one could hide forever, and very few secrets stayed hidden in the shadows.

Stella took another long sip of cocoa. Tomorrow she'd ask Slade for a couple of personal days. She had to do something. For fourteen years, she'd been waiting to take action. And now, at last, she had a lead. She wasn't going to waste it.

Rrring.

Stella reached for her phone.

Slade. Great timing.

But Slade's tone immediately told her now was not the moment to ask for personal time.

"Stella." She'd expected Slade's voice to be soft, relaxed. Comforting. It wasn't. "When you were in the basement with Rhodell, did he mention anything about Murfreesboro?"

Murfreesboro? The city?

"No, nothing. Why?"

Silence. "Yeah, that's what I thought. I just got word. Six people are missing in the Murfreesboro area."

"Jeez." Stella lifted a hand to her forehead. She stood, moved away from the window, and watched Scoot go behind a plastic treasure trunk. "You don't think it was Rhodell? Maybe he had another location?"

Had she spent the last day and a half filling in forms while people sat tied to chairs in some other basement somewhere? The thought made her want to vomit.

"No, I don't think so," Slade said. "These missing people don't fit Darwin Rhodell's type. They're all Caucasian, and half of them are related. And Stella?" He paused. "They all went missing on the same day."

Stella stopped pacing.

The same day?

Kidnapping was a complex crime. Killing. Robbery. They could be spontaneous and often were. But kidnapping took planning, research, and the preparation of vehicles and hideouts. To take six people in one day? That seemed impossible.

"Stella? You still there?"

She shook her head to clear it. "Yeah, yeah. I'm here."

"Good. Pack a bag. I'll need you and the rest of the team in Murfreesboro first thing in the morning."

"Yes, sir."

As the screen went black, Stella sighed. So, that was that. She wasn't going to Atlanta in the morning.

Sorry, Dad. Duty calls.

Just as Stella tossed her phone on the couch, her doorbell rang. Frowning, she crossed to her front door and peered through the peephole.

Hagen.

Stella's mind flew back to the drive from Hu Zhao's cabin to the motel, focusing on the moment they seemed to have found something in each other's company that took them out of the horrors of the moment. It even took them out of the horrors of their pasts.

Stella had just assumed those moments with Hagen were as fragile as snowflakes. They'd land occasionally and disappear without a trace.

Was that what this visit was about? Was he trying to make it snow again? Had her capture by Darwin Rhodell, however briefly, made something click in the way he saw her?

Stella swallowed. She wasn't in the mood for that kind of conversation. Not now. Not this evening. Maybe not ever.

Unlatching the chain and opening the door, she forced a smile. "Hey, Hagen. What's up?"

"I need to talk to you." Hagen's expression was serious. His jaw was set, his eyes unblinking. "About Joel Ramirez."

The End
To be continued...

Thank you for reading.
All of the *Stella Knox Series* books can be found on Amazon.

ACKNOWLEDGMENTS

How does one properly thank everyone involved in taking a dream and making it a reality? Here goes.

In addition to our families, whose unending support provided the foundation for us to find the time and energy to put these thoughts on paper, we want to thank the editors who polished our words and made them shine.

Many thanks to our publisher for risking taking on two newbies and giving us the confidence to become bona fide authors.

More than anyone, we want to thank you, our readers, for sharing your most important asset, your time, with this book. We hope with all our hearts we made it worthwhile.

Much love,

Mary & Stacy

ABOUT THE AUTHOR

Mary Stone

Mary Stone lives among the majestic Blue Ridge Mountains of East Tennessee with her two dogs, four cats, a couple of energetic boys, and a very patient husband.

As a young girl, she would go to bed every night, wondering what type of creature might be lurking underneath. It wasn't until she was older that she learned that the creatures she needed to most fear were human.

Today, she creates vivid stories with courageous, strong heroines and dastardly villains. She invites you to enter her world of serial killers, FBI agents but never damsels in distress. Her female characters can handle themselves, going toe-to-toe with any male character, protagonist or antagonist.

Discover more about Mary Stone on her website.
www.authormarystone.com

Stacy O'Hare

Growing up in West Virginia, most of the women in Stacy O'Hare's family worked in the medical field. Stacy was no exception and followed in their footsteps, becoming a nurse's aid. It wasn't until she had a comatose patient she became attached to and made up a whole life story about—with a past as an FBI agent included—that she discovered her love of stories. She started jotting them down, and typing them out, and expanding them when she got off shift. Somehow, they turned into a book. Then another. Now, she's over the moon to be releasing her first series.

Connect with Mary Online

facebook.com/authormarystone
goodreads.com/AuthorMaryStone
bookbub.com/profile/3378576590
pinterest.com/MaryStoneAuthor

Made in the USA
Monee, IL
18 August 2022